PRAISE FOR

Praise for *The Keeper of Secrets*

Thomas's writing comes alive when describing the glories of music and the alchemy of its extraordinary practitioners. She has also managed to portray the horror of life in Dachau with pinpoint accuracy and emotional conviction.

NZ Listener

Originally self-published as an ebook, gaining widespread popularity and rave reviews, *The Keeper of Secrets* is the culmination of years of meticulous research, for which the reader reaps the rewards. Prepare to be swept up in a captivating story that both entertains and informs.

Australian Women's Weekly

I can see why it's been so successful. *The Keeper of Secrets* is holocaust fiction with a difference, a compelling tale about a precious violin and the people who love, play and covet it.

Herald on Sunday

Praise for *Rachel's Legacy*

This sequel ... seamlessly weaves important historical detail into this saga of a single family riven and nearly decimated by the Holocaust. Of local interest is Thomas's compassionate rendering of the cruel prejudices inflicted on German refugees to the Antipodes. Ultimately, this lovely sequel, driven by the trajectory of characters rather than the fate of an instrument, will leave Thomas's readers eager for the follow-up to come.

NZ Listener

The weaving together of present and past makes for an enthralling read, and the author's obviously extensive research shines through, without being too overwhelming to the story.

Bay Weekend

Secrets and legacies in many different forms are important throughout and Thomas does a good job of conveying dramatically the importance that art can have in people's lives.

North and South

This book, at its core, is a celebration of heritage. It is about the importance of remembering the past, not for the purpose of learning from history's mistakes but simply to acknowledge that it happened and that each event has shaped and moulded our present.

Oamaru Mail

Praise for *Blood, Wine & Chocolate*

From the mean streets of the East End to the sparkling waters of Auckland, this tale of switched identities, vengeful obsession and lethal ingenuity is as addictive as chocolate with more twists than a corkscrew.

Bay Weekend

Be sure you have nothing else planned because this book will carry you away.

Greymouth Evening Standard

Thomas balances plot and character perfectly and her plot points are nothing if not creative. One character is dispatched with a wine bottle in a manner that will have you squirming simultaneously in delight and horror. Readers will finish this book looking forward to Thomas's next offering.

North and South

The wine and chocolate are described in loving and detailed terms, which will appeal to wine and chocolate buffs. Readers who enjoy thrillers will find this to be a page-turner that's likely to be consumed in a couple of gulps.

Otago Daily Times

ALSO BY JULIE THOMAS

The Keeper of Secrets
Rachel's Legacy
Blood, Wine & Chocolate

LEVI'S
WAR

JULIE THOMAS

HarperCollins*Publishers*

HarperCollins*Publishers*

Australia • Brazil • Canada • France • Germany • Holland • Hungary
India • Italy • Japan • Mexico • New Zealand • Poland • Spain • Sweden
Switzerland • United Kingdom • United States of America

First published in 2018
This edition published in 2021
by HarperCollins*Publishers* (New Zealand) Limited
Unit D1, 63 Apollo Drive, Rosedale, Auckland 0632, New Zealand
harpercollins.co.nz

A catalogue record of this book is available from the
National Library of New Zealand

ISBN: 978 1 4607 5962 2 (pbk)
ISBN: 978 1 7754 9130 9 (ebook)

Cover design by Michelle Zaiter, HarperCollins Design Studio
Cover images: Man © Mark Owen / Trevillion Images; background by Jan Rckert
/ EyeEm / Getty Images
Typeset in Sabon LT by Kirby Jones
Author photograph by Victoria-p.com
Printed and bound in Australia by McPherson's Printing Group
The papers used by HarperCollins in the manufacture of this book are a natural,
recyclable product made from wood grown in sustainable plantation forests.
The fibre source and manufacturing processes meet recognised international
environmental standards, and carry certification.

To my beautiful Georgios and Victoria — you brought such joyful noise and wonderful imagery into our lives and you died the way you lived, gently, with grace and dignity. And I hope that you both know how deeply you are mourned.

I come from a people who gave the Ten Commandments to the world. Time has come to strengthen them by three additional ones, which we ought to adopt and commit ourselves to: thou shall not be a perpetrator; thou shall not be a victim; and thou shall never, but never, be a bystander.

Yehuda Bauer, Professor of Holocaust Studies at the Avraham Harman Institute of Contemporary Jewry at the Hebrew University of Jerusalem, in a speech to the German Bundestag, 27 January 1998

LIST OF CHARACTERS

The Horowitzs
Levi Horowitz   The eldest Horowitz
Simon Horowitz   Levi's younger brother
David Horowitz   Simon's son
Cindy Horowitz   David's wife
Daniel Horowitz   David and Cindy's son, Simon's grandson
Dr Jacob (Kobi) Voight   Levi's great-nephew

Others
Major Richard Stratton   Army major
Lieutenant David Connor   Army lieutenant
Teyve Liebermann   Levi's saviour
Peter Dickenson   London bank manager
Margot & Fred   Levi's first landlords
Galina Slatkin   Levi's second landlord
Pierre   Levi's friend on the Isle of Man
George Ross   Jacob's lover

In Germany
Reich Minister Joseph Goebbels   Head of Propaganda
Count & Countess von Engel   Nazi party stalwarts
Reichsführer Heinrich Himmler   Head of the SS
Führer Adolf Hitler   Führer of Nazi Germany

SS-Hauptsturmführer Erik von Engel   Levi's friend
Karl & Elsa von Engel   Erik's parents
Eva Braun   Hitler's mistress

In Italy
Peter   Liberistas leader
Maria & Marcin   Partisans & Roza's parents
Roza (Elzbieta Krawczyk/Liswski)   Partisan
Fr Don Aldo Brunacci   Assisi network
Bishop Placido Nicolini   Assisi network
Colonel Valentin Müller   German Commander of Assisi

PROLOGUE

The National Archives
Kew, London

June 2017

'Prepare to meet a genuine hero,' Lieutenant David Connor said quietly. Then he went to the laptop and hit some buttons. After a few seconds' delay, the screen was filled with a black-and-white image of Levi Horowitz, a man of about twenty-eight. He was perched on a high stool and wore black shoes, dark-coloured pants and a white shirt. His hair was wavy and full around his head. He looked at the ground for a full minute, and then raised his eyes to stare into the camera. His awkward body was painfully thin and his face was gaunt, the skin stretched over bones that would have sliced through butter. His eyes were surrounded by a ring of darkness, the sign of extreme fatigue. He looked haunted, wary, as if he was longing to be anywhere but where he was.

'Good God,' Major Richard Stratton muttered. 'The man looks like a walking corpse.'

On screen the image moved and gave a dry cough, his hand to his mouth.

'May I smoke?' he asked in a thick Germanic accent.

Off-screen someone answered. 'Certainly, sir.'

A uniformed arm offered him a cigarette, which he put between his lips, then the arm leaned in again with a lighter. Levi nodded his thanks and took a deep pull on the cigarette. Smoke billowed out through his nose.

'My real name is Levi Horowitz and this is the story of my war. I shall recount it once, here, and then I don't want to speak about it ever again.'

Slowly Stratton pulled himself to his feet. He was tall, just into his fifth decade, with close-cropped red hair and a neatly trimmed beard, green eyes and a military bearing. His body was beginning to show the effects of his sedentary occupation as his muscles softened and his waistline expanded.

'Tell me again, who is this and when was it recorded?' he asked, signalling for the lieutenant to pause the video.

'A Jew, a refugee, called Levi Horowitz. It was recorded on his return to England in 1945,' Connor replied.

'And he spied, behind enemy lines?'

'Oh, he most certainly did. I think it might be better if Levi explains it for himself. He is fluent in English and he is honest, brutally honest.'

The major nodded. Stratton was in charge of the section of the military archive where the lieutenant had found a digitised and re-archived World War II interview. The decision to use the material, or not, would be his.

'Fair enough.'

'Sir, it appears that he sent information back from Germany which was ignored, dismissed, by his commanding officers. It doesn't reflect well.'

The major raised an eyebrow.

'Should we be concerned?'

'Judge for yourself.'

CHAPTER ONE

Berlin to London

11 November 1938

Levi Horowitz wasn't a natural soldier. He had never considered spending one second of the twenty-one years of his life in any of the armed forces. As the black Mercedes drew away from his family home and the forlorn group on the doorstep continued to wave goodbye, he was busy imagining a new life working in a bank in London.

Berlin had become an increasingly dangerous place for a Jew. The restrictions imposed by their Nazi rulers continued to pile up, new ones almost every day, and the night before his departure he'd witnessed the biggest pogrom for a hundred years. He and his younger brother, Simon, had been caught up in the midst of the shattering glass, the acrid smoke and the vicious batons of the storm troopers, and had found refuge with a gentile woman.

In the morning they'd taken their leave and made their way home. Simon had led Levi to the music shop of Amos Wiggenstein, a local luthier. He'd seen the violins burning in a pile on the cobbled street and Amos's assistant, Jacob, being beaten, and now he wanted to see what was left. They salvaged seven complete violins, carried them home in a wooden box and hid them in the attic of their house.

Violins were an integral part of their lives. Their papa and mama owned two, a 1742 Guarneri del Gesú and a 1640 Amati. Both Papa and Simon played the Guarneri and Levi played the huge Steinway grand piano.

And now he was being driven away from terror and towards safety. Did he feel guilty? Perhaps, a little. He had some of his family treasures hidden in a leather pouch in his armpit and some documents in a package strapped to his chest. He had layers of clothing on under the coat, and bending in the middle was difficult, nevertheless it felt like he was the guardian of centuries of family possessions. If those at home were forced to surrender their belongings, he carried a complete inventory and some of the most precious pieces of jewellery with him to sanctuary.

Not that that was probable. Papa was adamant that the people would throw out this little Austrian-born dictator at the next election and normality would be restored. Once again their lives would be full of music, dancing, tennis parties, shopping at the grand stores and having picnics in the Tiergarten. Levi couldn't help wondering whether if he was living a wonderful life in London he would want to return to his parents' home.

He looked like his mother rather than his short, round, ever-happy father. He was over six foot and lean, with a very straight back, long limbs and surprisingly elongated and delicate fingers. His hair was a rich auburn colour, cut close to his head so the curls were not so apparent. His skin was pale, but dusted with freckles, and his eyes were a light moss green, unlike his three siblings who all had their father's dark eyes, dark hair and swarthy complexion. At rest, his face wore a serious expression, thoughtful and reflective of his introverted personality.

He had been under the impression that he would be taken south to the Swiss border but the driver informed him that they were travelling north to the Danish border. Once into Denmark he would be met by a contact who would take him north to the coast and put him on a fishing boat for Sweden. From Stockholm he would fly to London. It all sounded very exciting. The miles were gobbled up by the quiet, comfortable car, and after a while he fell asleep.

'We've come to a checkpoint, Herr Horowitz.'

The voice roused him and he sat up. There were very bright lights ahead and a barrier across the road.

'They'll need your papers, sir,' the driver added.

He fumbled inside the pocket of his papa's woollen coat and pulled out the folded exit visa Papa's friend had given him.

'I have them here,' he said.

He rolled down the window and put the paper into a gloved hand that was thrust into the car. There was a full moment of silence. All he felt was impatience at the delay.

'Get out of the car please, sir.'

The voice was firm but neutral. Levi hesitated and then did as he was asked. His suitcase was on the seat beside him. The speaker was a soldier in uniform.

'Bring your case and follow me.'

'But why? My papers are correct —'

'Just follow my orders, sir!'

The man looked angry. Levi shrugged, bent inside the car and picked up his suitcase.

'I won't be long,' he said to the driver.

As he followed the soldier across the stony ground towards a hut, he heard the car engine fire. He spun around and watched the Mercedes make a wide U-turn and disappear into the blackness.

'Hey! Come back!' It was a cry of shock and anger.

'There are plenty more cars coming. This way.'

With reluctance, Levi did as the soldier said.

The wooden building was cold and draughty. The soldier pointed to a chair behind a table. 'Sit there, please.'

Levi put his suitcase on the ground beside the chair and sat down. The soldier picked up the case and put it on the table.

'Is it locked?' he asked.

Levi blinked. What was all this about?

'Yes, of course it is,' he said, trying not to let his impatience show.

'Do you have the key?'

'Yes, of course.'

'Then unlock it, now!'

He took the key from his trouser pocket and unlocked the two keyholes in the case. The soldier picked it up and took it with him. Levi heard a key turn on the other side of the door. The room was lit by a bright bulb hanging in the centre of the ceiling. Over to one side was a bench with a kettle and two cups and a bottle of milk. He got up and walked around. Behind the blind the one window was crossed with iron bars in a grid pattern. The door handle turned, but the door was locked.

He returned to the seat and slumped down. He hadn't

anticipated this. The car was gone, his exit visa and suitcase were in the hands of a soldier and he was locked inside a hut on the German side of the Danish border. The one good thing about his situation was that the valuables were hidden on his person. Still, it felt like an opportune time to pray, so he bowed his head and asked G-d to intervene and set him back on his road to London. A few minutes passed, the key turned in the lock and the door opened.

'Get up!'

This man was in plainclothes, a tight-fitting black leather coat and polished jackboots. He held the suitcase and a piece of paper in one hand. Levi rose to his feet.

'Where are you going, Jew?' The man snarling up at him was at least four inches shorter than himself.

Levi felt himself rise up to accentuate the height difference. He swallowed hard against his fear. As Jews, they'd been reviled in public for years and he had learned to show nothing.

'London. My papa got my exit visa from a friend in the government, he paid for it, and it's genuine.'

The man dropped the case to the ground and drew a pistol from his pocket. He was Gestapo.

'Genuine?' It was a sneer.

'Yes. My papa is an influential banker —'

The Gestapo agent gave a humourless bark of laughter.

'Your papa is a filthy *Jew*. And so are you, and you are trying to leave illegally. That is a crime. A crime against the Fatherland and against the Führer. Punishable by death.'

The pistol was levelled at Levi's stomach. So this was going to be the end of his journey, in a dismal hut in the middle of nowhere. No wonderful life in London, no keeping the family treasure safe. Where was his G-d? The G-d of Abraham and Moses and David. The G-d he worshipped every Saturday in the synagogue. His papa had taught him he was a child of this G-d, one of the blessed people.

Dissent seemed worthless, but Levi felt he had to try. 'It is not illegal! I have a government exit visa and a job in a bank in Lon —'

The Gestapo agent's face was puce with rage.

'Quiet! I don't want to hear your pitiful excuses. Take your clothes off.'

'What?' Levi was astonished.

'You heard me: take your clothing off.'

He hesitated a moment longer and the Gestapo agent cocked the pistol.

'Do I have to shoot you first?'

'No.'

Levi struggled out of his papa's coat and then the other layers of clothes he had put on. He was very aware that when he took off his woollen singlet the agent would see the pouch in his armpit.

'What is this?' The agent's eyes gleamed as he stepped forward. 'Take it off and hand it to me.'

Levi pulled the bag free and handed it over. The agent opened it and peered inside.

'As I thought, you are smuggling goods you are not entitled to.'

'Those are my —'

Levi's protest was cut off by the hollow click of the trigger. Nothing happened, the Luger jammed.

'Fuck!'

The Gestapo agent shook the gun and peered down the barrel. This gave Levi the seconds he needed. He reacted from pure instinct, springing across the dirt floor. His rising left arm blocked the gun as it hurtled towards his head and his right fist punched the agent square on the chin. His height advantage increased the power behind the blow and the other man staggered backwards.

'Filthy Jew!' he screamed and pointed the gun again. It clicked uselessly. This emboldened Levi and he charged at the agent, who was still reeling. Levi raised his knee and aimed for the man's groin, then caught him again with a right-left combination. The agent dropped to the ground like a dead weight. Levi knelt and felt for a pulse. The man was alive, just knocked out cold.

Levi scooped up the gun, the pouch, the piece of paper, his clothing and the suitcase. With a cat-like fluidity he ran for the door. It was unlocked, but as he closed it behind him he noticed the key in the outside lock. He turned the key, heard the satisfying click and threw the key into the forest. He hung the treasure back in his armpit and pulled his clothes back on, his numb fingers fumbling with the buttons, finally wrapping himself in the warmth of the coat. The other soldier was standing with his back to the hut, smoking a cigarette. Keeping to the shadows cast by tall trees, Levi ran past the guard-rail and into Denmark.

About half an hour later a car turned the corner and came sweeping down the middle of the deserted road. Its powerful headlights illuminated the path before it. Levi dropped his suitcase and waved his arms. Maybe it was a dangerous thing to do, but he'd never make the coastline in time to catch the boat to Sweden on foot. The vehicle slowed and came to a stop just ahead of him. He said a silent prayer and jogged to the car. The back door opened and he leaned inside.

'Hello. What are you doing out here on your own?'

It was a man, about the same age as his papa, in a black woollen coat with a fur collar. His dark eyes were kind and a smile played at the corner of his lips. Something about his face, the nose, the chin, was familiar.

'I'm ... I'm going to the coast. I have an exit visa. I'm going to Stockholm and then to London.'

Levi thrust the paper towards the man, who took it, unfolded it and glanced down. Then he looked up.

'Are you Benjamin Horowitz's son?'

Levi nodded. He didn't know if the fact this man appeared to know Papa was a good thing or a bad thing. He was pretty sure the traveller was a Jew, but he could also have been a Nazi sympathiser. Levi could feel his heart pounding with fear. The man indicated for him to get in.

'Climb in, young Mr Horowitz.'

Levi hesitated. What the hell, this was why he had waved the car down.

'Thank you. Do you know my papa?' he asked as he slid onto the leather seat and put his suitcase between his feet.

'I do, indeed. Moshe, keep driving,' the man instructed to the silent figure behind the steering wheel. Then he extended his hand towards Levi.

'I'm Teyve, Teyve Liebermann. I'm a shop owner, or I was. When things got bad your papa helped me to stay in business. Why are you going to London?'

'Papa has a friend there who will give me a job in his bank. I'm to take a fishing boat to Sweden.'

Teyve nodded slowly. 'It's a good plan, but a complicated one. I have an exit visa and I'm on my way to Copenhagen. From there I shall fly to London. My wife was supposed to come with me, but she refused. She doesn't believe the situation in Berlin will get any worse and she is so German, she says she couldn't live in London.'

His voice had a sad quality, and Levi wanted to console him.

'My papa thinks the same thing, but he decided to send me away just in case. When it gets better I'll come home.'

Teyve smiled. 'So will I. And reopen my shops! But in the meantime, young man, would you like to come to Copenhagen with me and fly to London?'

Levi frowned. What to do? Stick to the plan or trust this new companion?

'Do your parents still have those wonderful music nights?' Teyve asked. 'I remember your papa playing his violin.'

'I play the piano!'

Levi felt hope rising in his throat. Teyve studied him and then nodded. 'Ah yes, I think I remember you now. Chopin.'

Levi beamed.

'My favourite. Thank you, Herr Liebermann. Papa would be very pleased that I met you. I will accept your invitation.'

'Good.'

As Levi settled down into the firm seat he could feel the gun nestled in his pocket and prayed he wouldn't have to use it.

CHAPTER TWO

London

November 1938

The rest of the journey went without incident. Levi realised two things by the time they arrived in London. Firstly, Teyve was a very wealthy man, and secondly, Jews were not treated with the same disdain outside of Germany. It was like the old days. People called him 'sir' and took his coat and smiled with appreciation when he smiled at them. He suspected that some assumed he was Teyve's nephew and treated him accordingly.

He'd never been on a plane, and the flight from Copenhagen to Paris, and then on to Heston Aerodrome west of London, was an adventure. He took his cue from his companion, sipped his beer, and didn't behave like a refugee fleeing his traumatic homeland. The customs official at Heston was polite and deferential to Teyve.

'Are you going to open a shop here, sir?' The hand holding the stamp was hovering above the piece of paper.

Teyve beamed at the tired face looking up at him. 'Of course! More than one. And I will employ the best of British shop assistants to work in it.'

The stamp came down with a definitive bang. 'Very good, sir. Welcome to England.'

'Thank you.'

Levi handed his paper to the same man. Two impassive blue eyes scanned it and then glanced at him quizzically.

'Levi Horowitz.'

'Yes, sir.'

'How do you qualify?'

'I'm a banker.'

The man looked him up and down and smirked, the eyes had iced over. 'Are you old enough to work in a bank?'

Levi swallowed. Suddenly Teyve was beside him again, his hand resting on Levi's shoulder. 'He's with me. He has a letter to Mr Peter Dickenson of London's Marylebone Bank, who will employ him. His father, Benjamin Horowitz, owns one of the most esteemed banks in Berlin.'

Once again the stamp fell onto the paper and it was handed back to Levi.

'Very good, sir. Welcome to England.'

Levi wondered how many times a day the man said that sentence and what he really wanted to say. He smiled broadly at the official.

'Thank you.'

It was late afternoon and darkness had fallen. A chill wind blew across the field towards the car park at the aerodrome. Levi wasn't sure what would happen next. He braced himself to say goodbye to the friend of his father who had shown him such kindness.

'Where will you go now?' Teyve asked him.

Levi picked up his suitcase. 'There is a bus stop over there. I have some pounds, I will catch a bus into the city. Papa said there are Jewish organisations in North London who take care of refugees. If I can find one of them, maybe they will give me a bed.'

Teyve shook his head. 'Benjamin would never forgive me if I left you here to catch a bus into the unknown. No, definitely not. I am going to take a taxi to stay with a friend of mine, a man who has supplied my shops with beautiful clothing for many years. He lives in Hampstead. I'm sure he and his wife will be happy to accommodate you. And tomorrow you can go into London and find Mr Peter Dickenson of the Marylebone Bank.'

Levi made a mental note that he needed to make sure his papa knew how kind Mr Liebermann had been. When they were all safely back in Berlin, Papa would want to do something to show his appreciation.

Levi slept very well during his first night in England. His hosts were welcoming and their house was comfortable, much smaller than his home, but nicely furnished. They had a dog, a black Labrador, and Levi lavished attention on it. Consequently it slept on his bed, and its deep snore lulled him to sleep.

The next morning he was wondering whether to pack his bag when Margot, the lady of the house, knocked softly on his open door. She was almost as round as she was tall, and she smelled faintly of flour and dried fruit.

'How did you sleep, dear?'

'Very well, thank you.'

She brushed her large hands on her pinafore and smiled at

him. 'Don't feel you have to up and go. You're welcome to stay here until you get settled. Bobo loves you and would miss your company! I have a friend who runs a boarding house south of the river. She has several refugees there, mostly Jews, Europeans I think, and she knows how to cook what they like! Shall I see if she has a spare room?'

Levi felt a surge of affection and gratitude. 'Yes, please! You are all so kind. I wish I could explain what it's like at home. We don't socialise with fellow Jews because it's too dangerous to congregate together. When my mama goes shopping, some of the gentiles spit on her and call her names.'

Margot shook her head. 'It is all too shocking. Well, you're safe now, and if anyone is rude to you, you just tell my Fred. He was a boxing champion at school, you know — he'll give them what for.'

'Well, I never, fancy that, Benjamin Horowitz's son!' Mr Peter Dickenson was a lean man with a thick head of sandy-coloured hair. He was younger than Levi had expected, possibly around forty. Levi sat opposite the generous wooden desk and waited patiently.

'Your father says you have been working as a clerk in his bank?'

Levi nodded. 'Yes, sir. I started on the personal accounts, but Papa moved me over to some of the larger business accounts, some of them government ones. I did backroom stuff, not meetings with clients.'

And compared to what he really wanted to do he had found the work monotonous and lonely, but he wasn't going to admit that to his prospective employer.

'You are twenty-one.' It was a statement, not a question.

'Yes, sir.'

'Didn't fancy going to University?'

Levi hesitated. 'I wasn't allowed, sir. Jews are banned from higher education in Germany.'

Dickenson nodded abruptly. 'Of course. Sorry. How ridiculous. Your English is very good.'

'We had lessons as children. I speak a little French, Italian, but mostly I learned English. My Feter Avrum, my papa's brother, immigrated to America in 1925, and Papa promised us we could go and have a holiday with him if our English was good enough. I'm musical, and Mama says that languages come easily to those with a musical ear.'

'Can you write in English?'

'Yes, sir.'

'Apart from a job, what else do you need from me?'

Levi reached into his coat pocket and drew out a leather pouch. 'I have some jewellery here. Papa said I was to deposit it in your bank for safekeeping.'

Dickenson reached out his hand, and Levi passed the bag across the desk. He watched silently as the man opened it and examined the contents in the palm of his hand: rings, brooches, two solid silver snuff boxes, two miniature portraits of Benjamin and Elizabeth, his father and mother. When Dickenson saw the seven loose diamonds in the tiny black box he looked up sharply.

'You carried these with you?'

'Yes, sir. I hung the pouch over my shoulder, in my armpit, and it was taped to my side.'

Levi wondered whether to tell this man about the Gestapo

agent and how close he'd come to losing his possessions, but something told him it was better to keep silent for the moment.

'Do you have a list of these things?' Dickenson asked.

Levi unfolded two sheets of paper and handed them across. 'The first one is a list of what I have, the second is a list of all our family's possessions.'

Dickenson scanned the two lists, shook his head and folded them up. 'Let's hope no one takes any of them from your family. Very well, Levi. I can do that for you and we will find a position for you here. Do you have somewhere to live?'

'Yes, sir, a boarding house south of the river. You should know that there were ten diamonds. I am going to sell one to a jeweller in Covent Garden to give me funds and I have plans for the other two.'

Teyve was still living in the Hampstead house when it came time for Levi to move to his new home. His new friends at the bank had told him that refugees were given exit visas but not allowed to take more than a very little money with them. This had given him an idea. A way he could thank the people who had helped him. Before he left, he shook Teyve by the hand.

'I can't thank you enough for all your help.'

'Don't mention it, son, I'm sure Benjamin would do the same for me.'

Levi reached into his pocket and drew out a piece of paper. He thrust it into Teyve's hand.

'This is my papa saying thank you and go well.'

The older man looked at the crumpled piece of paper and frowned. Then he opened it and saw the loose diamond sitting in the centre. When he looked up his eyes were glinting with unshed tears.

'Thank you, my boy. That repays me more than you will ever know.'

He grasped Levi in a bear hug, and when they parted Levi smiled and nodded. Then he turned to Margot and her husband, Fred, who stood in the hall behind them, watching. Margot came forward and reached up for a hug. Levi bent down and obliged.

'Thank you so much for your kindness, you have made me feel at home.'

She put her hands against his chest. 'Oh don't be silly, dear. We know where you are and we'll see you again. You must come and keep Shabbat with us.'

Levi took her hand and put another piece of paper into it. She touched it with her finger.

'What's this then?' she asked.

'Open it and see.'

She opened the paper and saw the diamond. 'Oh my good Lord, you lovely boy!'

Fred joined her and stared at the stone.

Levi smiled at them. 'Take it to Covent Garden and sell it. They are desperate for good stones, so make sure they give you enough. See more than one jeweller, tell them you are comparing offers.'

Fred extended his workman's hand and enveloped Levi's long fingers. 'Thank you very much, son, much appreciated.'

'No,' Levi turned to look at the smiling Teyve, 'it is I who should be saying thank you. I will never forget any of you.'

CHAPTER THREE

London

1939

Life had fallen into place with what seemed like remarkable ease. Levi had a job and a place to live. The boarding establishment was a huge house on the edge of Richmond Park. The rooms weren't large, but the beds were comfortable and there were enough blankets to keep out the cold. The view from his window was green, large trees and an expanse of grass. It made him feel homesick for the back garden at home, and he liked to watch the birds perched in lines on the branches. He wrote a letter to his younger siblings, twins Rachel and David, and told them he'd named the birds after some of the older members of their synagogue. He knew it would make them laugh. He waited patiently for them to reply, and when they didn't he wrote again, stressing how much it would mean to him to hear news of his family.

His fellow housemates were a mixture of Hungarian, Czechoslovakian, Russian, German, Italian and French men. Most of them were Jewish, and they ranged from those trying to maintain their strict faith and life practices, to those who had been so assimilated they hardly went to Shul. Levi was one of the very few who worked in the same field he'd left behind in Berlin.

The front room had an upright piano, old and sturdy but in tune, and one or two men had brought precious violins and flutes with them. They formed a makeshift band and entertained the others with instrumental and vocal renditions of favourite tunes from their homelands.

Mrs Galina Slatkin, the owner, had inherited her house from her parents. She was a clever cook, and understood that some of her boarders craved garlic, paprika, herbs, beetroot, cheese and spicy sausage. No one asked where she obtained these magic ingredients from, but the fact that her brother had an illegal still in his backyard shed and made alcohol, and that she was adept at bartering, no doubt had something to do with her genius.

Levi found himself very happy there. He had the freedom to walk where he wanted and shop where he wanted, and no one swore at him or made him feel unsafe. When he smiled at shop assistants they smiled back and many called him, 'sir.'

There were no storm troopers with batons and no crude anti-Semitic slogans painted on buildings. He was allowed to own a radio and read books by Jewish authors. He found a Jewish doctor and a Jewish dentist, and both were happy to have him as a client. It made him realise how much had been ripped away from the Jews in his homeland, how normal his life had once been and what it felt like to be a valued member of your society. If he dwelt upon this injustice, he found himself becoming angry.

Five days a week he dressed in one or other of his two suits, a tie and a white shirt, polished black shoes and a fedora hat and made his way by bus into the city. The bank was in a cavernous and impressive Georgian building, and he loved the sound of the echoes in the vast marble entrance hall. His job was similar to the tasks he'd done back home, except the documents were in English, and the people around him were friendly and welcoming.

In March of 1939 a workmate, an accountant called Ted who came from Liverpool, invited him to a jazz club, Le Meridian, to watch an American band. Jazz had been popular in the USA since the 1920s, but was only just gaining a real foothold in England. Levi followed Ted down a flight of steps into a smoke-filled, dimly lit space. They ordered cocktails at the bar and took a table close to the raised stage. For Levi, jazz was fascinating, a world away from the classical music he had grown up playing, or the swing music he'd heard in the cafés of Berlin. The rhythms were infectious, his fingers and toes tapped in time and he felt a wave of joy.

'Don't look now, but someone is watching you,' Ted murmured. Levi glanced over his shoulder.

'I said don't look!'

'Where? What do you mean?'

'Over by the bar, nine o'clock.'

Levi sighed and frowned at his companion. 'How can I see if I'm not allowed to look?' he asked, trying to keep the exasperation from his voice.

'Honestly, you are so naïve! Take a sip of your drink and slowly turn around.'

Levi did as he was told. A woman sat at the bar nursing a whisky on the rocks and watching them. She was a buxom brunette, wearing a tight-fitting and low-cut dress. She smiled at him.

'Go over and talk to her, buy her a drink.'

Levi shook his head. He could imagine nothing worse than trying to make conversation above the music.

'Certainly not,' he said firmly, and took another sip of cocktail.

Ted sighed. 'Are you a homosexual, Horowitz?' he asked.

'What?' Levi felt the shock of the question like a fist to the solar plexus, immediately followed by acute embarrassment.

'For goodness' sake, Ted, what sort of question is that?'

Ted shrugged. 'Okay, so you're shy. Mind if I step in?'

'Why should I mind?' Levi asked.

'You might be planning to pick her up, wouldn't want to step on your toes.'

He looked across the table and recognised the smile twitching at the corners of Ted's mouth.

'You're teasing me. I don't understand your English ways. Go ahead, be my guest,' he said.

Ted stood up and gave him a mock salute. 'See you in the morning.'

Two nights later Levi went back by himself, and realised almost immediately that the pianist was unwell and struggling to keep up. At the first break he went up to the man playing the trumpet, who seemed to be in charge, and asked if he could have a chance to play the piano. The love affair was instanteous; the music flowed through him like an electrical charge, and by song number three he was improvising. The trumpet player came over at the next break.

'Billy wants to know if you can stay till closing. He'd like to go home if you've got this,' he said. Levi nodded and smiled. The trumpet player patted his shoulder.

'Thanks, buddy. You're great. We'll pay you.'

Several hours later Levi floated out of the club with some pounds in his pocket, the smell of smoke in his nostrils and the taste of whisky on his lips. Would he come back and play again? Try and stop him! The thought of his father's reaction made him smile.

On 1 September 1939, Hitler's army invaded Poland and everything changed. Within hours Levi was an 'enemy alien', not because he was Jewish but because he was German. He was horrified to find himself in a country at war with his homeland. At the boarding house, all of the German men gathered and discussed what to do.

'I think we should move away, get away from London,' said Gunther, his shaggy eyebrows drawn together in a worried frown.

'It may be even worse somewhere else. London has so many different races and people are used to that. If we go somewhere else, to the north, or into the countryside, we may be treated with even more hostility.'

The speaker, Michael, was a teacher by trade, working now as a baker's assistant. He was a very tall, sombre, quiet man who spoke with authority, and they were used to listening to and agreeing with him.

'I think Michael is right,' Levi added, 'Here we can blend in, especially if we don't talk much. We just need to be careful, go about our business and avoid trouble.' So it was decided, for the moment, that they would stay put.

Less than a month later they all got letters ordering them to appear before a special tribunal. All Germans and Austrians over the age of sixteen had to report and be assessed. Once again Michael quelled the panic and assured them that, as they had fled from Hitler, they had nothing to fear from his enemies.

On the day of his appointment, Levi dressed in his best clothes and put his papers in his inside pocket. He stood in front of his mirror and silently practised what he was going to say.

Levi stood in front of the three-man tribunal and watched them read his papers and the affidavit that Mr Dickenson had written for him. They didn't even look at him. The middle man slammed a stamp on his paperwork.

'You are a category C, no special risk. You are to be left at liberty. Next!'

Levi took the papers thrust towards him. 'Thank you, sir.'

He turned on his heel and walked out. A sense of relief flooded him, and he felt an urgent need to go home and see how his friends had fared.

All but one had returned with the same stamp on their documentation. Andros, an Austrian of Hungarian descent, had confessed links to the fascist party and was sent to a holding camp to await the construction of internment camps on the Isle of Man. Levi couldn't help but wonder why he hadn't just kept his mouth shut about his beliefs and retained his freedom, but he knew that Andros was a hot-head and believed that keeping quiet was akin to betrayal. Maybe his honesty was to be admired, Levi thought as he wrote in his journal about the day's events. If he held such loyalties, would he have been prepared to be interred for them? Would he give up the comforts of his life for ideals and principles? How patriotic was he? Would he exchange his freedom for a chance to serve the good of his country? To free it from the Nazi tyranny? The questions haunted him as he listened to the dinner-time conversation. There was much to think about in this ever-changing world.

So life continued as normal, except it didn't. Inside their haven the men felt safe and comfortable, and they knew the neighbours had been warned by Mrs Slatkin: any rude comments to her men and she would not be suppling bottles of the popular illicit alcohol. But travelling on public transport, and even the simple act of going into Hyde Park to eat lunch, was fraught with the possibility that someone would verbally assault them. The German men were particularly at risk, and Levi took to hurrying to the bank and keeping his head engrossed in his work until it was time to rush home.

Hitler had made overtures of peace towards Britain and France, but the English Prime Minister, Neville Chamberlain, rejected these, and there was an uneasy cloud over Europe as the Soviet Union bullied the Baltic states and invaded Finland. Levi followed the news closely, and wrote letters home urging his father to bring the rest of the family to London. Still there was no answer, and the lack of mail made him uncomfortably anxious. He told himself they were too busy trying to cope with their plight as Jews in a hostile environment, but at night, when he couldn't rationalise the silence, it kept him awake and he tossed and turned with worry.

Even with the risk of verbal abuse, life was better here than in Berlin. The German men in the house spent endless hours discussing what Hitler would do next and how little the English seemed to understand about this maniac and his obsession with ruling Europe, goaded on by his cohorts, Himmler, Goering and Goebbels. And always there was the fear of confrontation.

'Hello.'

Levi looked up from his book. An elderly man had sat down next to him on the bus. He nodded and smiled.

'Not joined up then?' the man asked cheerfully.

Levi felt a trickle of fear down his spine. If he answered, his accent would give him away. If he didn't, the man would become suspicious and keep asking. He shook his head. The man peered at him.

'What's wrong, lad? Cat got your tongue?'

'No.' It was very quiet, almost a whisper.

'Where are you from?' Surprisingly there was no note of accusation in the tone of the question.

He looked the man full in the face. 'Berlin.'

Too late. The expression hardened and the man looked him up and down. 'A Jerry! On our bus?'

Levi sighed deeply. 'Sir, I am a refugee, a Jew. My family is being persecuted by Hitler now, as we speak. I'm working hard and not troubling anyone. If we are invaded I will take my place to fight against my countrymen.'

The man snorted with derision. 'Like hell you will. My boy was killed by the Jerrys, at the Somme, in the last war. You could be a spy, sending messages back to those bloody Nazis.'

The bus swung into a stop. It wasn't Levi's, but he knew his best course of action was to depart. He stood up.

'I'm very sorry for your loss. Excuse me.'

He swayed slightly as he scrambled his way to the opening door.

'Bloody Jerry! Go home!'

The man's final words rang in Levi's ears as his feet found the pavement and people around him stopped and stared.

The worst incident by far was a sudden police raid on the house while they were all eating dinner around the table. It was Shabbat, their weekly celebration of the Sabbath, and it was clear that the raid was timed to cause the most offence and inconvenience.

'What do you want with us?' Gunther demanded of the officer who was left to guard them in the dining room while others searched the house.

The man shrugged. 'Be quiet!' he barked loudly.

'Don't worry,' Michael said gently, 'they're only doing their job. There is nothing to worry about.'

A loud noise from the rooms upstairs drew all their glances to the roof.

'What was —?'

The door burst open and the constable in charge rushed in. He was holding something in his hand. To his horror Levi realised it was his German pistol. He kept it well hidden and had forgotten it was there.

'Is anyone going to admit to owning this or do we have to arrest you all?' the Constable asked accusingly.

Levi stood up. 'I can explain. I was arrested and questioned by a Gestapo agent at the Danish border. The gun jammed when he tried to shoot me and I fought back. I took his gun when I knocked him out. I didn't know what to do with it, so I brought it with me. It has no ammunition.'

The constable checked the gun. 'Why did you keep it?' he demanded.

'I … I had forgotten I had it. I should have handed it in, I'm sorry.'

The officer walked over to Levi and studied him. For a moment no one spoke. Levi kept his expression impassive and his eyes locked on the other man's. In his chest his heart was thumping, and he breathed slowly to control his fear.

'You didn't shoot him?' the officer asked at last.

Levi was shocked. 'No sir, I punched him out cold, locked the door behind me and ran into Denmark. Besides, the gun was jammed. But I am no killer.'

Slowly the officer nodded. 'Nor are we. Did you hurt him?'

Levi ventured a small smile. 'I believe he would have been sore.'

There was a connection, an understanding between the two men. Levi felt a buzz of relief, this man wasn't going to arrest him.

The officer smiled back at him. 'All right, son, I believe you. But I'm taking this.' He pocketed the gun and held his hand out. 'Papers.'

Levi dug into his trousers pocket and handed them over. The man scanned them briefly.

'This incident will go on your official record, Mr Horowitz. But no further action will be taken at this stage.'

After they left, Levi sank down onto his chair. His legs were shaking under the table. Mrs Slatkin brought him a cup of coffee.

'It has a little something in it,' she said, 'to help with the shock. Why on earth did you have a gun?'

Levi looked up at her. Her eyes were concerned and kind, and for a moment he desperately missed his mama.

'I'm so sorry. I'd forgotten I had it.'

CHAPTER FOUR

London

June 1940

'Levi Horowitz?'

Levi looked up and saw a man in army uniform standing on the other side of his desk. His stomach lurched with a mixture of fear and the desire to run.

'Yes.'

Suddenly Mr Dickenson was beside the man, a worried frown on his face. 'What's this about, soldier?' he asked.

The officer looked him up and down. 'And who are you, sir?'

Dickenson drew himself up. 'The owner of this bank. What do you want with my staff member?'

The soldier ignored the question and turned back to Levi. 'Do you have your papers on you?' he asked.

Levi shook his head. 'No, not when I come to work.'

The soldier looked momentarily frustrated. 'You should carry them with you, but never mind. Mr Horowitz, you are to come with me. We will go to your place of residence and collect your personal belongings. Then I am to take you to Euston Station. There you will get on a train to Liverpool and then a ferry across to the Isle of Man. You will be interned at Hutchinson Internment Camp for the duration of the war.'

Levi rose to his feet and stared at the soldier. 'Why? What have I done?' Levi's voice sounded strangely small, and his throat felt very tight.

'This is outrageous!' Mr Dickenson spluttered, 'I will complain to your superior officer.'

Again the man ignored him and spoke only to Levi. 'The war in Europe is spreading rapidly, Hitler's armies are marching north, and the list of countries that have capitulated is growing. The government has enlarged the categories of people who should be interned. You now qualify under the category of enemy aliens who work in occupations that could be a risk to the British economy. Now, would you please come with me, sir?'

The impatience in his voice was clear. Levi threw a panicked glance at Mr Dickenson, who shook his head.

'Damn it, this young man is a *refugee* from the Nazis and he is *Jewish* — he's hardly going to be approached to work for them, nor would he agree to it.'

The soldier turned to glare at Dickenson. 'Nevertheless, the law is the law. And this young man is on record as possessing a German weapon. He is not as harmless as you may think. I must insist.' The voice was firm, final, and the hand on Levi's arm reinforced the message.

Dickenson sighed and pointed to the soldier. 'Do as he says, lad. We'll get this sorted out, don't you worry. I've got contacts and I'll make sure you're released as soon as possible.'

Levi nodded and grabbed his hat from the stand in the corner.

'I'm sorry to have to leave the wor —'

'It's not your fault! Don't be frightened, they won't hurt you. Will you, officer?' Dickenson asked. He glanced at the soldier who was waiting for Levi, and his expression was unmistakable.

'No sir, we won't hurt him or anyone else. We are not Nazis.'

The drive to the boarding house and then to the station was conducted in uncomfortable silence. The soldier gave him fifteen minutes to collect his belongings and pack his case. Mrs Slatkin was out, so he left her a note with his key and some extra money.

At Euston Station the solider put him on a train to Liverpool and told him he would be met at the station and transferred to the ferry.

'Don't even think about getting off somewhere along the route. The army will hunt you down.' Those words rang in his ears as he took his seat.

He'd read some vague reports of labour camps in Germany and prisoners being held in appalling conditions, so by the time he reached Lime Street Station his imagination had painted a very dire picture. Still, it was wartime and no doubt his family were enduring far more hardship. He'd almost stopped thinking about what could have happened to them, as some of the possibilities were horrendous and it was easier to block the options out, even if that layered still more guilt upon him. It wasn't truly fair for him to be enjoying himself as much as he had been. Perhaps the time had come to pay.

The ferry was full of men with suitcases all heading for the same place, so Levi just followed the masses, onto a truck and through the gates into the camp. The place was nothing like the hell-hole he'd pictured. The buildings were thirty-three commandeered hotels and boarding houses, all attached, in a row, facing a large grassed square in the seaside town of Douglas. The houses were white, with dark painted lintels and window borders, and all had bay windows and small gardens out the front. If it wasn't for the double row of barbed-wire fencing and the uniformed guards, it could have been a holiday camp.

First things first. They were photographed, then issued with an alien registration card which would have their photograph affixed to it.

Levi was shown to his bedroom, on the third floor of a house two from the end of the row. He sat on the single bed and looked around him. A cupboard, a chair and a bed, and a window with a sea view. Sunlight flooded the room and it was warm. Could be worse, could be a lot worse. A gentle knock broke his reverie. He turned towards the door and gasped with delight.

'Mr Liebermann!'

'Hello, Levi. We meet again.'

They shook hands and Levi sat back on the bed. Teyve took the chair.

'When did you arrive?' Teyve asked.

'About an hour ago. They came for me at the bank. Poor Mr Dickenson was so upset. He said he would make sure I was released as soon as possible.'

Teyve smiled and shook his head. 'Gentiles think they have such power over the government. They don't realise that it is preoccupied with preparations for war and we mean absolutely nothing. Personally, I wouldn't rush to leave here. It is a safe place.'

'How long have you been here?' Levi asked.

'Two weeks.'

'Why? Why did they send you here?'

The older man shrugged. 'I don't know. I'm German.'

'As if any of us would raise a finger for Hitler! It is ludicrous. I'm glad you're here,' Levi said. 'Tell me what it's like.'

Teyve frowned. 'I think they keep it as informal as possible, but many of the men resent being "locked up". There is frustration and depression and outrage at the injustice. People will bend your ear about how unfair it is. But I look upon it as an enforced rest, and when the bombs start to drop, I'll be safe. They won't waste bombs on us.'

'What do you do all day?' Levi asked, a hint of anxiety in his voice.

'First thing in the morning we all line up outside and they count us. To make sure no one has escaped in the night, I suppose. Where would we go? We're on an island! But they know us all by name and they are good men. Give them no trouble and they will leave you alone.

'There are days when we can go on a walk into the hills or down to the sea for a swim. The guards come with us, but it is easy enough to forget they're there. The sea is lovely and warm and refreshing. Or I spend time reading and planning my shops.'

'Do they have a piano?' Levi asked.

'Believe it or not, they have eleven! And the beginnings of an orchestra. There are two concert pianists and they give recitals. There are writers and painters and linguists and scientists, and even some mathematicians! They have lectures at night. You can learn a language or how to paint, or you could give piano lessons. Men have money and will pay to learn a new skill. It fills in the time.'

Levi was grinning. 'It sounds quite bearable.'

So began Levi's internment in Hutchinson Camp. At times he felt guilty because he enjoyed it so much.

Isle of Man, August 1940

The day everything changed began like any other. The men were woken by a sharp knock on their doors. They dressed and filed outside to stand and be counted. The just-risen late-summer sun warmed them as they stood in silence. After roll call they went to breakfast and chatted about what they planned for the day.

Levi joined his two best friends, Frank, a German poet from Cologne, and Pierre, a French-born painter who had grown up in Berlin, in the group going down to the sea for a swim. It was starting to turn cold in the evenings, and soon swimming would end until summer 1941, so they wanted to get in as much as they could. A guard accompanied them to the beach, but brought a ball for them to throw to each other and usually joined in. The water licked at Levi's body as he leapt through the waist-high waves, his arms raised and his feet struggling to keep him upright on the sand.

'Come on, dive in! Don't be a coward.' It was Frank. He gave Levi a friendly push as he passed him, sending him tumbling under the churning water. The taste of salt filled his mouth and nose, and as he rolled onto his back he could see the sunshine reflecting off the surface. He stood up, wiped his face and sent a spray in Frank's direction with the heel of his hand.

'Aha, if it's war you want, war you shall have.' Levi was laughing, and so were the men around him as they joined in the battle, using their hands and feet to send cascades of chilly water at each other.

Pierre dived at Levi, tackled him around the shins and pulled him under the sea. In seconds they were too deep to stand, and Levi found himself pushing against Pierre as he scrambled towards the surface. An arm around his chest pulled him back down, and then it happened. Just a second, there and gone. A pair of lips grazed his, the most delicate of kisses.

A surge of adrenalin rushed through his body. He opened his mouth in a gasp and water flooded in. He kicked away and broke out of the tomb, his lungs aching, burning with the lack of air. He gulped and spluttered. A few feet away Pierre surfaced, his dark eyes shining and a huge smile on his face. Without saying a word he launched himself towards the beach. Levi tread water and watched the head bobbing through the waves. What was that? What should he do? If he told the guard, Pierre would get into trouble and that was the last thing he wanted. Besides, it was his word against Pierre's, who would, undoubtedly, deny anything ever happened. Had it? Was it a trick of his mind? Was it what he wanted? Had he imagined it?

'Come on, Levi, time's up.'

It was the guard, standing further inshore, yelling at him and waving him in. With a sense of relief, he started towards the beach.

As always when he was confused, Levi headed for a piano to clear his mind as he played. *Étude 13. Opus 25 Number 1* by Chopin, a piece with delicate fingering that challenged him. Then into *Ballade Number 1 Opus 23*. That felt better! The music reminded him of his father and that sent him into one of his papa's favourite pieces, *The Goldberg Variations* by Bach. He went back to Chopin for the *Minute Waltz* and *Nocturne Number 2*.

By the time he finished he'd come to a decision. Pierre was just playing a silly joke, as he often did, and meant nothing. Levi would forget all about it and go back to worrying about more important things, like what had happened to his family and why he'd never had a response to any of his letters.

None of the lectures on offer that night interested him. Frank was playing cards and Pierre had gone for a walk, so Levi decided on an early night spent reading his book. It still gave him a thrill, as he read Ernest Hemingway's *Farewell to Arms*, to know that he was allowed to read a book that was banned at home and, what's more, a book that had been part of the mass book-burning their parents had taken them to in May 1933. Since arriving in London he'd gobbled up books banned in Germany: those of Bertolt Brecht, Sigmund Freud and many others.

About an hour after he'd lain down on his bed and started to read, there was a gentle knock on his closed door.

'Come in,' he called. Teyve often came to visit him around this time, and he enjoyed discussing the state of the war with his older friend. Newspapers were hard to get here, but the guards and the islanders were happy to tell them what they knew. The door was opened hesitantly. It was Pierre. Levi sat up and let the book slip to the floor.

'Hello,' he said. He wanted Pierre to know he'd forgotten all about what had happened in the sea, so he gave him an extra-large smile.

Pierre seemed relieved. 'Hello there. How is Hemingway?' He asked in French. They often talked in French.

'Very sad in places. What did you do this afternoon?' Levi asked.

Pierre sat down on the bed beside him. Usually his visitors sat in the chair, and Levi moved away to give himself more room.

'I wrote to Heinz,' Pierre said. Heinz was a German, only just nineteen, who'd been interred with them but had left two weeks previously to work on a farm in Kent.

'I know you miss him,' Levi said.

Pierre nodded and looked down at the bed. He picked at the quilting on the cover with his chewed nails.

'I do ... Levi?'

There was a moment's silence. Pierre raised his head and locked his gaze on Levi's. His dark eyes were round, with an air of innocence that reminded Levi of a puppy-dog. His olive skin tanned easily, and his teeth looked very white. For the first time Levi noticed the curls that sat on his neck, perfect circles of black hair. Something stirred in the pit of his stomach. He frowned. Did Pierre expect him to say something?

'Yes?'

'Did you know that Heinz and I were lovers?' Pierre asked quietly.

The question hung in the still air. Levi was shocked. It felt as if Pierre had kicked him in the chest. His breath came in a ragged gasp.

'No ... No, I didn't.'

Pierre shrugged and his body seemed to crumple a little. 'I guess not many people did. We were very discreet. Heinz said his papa would be so angry if he ever found out. He's an only child and he's expected to marry and provide grandchildren. Being homosexual is not in the family plan.'

Levi nodded thoughtfully. He could hear the sarcasm in Pierre's voice.

'I can understand why he was scared of that. My papa would probably be upset, too,' Levi said. As he spoke he wondered if this was true. Benjamin was a kind, caring man who was very involved in the lives of his children. Levi had seen enough of the fathers of his friends to know that this was not always the case. But this, this would challenge him. Levi knew it even as Pierre turned and took his hand in both of his.

'But they're not here!' There was a new urgency in Pierre's voice. 'And no one needs to know.'

Levi pulled his hand away. 'What? What are you suggesting?' he asked.

'I see the way you look at me. I know you feel the same way I do, even if you don't understand it. Levi, don't be scared. I can show you —'

Levi wanted to get up but the weight of the other man's body pinned the cover around him.

'No!' he said firmly.

Pierre put his palm up and touched Levi's cheek. 'Has no one ever touched you like this?' Pierre asked.

Suddenly Levi's mind was flooded with the memory of the last time he'd seen his childhood friend, Rolf, on the night of the Kristallnacht. Rolf had wanted him and Simon to stay with their friends, a group of gentiles, hiding in a broken café, waiting for it all to be over. Before the brothers left, Rolf had hugged him and put the palm of his hand on Levi's cheek. He'd known, without acting on it, that Rolf loved him with a feeling that was stronger than friendship. Life had intervened and torn them apart. He hadn't realised until Pierre touched his cheek that he missed Rolf.

'Yes,' Levi said softly, 'as a matter of fact someone has.'

Sometime later Levi lay with his head on Pierre's chest, watching the moonlight seeping across the window ledge. He felt a deep contentment.

'Will we survive this war?' Pierre asked suddenly.

Levi stirred. 'Of course we will, no one's going to hurt us here. We'll pass our days in relative comfort, and when the dictator has been crushed we'll find somewhere to call our own.'

'How about a farm in France? We could make cheese.' Pierre laughed.

Levi sat up and looked down at him. 'Cheese? Why on earth would you want to do that?'

Pierre shrugged. 'Don't all Frenchman make cheese?'

'You're not French, you grew up in Germany,' Levi said.

'Well, Germans eat cheese. The main thing is we can find somewhere away from judgement.'

The story paused at this point. Levi looked directly at the camera filming him in 1945. His expression was impassive, but his eyes were filled with sadness.

'The rest of that conversation is private. But I do carry with me the guilt of leaving Pierre so suddenly. War is like that. You find friends, lovers, and you lose them, to an order or a bullet, in the blink of an eye.'

CHAPTER FIVE

The National Archives
Kew, London

June 2017

Major Stratton raised his hand. The lieutenant pushed a button and the screen froze.

'So he was gay?' the major asked.

The lieutenant hesitated. 'As he says, that's private, but there is more evidence of it later. I hope you might be starting to understand sir, why his story could be so useful. He's very articulate.'

The major nodded thoughtfully. 'Did he marry? Does he have family, any descendants?' he asked.

'According to records he had a younger brother, Simon, who was interred in Dachau and survived. They moved to America in mid-1947. We would need to locate them and let them see this, get their permission, before we could use any of it.'

'Find them.'

'Yes, sir. Shall we continue?'

'By God, yes.'

Isle of Man, August 1940

As they walked back from the hills behind the camp, Levi resisted the urge to grab Pierre's hand and squeeze it. A strange mixture of emotions swept through him in successive ripples: joy, wonderment, fear, guilt, and trepidation for the future. This was all so new and so dangerous.

A few hundred metres from the camp a senior officer came around the corner and stopped in front of the descending group.

'Ah, at last. I need one of your men, sergeant. Horowitz, come with me.'

Something akin to an icy dread raced down Levi's back.

'Yes, sir.'

He glanced at Pierre and saw the concern.

The officer gestured towards the houses. 'Quick man, follow me.'

Levi extended his stride to keep up with the pace of the man ahead of him. As they neared the main hall, the officer pointed to the door. 'In there, you have a visitor.'

Levi's stomach turned over. Who? Someone from London? Mr Dickenson? Maybe even someone from home? He pushed down the sudden surge of hope. He opened the door and walked inside. The room was dim, the curtains drawn against the sunshine. Two middle-aged men were waiting for him, one smoking and the other twisting a pool cue in his fingers.

'Ah, Horowitz?'

Levi walked slowly towards them. His internal alarm system was ringing, but he had no option.

'Yes, sir.'

'Levi Horowitz.'

He nodded. 'Yes, sir.'

Both men were wearing suits, shirts and ties. They weren't military. One pointed to a chair. 'Sit down, young man.'

Levi sat on the edge of the chair.

'May we call you Levi?'

He nodded again, but this time said nothing.

'Would you like to smoke?' the man with the cigarette between his fingers asked.

Levi shook his head. 'No, thank you. I don't smoke.'

'Before we tell you what we want, I'd like to check a couple of things. How old are you?'

'Twenty-three.'

One man seemed to be doing all the talking. The other was now leaning on the pool cue and watching.

'And you worked in a bank in London?'

'Yes, sir.'

'How many languages do you speak?'

Levi hesitated. 'German obviously, English, some French and not so much Italian,' he said.

'Impressive. And you play the piano? Very well I'm told.'

'Yes, sir. I started to play when I was four.'

They glanced at each other.

'You're Jewish, but you don't look it.'

Levi smiled. Was this a good thing in their eyes?

'I look like my mother, northern German, and way back they were Catholic. An ancestor married a Jew and we became the Jewish line.'

'Did anyone ever mistake you for an Aryan?' the man asked thoughtfully.

'Not when I was with my family, but when I was by myself I remember a couple of people who were about to say rude things and then they looked closely at me and apologised.'

Both men nodded.

'When did you leave Berlin?'

'The day after the Kristallnacht. Papa got a visa for me.'

There was a silence while the men looked at him. He was growing impatient. 'What do you want from me?' he finally asked.

The man asking the questions drew on his cigarette and let him wait another moment. 'Do you know what has happened to your family?' he asked.

Levi felt another shock of dread and leaned forward. 'No! Can you tell me anything? I write to them, but I never get any letters back.'

'You father is Benjamin Horowitz who owns the bank on Pariser Platz.' It wasn't a question.

'Yes! Is the bank open? Papa had lots of government acc —'

The man held his hand up, palm towards Levi. 'No. It is our understanding the bank was closed, Aryanised, in November 1939. We have no idea what became of your family, but there is much deporting of Jews to labour camps in Germany and east, in Poland.'

Levi slumped back. The weight of his pain threatened to crush him into the seat. Losing the bank would have broken his papa's heart. Please G-d they still had the house and all the possessions, but that didn't really matter, not compared with their lives. He imagined the fear his younger siblings must have felt. How would David and Rachel, the twins, possibly cope if they were separated? The man with the cigarette gave a loud cough and the noise broke through his thoughts.

'So maybe they are in a camp, like me,' he said softly.

'Possibly, but I would venture to say that it is not as easy an existence as the one you lead.'

Silence again while Levi digested this comparison. 'So, what do you want from me?' he asked again.

'Levi, do you ever wish you could play a more active role in defeating the Nazis? Help to free your family instead of hiding away here?'

The question stung, and his green eyes flashed with defiance. 'Of course! Do you want me to sign up in the British Army? Or Air Force? When I was young I wanted to learn to fly. I would be very happy to enlist, even to bomb Berlin.'

The man with the pool cue spoke at last. His accent was different, like one of the men in the London bank; he was Welsh. His free arm swept around the room.

'If we wanted to recruit for the armed forces there are hundreds of men here, some more suited for that than you. No, indeed not. We have a special job for you, Levi, one that no one else can do.'

Levi struggled to keep the flood of negative emotion concealed. He wanted to be left alone to think about, and pray for, his family and to talk to Pierre, hear his soft words of comfort. He scrubbed his face with both hands and sighed deeply.

'Are you going to tell me what it is, or do I have to guess?' he asked, trying to keep the resignation from his voice. 'Have you come all this way to tell me that my papa's bank has been closed by the Nazis?'

'We come from the Special Operations Executive in London. You won't have heard of us, no one has. But we have a special commission from Prime Minister Churchill, to ... sabotage the Axis war effort. We need people with a deep understanding of Germany, the language and the country, and we drop them by parachute behind enemy lines —'

'Back to Germany?' Levi's tone reflected his shock and disbelief.

'Yes. Back to Germany. Back to Berlin. In uniform. Nazi uniform. Impersonating a Nazi officer and infiltrating their headquarters.'

Levi opened his mouth, but was genuinely speechless.

'You won't be sent in until you're ready. You get commando training in armed and unarmed combat, then you get tradecraft and security and some specialist skills depending on your mission, Morse code, parachute, demolition. By the time you are given a credible back-story and dropped on the outskirts of Berlin, you will be a fighting machine.'

He couldn't help it, he laughed. 'Me? A fighting machine? Who ... who am I supposed to fight?'

'No one. You are supposed to play the piano, as brilliantly as we know you can. And keep your eyes and ears open. Your musical skill will bring you to the attention of the generals, maybe even Hitler. He loves listening to music. Our intelligence tells us he is confiscating musical instruments from the cities they conquer and taking them back to Berlin. You report back on everything you overhear, and you stay ready to act when we tell you to. You won't be alone, there are others already in place.'

Levi looked at the ground, wondering how far he could push. What would they say if they knew his secret? A smile twitched at the corners of his mouth. *Do you really know what you're getting, gentlemen?* Did he want to help the English to defeat his own country, maybe contribute to the death of fellow Germans? It would mean leaving the safety of the camp and, probably, never seeing Pierre again. But, my G-d, what an adventure!

'And ... if you manage to find your family, boy, if they are still in Berlin, we will do our best to get them out and bring them here.'

Slowly Levi raised his head and looked at them. His face was slightly flushed and his eyes were glistening. He blinked.

'Then you have yourself a spy,' he said.

CHAPTER SIX

The National Archives
Kew, London

September 2017

The National Archives was an imposing construction of concrete, glass, fountains and water. The group of five walked at Simon Horowitz's slow pace across the forecourt and through the main doorway. David went up to the desk.

Cindy looked at Simon, who was bent over his stick. 'Are you tired, Poppa? Would you like a wheelchair?'

Simon raised himself up and looked around him. 'Let's ask him how far we have to walk. If it's a long way, I'll say yes.'

A tall man in an army uniform came through a door and strode towards them. David stepped forward and extended his hand. 'Major Stratton?'

The man grasped his hand with a firm shake. 'Mr Horowitz? I'm Major Richard Stratton. Pleased to meet you.'

'This is my father, Simon Horowitz, my wife Cindy, my son Daniel and my second cousin Dr Kobi Voight. Kobi's grandmother, Rachel, was my aunt.'

Cindy asked the major how far they had to walk and would it be okay to get Mr Horowitz Senior a wheelchair?

He agreed, left them for a moment and came back with one. Simon sank into it gratefully, and Cindy grasped the handles. The major led them to a lift and then down a corridor to his office. It was organised, neat and totally bereft of anything personal. At one end was a door through to another room, with chairs and a sofa pointing towards an impressive wall-mounted television set. The major indicated that they were to go through and take a seat in the next room, then stood in front of the screen and faced them.

'This recording,' he said, his expression sombre and his voice deep and resonating, 'had, literally, been forgotten among the thousands here.'

'When was it made?' asked Kobi.

'In 1945, here in London. These men and women gave great service to our country and risked their lives daily. Most did not return — they gave their lives for our war effort — but those who did were debriefed and the sessions were filmed. Some years ago the tapes were digitised to ensure they survived and then re-shelved.'

'Return from where?' Simon asked.

The major hesitated. 'Levi explains it so well, I shall leave it to him.'

Cindy squeezed Simon's hand. 'You are absolutely sure you want to see this? It's not too late to change your mind.'

He smiled at her and turned back to the major. 'I know what my brother told me about his war and it wasn't much. For decades he just said that my war was much harder. I was in Dachau. And he felt ashamed to compare his experiences to mine. That was his way, he was always putting himself down. Now I want to know the truth.'

Major Stratton sat behind them and watched as they absorbed the story. They were all transfixed, occasionally one or other of them gave a gasp of shock or a giggle of recognition. These were Levi's family, the people who had loved him all their lives. He'd died nearly three years earlier in Vermont at the grand age of ninety-five and, unbelievably, it appeared they didn't know the truth about his war. Stratton was about to change all that. He recognised that they were what stood between him and using this story for publicity.

The sofa was occupied by the two he suspected had the strongest opinions of the group. Simon Horowitz, Levi's younger brother, had survived five years in Dachau, then lived for decades as an American banker. Next to him was his daughter-in-law, Cindy, a striking blonde who looked like she didn't miss a thing and watched over the old man like a gaoler.

The leader was her husband, David, Simon's only child. He was the peacemaker and looked the most like Levi, his Feter (uncle). David and Cindy Horowitz's son, Daniel, was a handsome young man in his early twenties and a virtuoso violinist. Stratton's research had revealed that the family had lost a 1742 Guarneri del Gesú violin during the war, looted by the Nazis, and reclaimed it in 2008 so that Daniel could play it.

Dr Kobi Voight was an Australian art historian. His mother, Elizabeth, had been born to Simon's younger sister, Rachel, in 1942. Rachel had been a member of the famed Red Orchestra resistance network in Berlin and had died in Auschwitz. Her daughter had been raised by a Lutheran couple who'd immigrated to Australia in 1950, and she'd been unaware of her true heritage until quite recently.

The family was a collection of astounding stories of survival, courage and sacrifice, even before you added Levi's true history to their own. They were determined and stubborn and held onto their heritage. What would they say about making this new chapter of bravery public?

He let the video run until it reached the moment Levi accepted the role with the Special Operations Executive. He froze it and walked between them and the screen.

'I suggest we pause there for a moment. You need to take breaks in order to absorb it all, and there is more than you can see in one day,' he said.

'He never told us about these people, not Mr Teyve Liebermann, nor Margot and Fred, nor Pierre.' It was David who broke the silence.

Simon was frowning and rotating his empty cup between his hands. 'Papa had told us Levi was going to Switzerland and then to London. I think I assumed that was what happened and I don't think I actually asked him, but I'm sure he always said Switzerland. He told me about the Gestapo officer and that the gun had jammed and he'd fought back and escaped, but the rest ...' His voice trailed off.

'I wonder if Mr Liebermann had children, if he has descendants,' David mused, more to himself than anyone else.

The major nodded. 'I believe the shops are still owned and run by the family, his grandsons now. There are branches in several cities,' he said.

'I'd love to find out if they know about Levi. If his gift of the diamond helped to establish the stores,' said Cindy.

'Easy enough to find out,' David said. 'We just need to google the company and find out who runs it.'

She looked down at her hand and then smiled at Simon. 'Well, I know where one of the diamonds went. And I have always treasured it,' she said.

Simon smiled at David. 'One for your mother and another for your wife. That was the deal Levi and I struck.'

'G-d bless him,' said David.

'And I feel privileged to have them both,' Cindy said. She squeezed Simon's hand.

'Poppa, did you know?' Daniel asked suddenly.

'What? Did I know what?'

'About ... the men.'

'That Levi had slept with men? No, not for sure, but I suspected he might have. As far as I know, after the war he was celibate.'

Kobi spoke for the first time. 'Why?' he asked sharply.

Simon shrugged. 'It wasn't like today. Everyone just accepts it today. As they should. When Levi was young it was against the law. We grew up relatively conservatively, but for the last twenty years we were Reform Jews. He was pleased about that.'

Kobi stood up. 'Excuse me, Major, where is the nearest bathroom?' he asked.

'Last door on the right, end of the corridor,' the major said.

Kobi took the lift to the ground floor and headed out the door to the serene quiet of the pool and fountain. He sat down heavily on the edge of the concrete rim. His brain was spinning and he felt slightly sick. *So, Feter Levi, why didn't you tell me? Why didn't I ask you?*

The events in Berlin in July 2014 had made their way to the front of Kobi's memory. George Ross, the English investment fund manager who'd shared Kobi's passion for Dürer and explored the city with him. When it came to the point, whether to make the relationship physical, Kobi had made his excuses and run away. He could still hear George accusing him of being a boring old tease and sticking his head in books while life passed him by. At the time all he'd felt was relief ... but now the idea of seventy years of celibacy just seemed terribly sad. *Were you too cautious, Feter Levi, or were you lazy? Was it too much work? Who had you lost? Was the pain too great?*

'Thought I might find you here.'

He turned to see David sit down beside him.

'Sorry. I suppose you want to get on with the film —'

'No, it's okay. Everyone's recovering from Feter Levi's shocking revelations. Wonder what the army thought in 1945 when they heard that bit?'

'Whatever he did for them, he'd already done it, so they couldn't stand him down.'

There was a long moment of silence.

'Does it upset you?' David asked.

Kobi sighed. 'I needed a moment. No, it doesn't upset me. I wish to G-d I'd asked him and talked to him about it.'

David glanced at him. 'Why?'

'Because ... I don't like to think of him being lonely and not able to be true to his real self. And he kept so much inside. I'm just being sentimental.'

'Don't for a moment think you're the only one who wishes for a chance to talk to him about things ... which he ought to have been told. This family is riddled with secrets,' David said sadly.

'Is that supposed to make me feel better?' Kobi asked.

'It might, or at least not so alone.'

Kobi stood up. 'Let's go back,' he said, his voice brittle. 'They'll want to get on with it.'

David hauled himself up to his considerable height. 'Okay, if you're ready.'

CHAPTER SEVEN

SOS Training Base
The moors

October 1940

When Levi told his trainers about what had happened in the hut on the Danish border, they told him he had a strong inbuilt survival instinct. Most people had it, but not everyone could access it. This was a good thing; they could use it to create a person who reacted instinctually to dangerous situations. On his second day, they loaded his backpack with heavy kit and sent him running over the rough ground for miles.

'You have an hour to make it to this mark and back.'

He stared at the man in army uniform. 'And if I don't make it in an hour?' he asked.

'You do it again. Stop whining and … go!'

Halfway there, he stopped and vomited his breakfast onto the rough grass. He was tall and athletic and had always loved the sense of freedom running gave him, but this pace was relentless. The desire to finish inside the time drove him on and he made it by three minutes.

'You will do this every day until you can do it easily inside half an hour.'

As he mastered each skill, another was added. A week in, they'd put a pistol into his hand and taught him to stand properly and aim. It felt cold and heavy, and his first desire was to throw it aside.

'It will kick back and rise when you fire it, so you need to compensate for that.'

His hands were long and elegant and he found holding the gun came naturally. He practised and practised until he could hit a tin can in a tree at a hundred yards.

At night he lay in the bunk and thought about Pierre and life in the camp. How betrayed had Pierre felt? Once again he'd reached out and once again the object of his affection had been wrenched away.

And Levi turned his decision over and over in his mind. This wasn't something he had to do. He could have said, 'No, thank you, choose someone else.' Presumably they would have allowed him to stay in the camp, attending lectures, playing the piano, and enjoying his friendships.

So why had he embarked on this dangerous course, one that could, even most probably would, cost him his life? The local newspapers were full of the war, what was Hitler planning and what might happen if he invaded Britain. Levi had close-up, first-hand experience of living under the Nazi regime, and he knew that these people had no idea of what it would be like. The Jews he'd met in England reminded him of his family and friends prior to 1933, confident, smug and completely at ease with their life. A Nazi invasion would shatter their complacency. If his actions could change just one tiny sliver of history, make it harder for the Nazis for one minute, then it was worth it. Besides, the Special Ops men had promised that if he could find his family they would do their best to bring them to England. Did he trust these people with their smooth words? Not for a moment, but if he found his family then maybe *he* could smuggle them out. And what his spy masters wanted of him wasn't so much for the now, it was for the future. He wanted to be able to say that when he was given his chance to change the course of history, he took it.

A month into his training the hand-to-hand combat began.

'Today we begin one of the hardest aspects of what you have to learn. How to kill another human being, silently, efficiently and without hesitation.'

Levi didn't know what to say, so he nodded. The man he'd come to know as Harry, with no surname, was standing in front of him. Between them was a half-body mannequin. Harry picked it up and held it out towards Levi.

'Take this.'

Levi did as he was told.

'You approach him from behind and put your arm around his throat and then you twist his neck to the left until you hear his neck snap. Try it.'

Levi grasped the body with his left hand and twisted with his right.

'Further, man, harder!'

Eventually he heard the sharp crack.

'You will practise this until you can do it without having to think about how hard and how far to twist.'

After that came the lessons in pulling out a flick-knife and slitting a man's throat, from side to side, with enough pressure to cut the artery. He spent hours fighting with Harry on a bare patch of earth. Harry taught him how to punch effectively, how to thrust his knee and find the groin, and how to use his body to flip and lever another to the ground.

'Why are you doing this?'

The voice was sharp and sounded angry.

'Because ... I —'

'Not fast enough! I need an answer. Why are you doing this?'

Levi peered into the bright light that shone into his eyes, but he could see nothing of the figure seated across the table.

'To be part of the war effort.'

'What part? What war effort?'

'Fighting Hitler, defeating Germany.'

'But you are German!'

He sighed. 'I am from a Germany that doesn't exist anymore. The Germany I know doesn't imprison and murder her own innocent citizens.'

'So you don't believe in the ideals of the Nazi party?'

'No!'

The light switched off to reveal an army officer. 'Well we need to change that. We need to make you a loyal and proud Nazi supporter,' he said.

* * *

Part of everyday was spent studying photos of the German high command and learning their names and back-stories. His handlers flung taunts in his face about Jews. These he was used to; however, now he needed to learn not only to listen to them impassively but to actively join in. And he practised the piano, learning the music of Richard Wagner, a fervent anti-Semite who his father had banned, and who was a favourite of Hitler's.

One of the more embarrassing issues they needed to address was the fact that Levi was circumcised. His handlers told him that most German men, who were not Jewish or Muslim, were not circumcised, and the Nazis used this as a way of 'exposing' men who didn't look Jewish. Their answer would be to supply him with a letter from an authentic German doctor, stating he'd suffered from phimosis as a boy. It was a condition where the foreskin of the penis became very tight and could not be retracted, and circumcision was the most common cure. The letter would be on his records, but that wouldn't save him if he needed to explain his circumcision under interrogation. It was imperative he kept the letter with him and didn't lose it: his life could depend on it.

As the weeks passed he felt himself changing, hardening. The lessons were not easy to learn, and many went against his basic character. He spent nights weeping into his pillow and wishing he was home in Berlin. Until one day that stopped. One day he realised that if he didn't embrace this new persona and the skills he would need, he simply wouldn't survive. From that day on he started to become what they needed him to become, a trained assassin and spy.

Berlin, December 1940

Three months later Levi was parachuted into Poland, to lend credibility to his back-story of having come from the Eastern front. He stepped off a train from Warsaw at the Berlin Hauptbahnhof, clutching a brown leather suitcase in his right hand. He wore the dress uniform of his new identity, Hauptmann Werner Schneider. British intelligence had created a rock-solid cover for him, and the relevant documentation had been inserted into German records. He was born in Cologne on 25 June 1919 and his father was an army officer still serving on the Eastern front, his mother a housewife. He had an elder sister, Lisle, who was married to a non-enlisted officer fighting in France, and a younger brother, Hans, who was in the Hitler Youth and was still at school.

Werner was a Hauptmann, or captain, in the German Luftwaffe, the air force. The equivalent rank in the RAF was flight lieutenant.

His record showed he was twenty-three, six foot one inches tall, Lutheran, spoke German, English, French and some Italian, loved to read and was accomplished at chess, played the piano expertly and was an experienced pilot. One of moles in the German Luftwaffe HQ had placed his file before a senior official in the propaganda office and suggested he would be a useful addition to the Berlin staff. So here he was, on a cold December day, waiting for a staff car to take him to his new quarters in his old home town. As he stood on the platform and listened, he let his brain become accustomed to hearing a barrage of German again, some of it humourous and conversational, some of it barked briskly, and still more as a shouted command. His eyes darted from left to right and the scene sunk in: uniforms both military and Nazi, older men in suits and hats, plain black dresses and coats on the women, stacks of luggage and no porters, very few children. People exchanging salutes and hurried greetings. There was something different about the place, an unspoken sombre, desperate atmosphere. It was a city on edge, a city at war.

The needles of driving heat stung as they bounced off his skin. He rotated his body under the steady stream of invigorating water. His arms and legs were muscular and strong after the unrelenting training, his hair was very short and his eyes had a coldness his family would not have recognised. On the bed lay his military uniform — white shirt, grey tie, brown belt, grey wool jacket and trousers, and black cap. The jacket shoulders carried the Hauptmann insignia, with its two stars. An iron cross on a ribbon lay beside the shirt, ready to be fastened at his throat.

The first time he'd tried the uniform on it had made him physically sick to see himself in the mirror. There were few things he now loathed more than a Nazi, a military puppet of this repugnant regime, and the thought of dressing up as one was beyond repulsive.

But the trainers had done their work well. They'd taunted him with cutting and crude words about Jews until his non-reaction became second nature and he joined in the jests. They'd taught him to press his fingernails into the palms of his hands to distract his brain when he felt fear or revulsion. Finally they'd put him in the cockpit of a captured

Messerschmitt Bf 109 and taught him to fly. He wouldn't survive in aerial combat, but if he had to prove he was a pilot or have a detailed conversation about flying, he could do that.

It had all come to this. His first morning in Berlin as Hauptmann Werner Schneider. In ninety minutes' time he would report for duty in the propaganda ministry and start translating English news reports. And if his training was sufficient and he kept his wits about him, he'd survive.

His hand reached for the tap and he turned the water off. The bathroom was cold and stark, and he shivered as he grasped for the thin towel. He rubbed the steam off the small mirror and extended his right arm into the air with a straightened hand.

'Heil Hitler!'

The words echoed through the silence. He sighed and began to rub himself down.

'Hauptmann Werner Schneider, sir.'

Joseph Goebbels looked up from the book he was reading. The tall man stood beside Goebbels' secretary, his cap under his arm. Goebbels sighed and extended his arm. 'Heil Hitler.'

The young man reciprocated, clicking his heels together.'Heil Hitler. It is an honour to meet you, Reich Minister.'

Goebbels had a narrow face with sharp features, large dark eyes and a high forehead. His lips were thin and seemed set in a perpetual snarl, as if he rarely smiled. On his right arm, above his elbow, he wore a black band with the swastika in a white circle. He studied the Hauptmann.

'Brunhilde tells me you play the piano, is this true?' he asked lazily. It was the resonant voice Levi had heard on public radios and on propaganda films in the years leading up to his flight to England. He was swamped by the sudden memory of the book-burning his father had taken him to in May 1933. They'd been close enough to see Goebbels standing behind the microphone on a podium draped with a Nazi flag. The burning of books had distressed his father deeply, and when the Reich Minister had started to rant about the trash and filth of the Jewish literati, Benjamin had taken his family home. Levi remembered his parents scoffing at the little pervert with the club foot and jug ears who seemed to be in charge of what the people of Germany believed. What would they say if they could see their eldest son now, he wondered?

'Yes, Reich Minister.'

'Good. We have social evenings, you can play for us sometimes. And you speak some foreign languages?'

'Yes, Reich Minister — English, French and some Italian.'

'Where did you learn to do that?' Goebbels frowned at him, and Levi thought he sensed a whiff of suspicion.

'I am musical and I have an ear for languages. My parents paid for me to have lessons, as extra learning, when I was at school. I was going to go to university and study languages, but I joined the Luftwaffe instead. I wanted to defend my country.'

Goebbels nodded and waved a hand towards the door. 'Very good. Brunhilde will show you to your desk.'

It was a dismissal and Levi was grateful for it.

* * *

His desk was in a small office all of his own. This surprised him; he had not expected such privacy. The relief that he'd have his own place to retreat to made him feel guilty — this was not what he was here to do. If he was to overhear conversations he would need to find excuses to mingle with the others in the department.

On his desk was a stack of newspapers that he recognised immediately. English dailies.

'Read these and translate anything that is significant into German,' Brunhilde told him.

He sat down in the chair behind the desk. The secretary scowled at him.

'Don't get too comfortable, if we get short of pilots you will find yourself back over the skies of the enemy.'

With that she turned and left, shutting the door behind her. Levi pulled the first paper from the pile. It was only six days old. *The Times*. It felt like a familiar friend, and he smiled as he started to read. So far, so good.

Levi lived in a studio apartment on the top floor of a large complex in Mitte, the centre of the city. He was surrounded by other officers. They ate together in a hall on the ground floor. It was one of the few opportunities he had to read the men around him. His training had taught him to be alert to any signs of discontent, a stray word or expression that could indicate a person who shared his hidden sympathies. But he learned quickly that the men were guarded and hard to read.

He had handed his ration book into the kitchen, as instructed, on his first day. According to the book he was allowed a pound of meat a day, but he knew that some of that

went to barter for products from the occupied countries —
cheese, fresh eggs and chocolate. The food on his plate was
from a typically German diet, dark rye bread, potatoes,
pork, sauerkraut, spaetzle, soup, rice or tinned fish. Dinner
was accompanied by a small stein of beer. His training had
finished what life in the internment camp had begun, helping
him to ignore the kosher rules he'd grown up with, but it still
felt strange. Any behaviour that looked even vaguely Jewish
was dangerous, and he found it hard now to remember
passages from the Torah that had been deeply engrained in
his consciousness.

He glanced around at the other heads bent over their
plates, engrossed in their food, and said a silent prayer to his
G-d.

'Forgive me for these transgressions, they are done in the
quest of a higher goal, as my forefathers have done in
the ancient of days,' he prayed and then attacked the food
with gusto.

It became a routine, sleeping on the narrow single
bed, showering, and dressing in the hated uniform, eating
breakfast and discussing the war with his fellow officers, and
then walking to the propaganda ministry. His day was full of
reading English newspapers. It kept him in touch with what
was happening in his adopted country, and it helped him to
believe that there would be an end to the madness that had
engulfed his homeland.

He felt guilty about how easily he'd followed the command
of his trainers and taken up smoking. Most of the other
officers smoked cigarettes, and it was a convenient way of
striking up a conversation. Without even trying he'd begun

to enjoy the habit, although at the back of his mind he could sense his parents' disapproval.

In the last days of his training they had addressed him only as 'Werner', and he knew that any hesitation in answering to that name could cost him his life. But would he ever *think* like Werner? He could live this life, sleep, eat and talk this life, but somewhere deep inside he rejected Hauptmann Werner Schneider. He was Levi Horowitz and he was a Jew. That knowledge would keep him sane.

Three weeks later, Levi was told his presence would be required that evening at the home of Count and Countess von Engel, Nazi party stalwarts who lived in the southern outskirts of Berlin, in Wannsee. A staff car would call for him at 6 pm promptly. He made sure his uniform was pressed, everything that could shine was gleaming, and he could see his face in his shoes.

His anticipation and nerves grew as the car chewed up the miles to the villa. He went over the well-rehearsed plan in his head. This was where Werner, the loyal Hauptmann, and Levi, the Jewish classical pianist, finally came together. His thoughts raced and he counted slowly to ten, breathing in and breathing out methodically.

'Be with me,' he prayed, 'keep my fingers nimble and my ears and eyes open to anything that will help to end this hell.'

They arrived at a substantial home, lit with golden light, on snow-covered lawn that cascaded gently down to a reed bank around a deep lake. Graceful swans paddled in unison across the ruffled water. Tall trees shuddered and shook in the wind, making a significant amount of noise. He thanked the driver and knocked on the servants' entrance door, stamping his feet while he waited for it to be answered.

The salon reminded him of the music room in his family home. At one end was a large Steinway grand piano and at the other was a marble fireplace, with a dancing orange blaze throwing out fierce heat. The walls were covered in silk paper, decorated in gold and green peacocks. There were several chairs and three sofas grouped in conversational circles around long coffee tables. It was obvious that the music was to be background entertainment rather than a recital. That was a relief to Levi. He hadn't played the piano since his training regime, and it would be good to get back to it without being the centre of attention.

Countess von Engel approached him as he was examining the keys. 'It was tuned just last week,' she said.

He turned and saluted her. 'Heil Hitler, Countess.'

She waved a hand in his direction. 'Yes, yes. Everyone will gather here after supper for coffee and pastries. What can you play for us, Hauptmann?'

Levi hesitated. 'What would you like, Countess? Chopin, Bach, Beethoven, Mozart, Liszt, Debussy, Brahms ... and I can play jazz.'

The countess smiled at him. She allowed genuine warmth into her expression, which perhaps explained the character lines developing around her eyes and mouth.

'I think some of our guests would object to jazz. The Führer calls it alien music,' she said. She leaned in closer and lowered her voice. 'Although, between you and me, Hauptmann, I have no doubt it is played in some of the cabarets, clubs and bars that many of our guests frequent. As far as the classical composers ... well, you know you can't play Mendelssohn, he was a Jew. Did you know Mozart had a Jewish librettist and of course, Handel used Old Testament texts for his Oratorios?'

He could feel himself returning her smile. She had the most wonderful cornflower-blue eyes and they twinkled in fun as she ran her elegant hand over the top of the piano. The rings on her fingers glistened in the candlelight.

'Wagner would be fine. Do you know the Horst Wessel song?'

He frowned and shook his head. 'No, Countess. I'm sorry, I don't.'

'Oh, thank goodness, it is absolutely awful! It's all about a young Nazi lad murdered by a thuggish gang of communists. I ask you, what kind of subject is that for music?'

He couldn't help but laugh. 'I'll try and stick to the German composers and if anyone objects to a piece I can stop playing it.'

She patted him on the arm. 'Good boy, have a little practice and we'll see you later.'

They filed in with glasses in hand, conversation tinkling like wind chimes. The women wore simple gowns in silks and velvets, while most of the men were in military or Nazi uniform. The countess came over to the piano.

'And here we are, young Hauptmann. What will you start with?' she asked.

'Perhaps a little Chopin?'

'Excellent.'

She clapped her hands loudly until the crowd of around twenty-five stopped talking and turned towards her.

'There is coffee on the sideboard and a selection of pastries, German-made I assure you, nothing French about them. And this is Hauptmann Werner Schneider from the propaganda ministry. Thank you, Joseph, for lending him to us.'

She gestured to Goebbels, who gave an uncomfortable nod in return.

'He comes highly recommended, so spare an ear for his playing,' she added.

Levi launched his right hand into the opening notes of the *Minute Waltz*. His fingers flew over the keys and the melody spilled out. It felt so good to be playing for an audience again! The piano had a wonderful rich tone and the crowd stood watching, hypnotised by the speed and the sound, until he finished one minute and forty seconds later. Spontaneous applause rang out around the room. He stood up and gave a small embarrassed bow, then sat down again.

Next was Beethoven's *Für Elise*, another well-known piece, then into the *Moonlight Sonata* first movement and Mozart's *Turkish March*. The countess stood off to one side and watched her guests mesmerised faces with a sense of triumph. It wasn't easy to find a new musical sensation with so many men being drafted into the armed forces or leaving the city for exile overseas, and this discovery would bring pleasure to the military elite and reflect well on both the count and herself. Her husband appeared at her elbow and whispered in her ear.

'We must get him to play for the Führer. Adolf will be delighted by him,' he said.

She nodded and put her finger to her lips. 'Shhh, I don't want to miss a note.'

When he came to end of the *Turkish March* a woman stepped out of her group and raised her coffee cup.

'Superb. Could I make a request?' She asked.

Levi smiled at her. 'Certainly, if I know it, it would be my pleasure.'

'Franz Liszt's *Hungarian Rhapsody Number Two*.'

Levi raised his eyebrows. 'I can see you want to test me. Let me see if I can remember it. I have to confess it is a long time since I've attempted this piece.'

But it was like riding a bicycle down the tree-lined street of his childhood. In an instant he was lost in the low, powerful notes, followed by the intricate runs for the next seven minutes. As he hit the last chord a huge roar of applause filled the room. Again he stood up and gave a self-conscious bow. The countess approached the piano.

'You are far too good for background music, Hauptmann. You will be the talk of Berlin by tomorrow morning.'

He couldn't help his stricken look. 'Oh, I hope not, Countess. I'm not very good at being the centre of attention.'

She laughed. 'Well you should be less talented then —'

'Countess, please introduce me to your new discovery.'

The speaker was a short man in military uniform, wearing the rank of Reichsführer, with rimless glasses, cold eyes and a small moustache. The countess stepped back to allow him to come closer. In person he looked more sinister than the photos Levi had been shown by his trainers.

'Reichsführer Himmler, this is Hauptmann Werner Schneider. And Hauptmann Schneider, this is the brilliant Reichsführer Heinrich Himmler. He is the head of the SS and is the genius behind the Aryanisation of Poland.'

Himmler gave a small nod in her direction.

Levi thrust his right arm in the air. 'Heil Hitler, Reichsführer,' he said. He was acting on pure instinct. It was for moments such as these that his coaching had prepared him, he realised. An icy wave spread through his gut, something between nausea and the desire to rip the man's throat out.

Himmler returned the salute.

'Heil Hitler, Hauptmann. Your playing is exquisite. I shall be telling the Führer about you tomorrow and you can expect a summons.'

Levi used every ounce of self-control to give Himmler a small smile. 'The honour would be great, Reichsführer.'

Himmler nodded in satisfaction. 'A word of advice, practise your Wagner. The Führer loves his Wagner.'

With that he turned on his heel and walked away.

'He's a strange man,' the countess murmured almost under her breath, 'but immensely powerful. He believes in homoeopathy and herbs. He told me all women should eat raw garlic. Between you and I, my husband suspects he's a complete crackpot, but you should cultivate his patronage.'

Levi wanted to shudder, but instead he smiled. 'Thank you, Countess, your patronage is all I desire.'

A slight blush rose in her very fair cheeks. 'Why Hauptmann Schneider, I do believe you might be flirting with me.'

Levi bent his head. 'Guilty as charged. I'm afraid I shall have to hide my true purpose.'

CHAPTER EIGHT

Berlin

Christmas 1940

Levi played at two gatherings at the von Engels' home before Christmas, but the Führer was nowhere to be seen. He did his day job as diligently as he could, and waited for people to trust him enough to speak their true feelings about the war. However there was a pervading sense of paranoia, mistrust and fear, which was, in itself, something he knew would interest his spy masters.

The von Engels invited him to spend Christmas with them. He arrived by staff car in time for the Christmas Eve tradition of dressing the enormous pine tree with ribbons, wooden ornaments and candles. Then the family and their invited house guests sat around the magnificent fire in the salon, drinking mulled wine and eating spiced cookies, and exchanged gifts. He'd taken Reich Minister Goebbels' advice and bought a small bottle of French perfume for the countess, a copy of *Mein Kampf* bound in leather for the count, and a whole wheel of cheese from the black market for the kitchen. His presents met with much delight, and he received a pair of wool-lined leather gloves and a bottle of Cognac in return.

The food amazed him. Christmas breakfast was a selection of cold meat and salmon, cheese, fruit, boiled eggs and bread rolls. He wanted to ask if there really was a war on, but held his tongue. The Lutheran church service was a minefield, but he followed the people around him and stood, knelt and repeated the phrases in the book when they did. They stopped on the way home for a snowball fight, then he played the piano and they all joined in, singing carols and favourite songs. Silently he thanked the foresight of his trainer who had taught him some Christian carols, just in case. It was the small details like that which could have blown his cover.

At lunch he was seated next to SS-Hauptsturmführer Erik von Engel, a nephew of Count von Engel. Erik held the corresponding rank to Levi's cover, but was in the Waffen-SS and worked in the office of Himmler. He was four months older than Levi, six foot, muscular, blond and blue-eyed, a poster boy for the German Volk. In spite of himself Levi quite liked the man. He had a quick wit and a ready smile.

Over glasses of wine, a plate of roast goose, bread dumplings, red cabbage, fried potatoes and an apple-and-sausage stuffing that Levi could have eaten until he popped, the two men talked about their families. Erik's father was Count Engel's younger brother and lived on a farm on the outskirts of Munich. He'd been highly commended in World War One and had served in the North Atlantic from 1939 to January 1941, when he'd been injured in a firefight between his destroyer and a British freighter and had come home to recuperate. Levi could tell that Erik was proud of his work in the SS, but knew better than to discuss it at such an occasion. He made a mental note that this was the kind of friend

'Werner' would have. But not the kind of friend a Jew like Levi would have, so how far was he willing to go to fit into this new world? As he watched the charismatic, handsome young man holding forth about the victories of the Third Reich and the joys of life in Berlin, Levi felt as if this was an important decision. Erik's job was thoroughly repulsive, but the man himself, something about him, meant Werner simply couldn't look away.

On a bitterly cold day Saturday in early January, Levi felt confident enough in his assumed role to take a tram ride to the Brandenburg Gate. Between each column hung long red flags with white circles and black swastikas in their centres. On either side of the structure stood red towers, festooned with more flags. Levi looked at them for several minutes. He was suddenly engulfed by memories of family visits to the square and summer picnics in the Tiergarten. He could see his twin siblings on their roller skates trying not to bump into other people, and Simon, forever waiting for the promised trip to the luthier's shop off the Friedrichstrasse, and behaving like a sullen teenager.

Eventually he thrust his gloved hands deep into his coat pockets and trudged off towards the street they had called home. The house looked the same as ever from the outside, graceful and solid. It had seven bedrooms, large formal rooms and a warm, welcoming kitchen. Oh how he longed to be back in that kitchen, sitting at the table, drinking coffee with his parents and listening to his siblings squabble! Just seeing the familiar shape of the place was enough to bring tears to his eyes.

If they were still there they'd be returning from Shul soon, in a tight group, hurrying to get away from the anti-Semitic sentiment that emanated from the government and ruled the city. Levi was horrified by how far this hatred had spread and how intense it had become in his absence. Every day he saw examples, from Hitler Youth to soldiers and Nazi party officials, from the SS storm troopers to ordinary people who felt they had free rein to swear at, and spit upon, the Jews who ventured out onto the streets. On one occasion he'd witnessed soldiers who wanted to cut off the ear locks of male Orthodox Jews. The people who'd been their neighbours for years had happily supplied the scissors. It took every ounce of self-control to stay silent and pretend to be one of the persecutors, a kind of hell he hadn't been adequately prepared to suffer.

He stood across the road, his coat collar turned up and his cap pulled low over his eyes. But no one came in or out of the house. He was sorely tempted to walk up to the front door and knock. He could say he was looking for someone if a person other than his family ... but what if they were still there? It would break his mother's heart to see him in this uniform. The words of the men who'd recruited him rang in his ears. If he could find them, if they were still in Berlin —

Suddenly the large front door swung open. Levi took a sharp breath. A man in an army uniform stepped out and put his cap on. His jacket was covered in braid and medals, he was a high-ranking officer. A plump woman came to the door and kissed him on the cheek. They lived there. In his house. He was unprepared for the fury that rose up from deep within, a bitterness he could taste in his mouth, swiftly followed by the horror of what this meant. If his family were not here, where were they? It was more than he could bear, so he turned and walked back towards the tram stop.

He'd thought about visiting Maria Weiss, the gentile woman who'd taken him and Simon in on the night of the Kristallnacht. Maybe she would know something. If his family had been tossed out they could very well have gone to Maria for help. But it was too dangerous, for them both. She knew him to be a Jew and he knew her to be a sympathiser, and that simple knowledge could get them both shot.

As he walked, with his eyes downcast and his fists clenched in his pockets, he prayed for his family. Surely G-d would keep them safe until this hell was over and they could all be reunited again? Maybe the house was gone and with it all the possessions, but nothing mattered more than life and that they could start again. He thanked G-d for the jewellery waiting in Mr Dickenson's bank vault in London. His papa's foresight would mean there was something left to help them get back on their feet. No wonder there'd been no response to his letters.

Why had he not tried harder to contact them and persuade Papa to bring them to London? What had happened to them while he'd been safe and enjoying his London life? The questions came thick and fast, and they made him feel sick. Guilt, grief, fear and helplessness. His mind was a swirling muddle as he sat impassively on the tram, careful to give nothing away.

Berlin, February 1941

Levi was still processing the knowledge that his family had disappeared, and that it was too dangerous to try to track them down, when Joseph Goebbels paid a visit to his office. He was deep in the translation of an article on the siege of the city of Tobruk in Libya.

'Hauptmann Schneider.'

Levi looked up, saw who it was and jumped to his feet. 'Heil Hitler, Reich Minister.'

Goebbels returned the salute. 'Heil Hitler, Hauptmann. I have news. Tomorrow night you are to play at a gathering at my house which will be attended by the Führer himself.'

Levi felt his stomach heave. 'Thank you, Reich Minister. I feel deeply honoured.'

Goebbels nodded. 'He is looking forward to hearing you. A car will call for you at 6 pm. Be ready.'

'Yes, Reich Minister.'

But the man had already turned and walked away. Levi slumped down onto his chair. It was as his handlers had said, his piano skills had given him access to the highest ranks of the Nazi party. Now it was up to him to exploit this situation and work himself into a position where he could learn important information. Or, he could just play the piano.

Levi had spent the intervening hours preparing himself mentally for this moment. He knew what he had to portray, and he knew what he would probably feel. His training would do the rest. He was standing beside the piano when the group walked in. Hitler was in the centre, wearing a brown jacket with an iron cross embroidered on the left pocket and a red arm band with a swastika in a white circle above his elbow. He was surrounded by men in uniform. Levi carried the image of the man burned into his brain, medium height, slight build, dark hair parted on the side and the rectangular moustache on the top lip.

Hitler walked straight up to him. Levi saluted.

'Heil Hitler, Mein Führer!'

Hitler stared at him for a full minute. 'It is good to finally meet you, Hauptmann Schneider. I have heard much about your piano playing.'

The eyes were large and intensely blue, a clear blue, and they held Levi's gaze. Everything seemed to stop, everyone seemed to be waiting for him to respond. He was held by those eyes. Finally he gave a small bow.

'I am deeply honoured, Mein Führer, and I hope I live up to your expectations.'

Hitler waved towards the chairs in rows facing the piano. 'We will keep you from the keyboard no longer,' he said, and walked over to a seat in the centre of the room. The rest of the crowd followed and when he had settled, they sat down.

Levi started with *Fantasia for Piano in F Sharp Minor* by Wagner. It was a melancholy piece, filled with strident chords, and went for nearly fifteen minutes. At the end Hitler stood and applauded, so everyone else followed suit. Levi wasn't sure what to do, but felt he should acknowledge the response. He rose and gave a small bow.

Then for dramatic effect he went into Beethoven's *Fifth Symphony* and from there straight into the andante of Mozart's *Piano Concerto Number 21*, lush and melodic.

Once again the Führer responded with a standing ovation and the crowd followed his lead. Levi bowed again.

'Is there anything in particular you would like me to play, Mein Führer?' Levi asked.

Hitler smiled. 'I am fond of "Song to the Evening Star" from Tannhäuser, *Isolde*'s "Liebestod", and one always loves to hear "The Ride of the Valkyries". You know, I first heard Richard Wagner when I was twelve years old and I went to a production of *Lohengrin* in Linz. I was in the standing-room section of the theatre and I stood for the whole production. I was captivated. The man was a genius and he believed in the Volk. He understood the evil of the Jew.'

Levi nodded. 'I can play those pieces for you, Mein Führer, and also perhaps "Elsa's Bridal Procession"?'

Hitler beamed. 'You have pleased me exceedingly, Hauptmann Schneider.'

Levi caught the expression on the face of Goebbels as he sat back down. It was one of euphoria, almost ecstasy, at the fact that he had provided his Führer with someone who had pleased him exceedingly. Levi closed his mind to his furious thoughts and concentrated on playing the music. The long hours during his training had paid off and he could let the music flow from his fingers as if it were Chopin or Beethoven. One after another the Wagner compositions Hitler had requested filled the room. At the end of the set there was another standing ovation.

Hitler turned to Goebbels. 'I want the Hauptmann available to play for me whenever I require him,' he said.

'Of course Mein Führer, he will be on standby twenty-four hours a day.'

Hitler nodded. 'And increase his wages.'

'Of course, Mein Führer.'

Hitler walked up to Levi and extended his hand. It felt soft, but the handshake was firm enough. 'Thank you,

Hauptmann. You are a credit to the Volk, and your talent is a symbol of the purity of your race.'

Levi supressed a smile and looked into the hypnotic blue eyes. 'Thank you, Mein Führer. I shall never forget your words.'

'Naturally.'

Hitler turned and walked from the room, followed by the rest of his entourage.

Three hours later Levi was under the shower in his bathroom. He had a scrubbing brush in his hand and was rubbing his body with vigour. Somehow the hot water helped to wash away his guilt and disgust.

'Forgive me, Papa,' he whispered.

CHAPTER NINE

Berlin

March 1941

Levi's dead drop — for any information he wanted to send back to London — was a club on the Friedrichstrasse. He went there regularly with a group of men his own age, some from the propaganda ministry and some from the Luftwaffe. It was a dimly lit, smoky room with a bar, a dance floor and a small stage for bands to play live music.

If he had anything to report he went to the bar and ordered a straight whisky on the rocks, with five blocks of ice. Then exactly twenty minutes later he would excuse himself from the table of laughing men, several with women on their knees, all enveloped in a cloud of cigarette smoke. He would go to the men's room and take the last stall in the row. The back wall of the cubicles was brick, and the fourth brick from the cistern was loose. He would pull it out, place his package behind it and replace the brick. Then he'd use the toilet, flush, wash his hands and return to the table.

By March 1941 he'd used the drop twice, once before Christmas and once after. The second time he'd told his handlers about his new close friend. SS-Hauptsturmführer

Erik von Engel, the nephew of Count Engel, was the kind of colleague that Werner would cultivate, a man with an important job and a strong sense of party loyalty. More importantly, Erik was delighted by the work his boss, Himmler, was doing and his tongue could be loosened after a couple of steins of beer. Most specifically, Erik told Levi about his role in Poland in 1939.

'The Einsatzgruppen was such an efficient force,' he said. 'You know, the documentation says we eliminated sixty-five thousand undesirables. Now they call us death squads.'

Levi raised an eyebrow. 'Define undesirables,' he said.

Erik shrugged. 'Intellectuals, communists, Jews. We shot a lot of Jews. But some we rounded up and put into ghettos. Many wouldn't walk, so we dragged them along the ground. If they stumbled we hit them with rifle butts or kicked them. And they stood at the edge of pits, their hands in the air, and we shot them and covered their bodies with lime. Children were torn from their mothers and they screamed at the top of their lungs.'

Suddenly his face lost some of its colour and his eyes seemed empty. He looked away. 'I can still hear that terrible screaming, at night when I try to sleep. And the shouting of the guards, the gunfire, the dogs barking, such a conflagration of noise.'

Levi said nothing. But the flash of humanity surprised him, even touched him. He wondered how Erik would respond if Levi offered the opinion that he should listen to his conscience, that all human beings were the same, that they felt the same terror and shame. That a Jew was no more an undesirable than Erik was. But that was a viewpoint Levi would hold; Werner would not. Erik pulled himself up and leaned forward. 'I've got a special new job, Werner.'

Levi feigned nonchalance. 'I still pity you not working in propaganda,' he said. 'We shape the attitudes of the people. We determine what they read in the papers, what they hear on the radio, the films they see.'

Erik snorted. 'That's nothing. Reichsführer Himmler is brilliant. He has commissioned a whole plan for the East. It will take us a year of work just on the plan, but it will mean all the Baltic states and the Ukraine and Poland, they will all be resettled by Germans. Ten million Germans!'

'What about the people who currently live there?' Levi asked causally.

'Oh we'll send them further east, use them for slave labour, or starve them, whatever. They don't matter. It'll take twenty years, but just imagine, Werner, a group of countries that extends the German border over six hundred miles east! When he is ready to put it to the Führer he says that it will be met with much rejoicing. And I am going to be part of it!'

Levi decided this was information his handlers would want to hear so he visited the club, ordered his whisky and made the drop. Erik was in the group who were out socialising together, and Levi gave him an extra big smile as he sat down again. Three hours later they stumbled out into the spring night air. Some of the men had their arms around the shoulders of women who made their living sleeping with the officers. They shouted their goodbyes to each other and went their separate ways.

The evening was clear and crisp, so Levi decided he would walk down to the river and stroll its banks for a while. The streets were almost empty apart from soldiers and men in Nazi uniforms. During the daylight hours he often saw people combing the city for discarded food, and he knew that in the winter they'd be looking for wood to burn as fuel. A strong part of him wished he could take the unwanted food from his lodgings, which was sent to a pig farm in the country, and distribute it to the hungry on the streets, but he knew it was impossible. Behaviour such as that would bring unwanted attention and undermine his cover.

A young woman on a bicycle passed him, her head down and her feet pumping the pedals. He noticed the basket was full of sheets of paper. Was she out plastering the city walls with resistance posters, he wondered? The Gestapo were on the lookout for such individuals. Should he stop her, warn her, tell her not to be so stupid and to leave the resistance to those who could do something concrete to oppose this regime? Too late. He watched her disappearing figure and hoped she would stay safe.

He ambled on. There was a bright moon and the buildings and trees were clearly visible. The River Spree gleamed silver in the moonlight. He turned a corner to walk back towards town and almost bumped into a group of four soldiers, their arms around each other's shoulders, staggering back to their beds.

They hurriedly disentangled themselves, stepped aside and saluted. He returned the salute and was about to move off.

'Levi? Is that you? You're a Hauptmann?'

He froze. He swung round and recognised Rolf. The years fell away and he saw the eager childish face beaming at him, brown eyes glistening with mischief and hair sticking up on end. This grown-up version was horrified and confused. It was Levi's worst nightmare, someone who knew him.

He shook his head. 'I'm sorry, you have me confused with someone else. I am Hauptmann Werner Schneider,' he said briskly.

'What? Who? I'm … I'm sorry, I thought you were —'

The others pulled him away. Levi stood stock still and gazed at them as they disappeared up a street. When they were out of view he put his head down and walked briskly back along the river bank. The panic subsided, replaced by a quiet certainty. It was a huge city, with thousands of soldiers, the chances of running into Rolf again were negligible.

Ten minutes later a hand pulled hard at his jacket.

'Levi? It is you, isn't it?'

He turned. Rolf was on his own. Levi's heart sank. He smiled warmly at the man and opened his arms for a bear hug. Relief flooded over Rolf's face. They embraced. Levi pulled the flick-knife from his trouser pocket and in one swift movement he cut Rolf's throat. There was a short strangled cry, then the body slumped against him and he dropped it to the pavement. He knelt and took the watch from Rolf's wrist and the wallet from his uniform pocket and hurled them both into the river. Without looking back he dissolved into the shadows cast by the buildings and sprinted home.

* * *

His feet pounded the cobblestones and his breath came in ragged gasps. Somewhere deep in his stomach he could feel the vomit starting to rise. Acid flooded his mouth and he stopped long enough to empty his stomach onto the pavement beside a building. His hands trembled as he supported himself against the cold stone.

My G-d, what have I become? What have I done? This is a possibility I was trained for, but what am I? No better than Himmler and his death squads who have no respect for human life. Once again his stomach heaved and he coughed and wiped his mouth with the back of his sleeve. *Rolf was like a brother to me once. We planned our futures, we would go to university together, raise our families and be life-long friends. What was his crime? Nothing. He recognised an old friend and for that he had to die.* Tears sprung from his eyes as he pulled himself away and continued to run. He needed to put as much distance as he could between himself and this evil deed.

How will I live with this? Was it Werner who did this thing, or was it Levi? Can I even tell the difference anymore?

Berlin, November 1941

On 7 November, Levi was awoken by the sound of bombs exploding as they hit the ground. The sudden jangle of air-raid sirens pierced through the other noises and he leaped from his bed and pulled on his uniform. His freezing fingers wouldn't push the buttons through the holes and he cursed as he tugged on his huge winter coat.

The nearest shelter was a short jog down the road. His fellow officers were running with him, in various stages of undress.

'Damn the English,' one of them muttered as he drew level with Levi, 'damn them to hell.'

The shelter was cold, musty and very crowded. Babies were crying and people spoke in hushed whispers as the thuds continued above. Eventually the all-clear sounded and they went back to their beds. There was practically no damage to buildings in his area, but Levi could imagine the reaction of the Führer. He would want revenge.

Berlin, December 1941

'I shall eliminate the Soviet Union as a military power and exterminate the scourge on civilisation that is communism. I shall open up vast tracts of land for the German people where they can live in freedom and prosperity. And we will mine the ground that is so rich in natural resources, it shall all belong to the Third Reich.'

It was almost as though he was talking to himself. Levi sat very still and looked at the piano keys.

'Do you not think those are admirable goals, Hauptmann?' Hitler asked. They were alone. Levi had been playing the Führer's favourite pieces of Wagner for him. Hitler said it relaxed him and helped him to plan and strategise while he listened.

'I do indeed, Mein Führer, but I expect nothing less from your brilliant mind.'

Hitler sighed. 'True, but you know, it is a heavy burden to bear sometimes. Being the only one who sees the future with such clarity. My generals are all idiots — unless I tell them exactly what to do, they flap around like fish on a slab.'

Levi smiled. 'A very imaginative description, Mein Führer.'

'Why can't they all be as successful as Greece, Yugoslavia, and Crete?'

Levi wasn't sure whether he was supposed to answer these questions. At the forefront of his mind was the mercurial personality of the Führer, which could turn from companionable to enraged in an instant.

'Do you know about what happened on the beaches of France, Hauptmann?' Hitler asked.

It was always better to plead ignorance until you knew which tack the conversation was taking.

'No, Mein Führer,' he said.

'We had them pinned down, and we halted our advance. Not my order. I trusted FieldMarshall von Rundstedt, and the enemy escaped. We could have forced Britain to surrender ...' his voice trailed off.

Levi waited for a moment to make sure the Führer wasn't going to start again. 'I hear good things from the Eastern Front, Mein Führer.'

Hitler scowled. 'They think their counter-offensive will work. That bastard Stalin thinks he'll hold onto Moscow and Leningrad. Just wait till the summer: next year will be a glorious one for the armies of the Third Reich.'

'I read the newspapers of the English and they are scared. No matter what Churchill says publicly, Mein Führer, its plain they know they are no match for you,' Levi said.

Hitler smiled. 'I'm very glad to hear that, Hauptmann.'

Levi didn't answer. Instead he started to play Wagner's *Piano Sonata in A Flat*, very quietly. Hitler closed his eyes. When the piece was finished, he sat on the edge of his seat.

'I admire Wagner more than I can tell you. Did you know he wrote an essay on Judaism in music?'

Levi shook his head. 'No, I didn't know that, Mein Führer.'

Hitler nodded. 'I think about him when Reinhard is droning on about his final solution.'

Levi's hand shook momentarily. 'Final solution to what, Mein Führer?'

'The Jews. He has this plan, he's going to hold a meeting about it in Wannsee, or so he tells me. He knows I want to eliminate the Jews, rid the continent of their filthy presence, and he says his plan will kill eleven million. Well, I shall put Himmler in charge of actually doing it, Heinrich knows how to get things done. Reinhard has an iron heart and he is a master of killing, but Himmler is the man for this.'

Levi could feel his stomach churning and for one awful moment he thought he was going to be sick, but he took deep breaths, pressed his nails into his palms, and it passed. Hitler seemed to have forgotten he was there. He was murmuring about the plan to exterminate the sub-human races, as if to reassure himself. Finally he looked over at Levi and waved his hand.

'That is all for today, Hauptmann, you may go now. I'm tired.'

The National Archives
Kew, London, September 2017

There was a stunned silence in the room. Suddenly Cindy Horowitz burst into tears, covering her face with her hands.

Her husband, David, rose swiftly and went to her, pulled her to her feet and embraced her.

Simon made a strange choking noise in his throat. 'If I couldn't see him as he said all this, I would refuse to believe it,' he said softly.

'He was doing his duty, for his adopted country,' David said, his voice firm and resolute.

Simon looked up at him and shook his head. His dark eyes were full of pain and anger. 'No, David, didn't you hear him? He murdered Rolf! My brother, my gentle Levi, murdered his childhood friend. In cold blood. The man I knew wouldn't swat a fly!'

David frowned. 'He had no choice, Poppa. If Rolf had reported him he'd have been shot as a spy, or sent to a death camp as a Jew.'

Simon sighed. 'Sometimes it is hard to remember what those days were like.'

Daniel shifted in his seat. 'Aren't we forgetting something?' he asked quietly.

They all looked at him.

'What?' his father asked.

'Well ... he fooled them. Imagine that! He sat and played the piano for Hitler and no one knew he was a Jew! What would Hitler have said and thought and done if he'd known that he was talking about his plans to a Jew?'

Major Stratton stood up and walked in front of the screen.

'Daniel is absolutely right. What Levi managed, where his piano playing took him, is astounding,' he said.

'Did he sent that information back? Did it make any difference?' Kobi asked.

Major Stratton hesitated. 'That's a very good question. In recent years we have uncovered evidence that suggests some were aware of what was happening in the camps, but not the extent. The codebreakers at Bletchley Park had some idea about the horrors of the Eastern Front, and in 1942 there was a report from inside the Warsaw ghetto. Numbers, methods and quite detailed information, but it was ignored, I'm afraid to say, because the organisation that supplied it was a socialist one.'

'What could they have done, anyway?' David asked. 'Bombing the camps would have just killed more people. People like Poppa, who survived.'

'Exactly. Churchill did propose bombing Auschwitz, but he was overruled. In December 1942 the Allies issued a proclamation condemning the "extermination" of the Jewish people, but I can't tell you what happened to the information Levi sent back,' Stratton said.

'So he risked his life for nothing,' Cindy had a sob in her voice.

Stratton shook his head. 'Oh no, he went on to achieve much more than piano playing and listening, we've hardly begun the story. But I think, perhaps, that is enough for today. How do you feel about resuming tomorrow, Mr Horowitz?'

He was looking at David, who glanced at his father. Simon's expression was a mixture of bewilderment, grief and exhaustion. David nodded. 'If you're happy for us to come back tomorrow, I think we could all do with a rest,' he said.

'Of course. Can I organise a car to take you back to your hotel?' Stratton asked.

'I would be extremely grateful, thank you.'

Stratton smiled at him. 'It is the least we can do.'

CHAPTER TEN

Berlin

March 1942

The streets were running with blood. Thick and red it trickled between the cobbles and fanned out from the corpses. Levi ran from body to body. When he rolled them over each had their throat cut and each had the face of Rolf, the smile frozen in the rictus of death. The blood covered his hands and dripped from his fingers. He raised his head and cried out.

'May G-d forgive me, I am not a monster.'

Suddenly he jerked awake and sat bolt upright. Sweat ran down his face and he was shaking. It was yet another nightmare. He hesitated to go to sleep. Would he ever move on from that night?

Levi's world revolved around the newspapers, playing the piano, both at gatherings for leading Nazi officials and in private for the Führer, leaving information at the club for his British handlers and a growing friendship with Erik von Engel. In March, the young SS officer invited Levi to come home with him to Munich to meet his family for a week's leave. Reich Minister Goebbels reluctantly allowed him to go. He was a valuable asset and hadn't had a break from his work since his arrival in December 1940.

Erik's parents lived on a farm beyond the city. His father, Karl, had been an officer in the Navy. His wife, Elsa, had been a model and a cabaret singer before her marriage and was a stunningly beautiful woman. She was Karl's second wife and not Erik's mother, who'd died when he was ten.

On a warm spring day, Erik and Levi accepted Karl's advice and took a picnic into the fields. All around them the forest rose at the edge of the grass, dark and quiet. Erik lay on his back and watched the clouds skid across the sky. Levi sat beside him, his legs stretched out and a rye-bread sandwich in his hand.

'Have you read how well the war in the Pacific is going?' Erik asked. 'Japan occupies more territory every month and the Americans seem remarkably unprepared. I think they would make lazy sailors and soldiers.'

Levi nodded. 'I think the Führer is pleased. And the battle at Kerch really made him smile. Such a rout! It bodes well for the summer offensive in the Soviet Union. He believes we will defeat the communists by the end of the year.'

'Good job. Imagine a world with no communists and no Jews and millions of miles of land occupied by Germans.'

Levi munched on his sandwich. Erik sat up.

'Are you happy, Werner?'

Levi turned and looked at him. 'What do you mean by that?' he asked.

Erik's face was unusually inexpressive, but his colour was high, bright dots on his cheekbones, and his blue eyes looked innocently at Levi. 'I mean … Well, I've never seen you with a woman. When we go out to the clubs and cabarets, you leave on your own. Do you ever sleep with anyone? Have any fun?'

Levi hesitated. This was dangerous territory, perhaps the only thing he was unprepared for.

'I'm busy with my work and my music —'

'Are you homosexual?' Erik asked.

The question hung for a split second too long in the warm summer atmosphere. Levi looked down. He needed to deflect this discussion and get back to talk about the war. He needed to concentrate on why he had allowed this unlikely friendship to blossom. The idea of an intimate relationship with a man who'd murdered Jews should revolt him. He waited for that emotion to rise and smother this dangerous possibility.

'I think your reluctance to answer tells me what your words do not,' Erik said softly.

'Would it make a difference? Would you feel you had to report me?' Levi asked. 'And I'm not admitting to anything.'

Why did I ask that? Why didn't I just deny the question, the accusation? What am I doing?

Very slowly Erik leaned over and kissed him softly on the lips. The shock of reaction was familiar, if almost forgotten. Levi pulled away.

Erik smiled at him. 'What are you afraid of?' he asked.

'Your father —'

'Is busy in his office.'

Once again Erik leaned further towards Levi and kissed him. It took Levi a moment to respond. The roaring in his head blocked out all the warning bells as he kissed Erik back.

As Erik moved closer towards him he held up a hand, palming facing outwards.

'What?' Erik asked, frowning in bewilderment.

'There's something I have to tell you. You might get the wrong idea.'

Levi rubbed his mouth with the back of his hand.

'You don't want me?' he asked.

Levi shook his head.

'No, not that. I … I had a condition, when I was a child. And I'm …' his voice trailed off.

Erik shrugged. 'What? You're impotent?'

Levi gave a half laugh. 'No! Nothing like that. I'm circumcised. It wasn't, well my parents, they had no choice.'

Erik smiled and put his hand up to touch Levi's cheek.

'Did you think I might suspect you were a Jew?'

Levi nodded. 'I wasn't sure what you'd think. I just didn't want you to get the wrong idea about me.'

Now Levi had a much more dangerous line to walk. As if he wasn't at risk enough, he'd added a sexual relationship that would, if it was uncovered, have them both sent to a concentration camp. How could he contemplate having feelings for this man, a death squad member? And if love was incomprehensible, was lust irresponsible? The potential for him to sleep-talk, betray something from his subconscious mind, was suddenly a dangerous reality and one he had no way to counter. Levi looked at himself in the mirror.

I'm a Jew and a homosexual and I'm wearing a German military uniform. I am in the presence of Reich Minister Goebbels daily and often in the presence of the Führer, himself, sometimes alone. If I told my superior I felt at risk on the streets he would allow me to wear a side-arm and I could use that to assassinate the Führer. If I took that step I would then have to kill myself as the punishment would be more than I could bear. And what purpose would it serve? I, myself, am of more value alive, making mental notes of all I hear and see and reporting it back. I have to believe it makes a difference. That someone, somewhere, is creating better policy because of the risks I am taking.

He sighed deeply and put his cap on. A long time ago, in another life, a teacher at school had given him a book of Shakespeare to read in English. Most of it had been too hard for his limited understanding of the language, but one phrase stuck with him and seemed so appropriate.

'Once more unto the breach, dear friends, once more; Or close the wall up with our English dead!' he said in English.

Levi had thought about the possibility that he would be called upon to take part in abusing Jews, but there were so few Jews left at large in Berlin he'd decided it was something he might, with luck, avoid. Still, he'd mentally dissected the potential and how he should handle it. When his luck ran out and it happened, he was taken completely by surprise. It was a Saturday and he was on his way to a biergarten with Erik and three other friends. About half a mile from their destination they saw a group of orthodox Jews, men and women, walking at a rapid pace, presumably on their way home from the nearby half-ruined synagogue.

Many Jews had been rounded up and shipped to the camps in the East and it was rare to see them on the streets. These must have some kind of special stamp on their papers; the men engaged in work vital to the war effort.

Erik reacted immediately. 'What are they doing still at liberty?' he asked.

'Disgraceful! What are we going to do about it?' one of their friends responded. The two men grinned at each other and sprinted across the street. Levi stopped. He could see them talking to the Jews, asking for papers. The group was immediately engaged in an argument.

'Come on, we can't let them have all the fun,' another of his companions pulled at his arm. Reluctantly Levi followed till he was standing beside Erik.

'There has been an oversight. We need to escort these fine people to the central collection building,' Erik said, 'otherwise they might miss their train and we wouldn't want that to happen.'

One of the other officers spat at them. 'We don't want them taking up air that we could be breathing,' he said.

Levi looked at the group, three men, two women and two children, huddled together, their faces white and their eyes large with fear.

'But before we do, there is some sport to be had,' another officer said, laughing, drawing a knife from his trouser pocket. He pulled one of men out of the group and cut his ear locks off close to his head. Then he elbowed the man in the stomach and pushed him back into the group. The man was bent over gripping his torso in pain. Every fibre in Levi's being wanted to help, but he dug his fingernails into the palms of his hand and said nothing.

'Here you are,' the officer was handing him the offensive scissors.

'No, thank —'

'Oh come on Werner, don't be a spoilsport. No one will report you and even if they did, you'll only get a pat on the back from Reich Minister Goebbels,' said Erik.

Levi took the knife and pulled another of the men from the pitiful huddle. He was a younger man and he stood silent, his hands by his sides. But instead of keeping his eyes downcast as the other man had, he looked Levi square in the eye. There was a note of silent, furious accusation in the brown eyes as they gazed deep into Levi's. *What am I doing? Will my G-d ever forgive me these atrocities?* Levi grasped the ear locks and cut them through, one at a time. Then he pushed the man back towards his family and handed the knife to Erik.

'What? No punch?' Erik asked him, smiling broadly.

Levi shook his head. 'Maybe I'm a coward, but I don't hit unarmed men,' he said softly.

Erik's smile vanished to be replaced by a scowl of anger. 'Careful my friend, attitudes like that will have you branded a sympathiser. These are not men, they're rats, vermin. Or have you not been listening to the Führer?'

Levi shrugged. 'As you wish,' he said and pulled the young man out onto the pavement again. He hit him with a hard right-handed punch and the man was felled.

Erik gave a loud burst of laughter. 'Excellent!' he yelled, and cut the ear locks from the last of the male Jews.

* * *

'Werner, I want you to meet a friend of mine. He works at the Luftwaffe headquarters. This is Hauptmann Harro Schulze-Boysen,' Erik said.

Levi shook the outstretched hand. The man was tall and lean, his features chiselled, his colouring pale, his smile wide and his gaze spellbinding.

'This is my dear friend, Hauptmann Werner Schneider.'

'Heil Hitler, Hauptmann,' Levi saluted.

'Heil Hitler, Hauptmann,' said Schulze-Boysen with a touch of amusement playing at the edge of his thin lips.

'Harro works in the intelligence division of the Air Ministry. He does what you do, he analyses foreign press reports.'

Levi nodded. 'So you speak English?' he asked.

Schultz-Boysen smiled. 'I speak and read French, English, Norwegian, Dutch, Swedish, Danish and Russian.'

'Goodness me, it makes my English, French and a little Italian seem very insignificant.'

'I spent time in England during my childhood and in Scotland. I have an ear for languages.'

Erik was watching them and something caused him to frown. Levi wondered momentarily about the Hauptmann's sexuality.

'Harro has the most amazing wife, her name is Libertas and her mother is the daughter of a Prussian prince. They live in Charlottenburg,' Erik said, his enthusiasm for this couple plain to see.

Harro nodded. 'You must come over for tea one night and bring Hauptmann Schneider. My wife works in film and we have a wonderful group who party with us regularly. You'd both be most welcome.'

Levi spent the rest of the day thinking about Hauptmann Harro Schulze-Boysen. He wasn't sure why, but for the first time something had triggered his inbuilt sense of someone who shared his real feelings. There was something about the way the man made the salute, as if he detested doing it, something about his bearing. Could he be a potential ally? Could he be turned for the English? He was from an aristocratic family, Prussian, military, as was his wife, and Levi knew that many of them were less than happy with the Nazi regime and its hideous policies. But how to approach the matter? How to get him really talking about the war and gauge what his feelings were? He would press Erik, he decided, and express his eagerness to take up the offer of dinner at their Charlottenburg home.

'Tell me about Schulze-Boysen,' Levi said. Erik stirred and turned over to look at him. They were lying in Eric's rumpled bed in his apartment.

'What do you want to know?' Eric asked.

'How long have you known him?'

'About a year. We were introduced by my cousin, Fredrick, he also works in that office, for Goering.'

'He's very smart.'

Erik nodded and smiled. 'If you fancy him, you're out of luck, he's a ladies man.'

Levi looked at his lover and smiled back. There was something about the clear blue eyes and the blond hair. 'Why would I fancy him? He's too old for me.'

Erik laughed. 'But he interests you. Why?' he asked.

'I don't know, maybe because he's so smart. But I would like to take him up on that invitation, go over one night for tea.'

'They have wonderful parties, drinking, dancing, and discussing politics. I'll tell him we want to come.'

Levi nodded. 'That would be excellent. Maybe I could play the piano for them and people could dance.'

Erik shook his head, amusement playing at the corners of his mouth. 'I don't know what to do with you, Werner, the things you do to avoid dancing.'

It had started out as a convenience, a way to information. He learned interesting insights into what Himmler was planning from Erik and passed them on to his handlers. He was using the young man for his own ends. But it warmed him to the core to be held by another on cold nights, to feel another's heart beat and steady breathing. And the more time he spent in Erik's company the more emotion he felt, in spite of himself. He knew passion was dangerous and could compromise his situation, so he did his best to supress it, deny it, ignore it. But still, the idea of taking Erik home and introducing him to his parents, to Simon and the twins, to the life they could have after the war, crept in at the corners of his mind when he wasn't concentrating. It was a confusing image and one that led to treacherous thoughts. So he had to reprimand himself, remind himself it wasn't real. He wasn't a German officer, he wasn't Werner. This was the fantasy and it wouldn't last after the war. He was a Jew. His race was an anathema to Erik, and had he known the truth he would have drawn his pistol and shot Levi between the eyes. That was the cold, hard truth.

His reverie was broken by the arrival of Brunhilde with a message. 'Reich Minister Goebbels requires your presence in his office, immediately,' she said.

As always the sliver of fear, of panic, of impending danger flickered in his stomach and crawled its way up his spine. 'Of course,' he said, standing and following her.

'Heil Hitler, Reich Minister,' he said.

'Heil Hitler, Hauptmann. Come in and close the door.'

Goebbels pointed to a chair across from his large desk.

'Tell me, what do you know about the Berghof?' he asked.

Levi frowned. He should feign ignorance, it was always safer.

'Nothing, Reich Minister.'

'It is the Führer's vacation home, in the Bavarian alps, near Berchtesgaden. He entertains there, and it has occurred to him that he would like you to play the piano for his guests. You are to leave tomorrow by air. There is a landing strip close to the house, and you will stay until the Führer orders your return to Berlin. Is that understood?' Goebbels gave him a rare smile. 'This is a particular honour, Hauptmann, and I know you will appreciate that the Führer is displaying his trust in you.'

'Yes, Reich Minister.'

'It is so obvious that you must never repeat anything you hear that I have never felt the need to emphasise that to you.'

Levi gave a small nod. 'Thank you, Reich Minister. Sometimes the Führer will make a comment about the war when I play for him and I am aware of the need for discretion.'

'Indeed. Your promotion and your talent reflect well on me, and I hope your remuneration demonstrates that.'

'Indeed it does, Reich Minister. I am, as always, very grateful for the opportunity.'

Goebbels gave the customary wave of his hand. 'Very good. You may go home and make your preparations. I am told the car will call for you at 10.30 am tomorrow morning and the plane leaves at midday. I will see you there in a week's time.'

He barely had time to send Erik a note, to let him know what was happening, and to make a hurried visit to the club to inform his handlers that they would hear nothing more from him until he returned to Berlin. Was this a good thing? It felt like another adventure. Another opportunity. But if he was uncovered there would no chance of escape, no option but the bullet.

CHAPTER ELEVEN

The Berghof

September 1942

The chalet was surrounded by a large terrace, which sported big canvas umbrellas, giving the place a 'holiday home' atmosphere. The Führer himself had decorated the interior. The dining room was panelled in cumbria pine and held a table that seated sixteen people, with an ornate light fitting that ran its length. Levi's favourite room was what the Führer referred to as the 'Great Hall'. At one end was a massive marble fireplace with a heavy mantel. At the other was the piano. Its most extraordinary feature was a picture window which could be lowered into the wall to give an open-air view of the Alps. It was a beautiful and restful place, full of antique furniture and art, and lovingly looked after by an army of housekeepers, gardeners, cooks and domestic servants.

One of the bathrooms had a wall of red tiles, each bearing a black swastika in a white circle. Most of the rooms held caged canaries, which would whistle on command for Levi. His bedroom featured a window with a lovely mountain vista, an enormous and comfortable bed and two water-colour sketches by the Führer on the walls.

Nearby were the airstrip and other houses that had been built by the Nazi elite. Field Marshall Goering and Reichsführer Himmler both had homes there. Like Hitler, they spent most of their time in Berlin, but accompanied him to the Berghof when the Führer decided to decamp to his retreat. A barracks adjacent to the Führer's home on the mountain housed a contingent of his private guard, the SS-Leibstansarte Adolf Hitler. They patrolled the grounds with dogs on chains and rifles at the ready, and every time they encountered Levi they saluted him. His knowledge of their ignorance made him smile as he offered a salute back.

His days revolved around the requirement for him to play the piano when guests requested it. Otherwise he read what few books the censors allowed, walked the trails that led up into the mountains, wrote to Erik and talked to the staff.

It was his first encounter with Hitler's companion, Eva Braun, and her sister, Gretl. Eva was an interesting woman. An archetypical Aryan with her bright sapphire eyes and bouncy fair curls, she wasn't a conventional beauty, but there was something about her face when she smiled that stopped Levi in his tracks. He liked to play with her two Scottish terrier dogs, Negus and Stasi, and she often joined him on the terrace to throw balls for the dogs. When the Führer was away, Levi exercised his German Shepherd, Blondi. Eva's younger sister, Gretl, was a smoker and a flirt. Her hair was darker, almost auburn, and her animated face seemed never far from laughter.

On a gorgeous day in early September, Levi was practising a Beethoven piece that he wanted to surprise the Führer with when he returned from Berlin. The door was flung wide and Eva came storming in. She was obviously angry.

'Damn it, Werner! Where is the loyalty? He has given everything for this country and people still betray him.'

Levi stood up. 'What has happened?' he asked cautiously. Her emotions alarmed him, it wasn't like her to be this roused.

'I've just spoken with Fritz and he tells me there has been a major resistance cell uncovered in Berlin. People Adolf knew and trusted.'

Levi swallowed hard. 'Who are they?' he asked.

'Some Luftwaffe officer on the intelligence desk. His wife worked for Herman and he had championed her! An economist in the Economics Ministry and his wife, who is an American, and lots more. They're rounding them up and starting the interrogations. Fritz says that they will die, all of them.'

Levi sat down. Perhaps he was closer to danger at this moment than ever before.

'What have they been doing?' he asked.

'Some printing of posters and leaflets, putting posters up around the city. But much worse than that, spying for the Russians! It was some coded radio messages that gave them away, we broke the code of signals sent to Moscow. How could they possibly want to help that dictator, Stalin? He's such a monster.'

'Do you remember the name of the Luftwaffe officer?' he asked.

She turned and stared at him. 'Why?' her tone was vaguely suspicious.

'I think I might have met him once.'

'No, but it was a double-barrelled name. His mother-in-law is a close friend of Herman's, and Fritz says that Herman is almost apoplectic with rage. I think he spoke lots of languages, the officer, so Herman brought him into the Luftwaffe HQ. And his wife had worked in film. Does that ring any bells?'

Levi nodded. 'Yes, I'm sure I met him. With a friend of mine, a nephew of Count von Engels who is a Hauptman in the SS. Erik works as an aide for Reichsführer Himmler.'

She shook her head. 'Well thank goodness he didn't corrupt you! Adolf will be furious, but so hurt as well. He wants the people working for the Third Reich to share his dream. He has such plans for our nation, and these people, working for the Americans and the Soviets, they are worse than scum. I would send them to the camps but they won't, they'll try them and pass down judgment and then hang them or guillotine them. I think that's too good.'

She flopped down in one of chairs. 'Play me something, Werner, cheer me up.'

'What would you like?' he asked; his heart was pounding in his chest and his palms felt sweaty.

'Something light — Chopin.'

'Of course, Fraulein.'

The thought rumbled through Levi's head like a freight train. It was night and he was lying in bed gazing up at the roof. The Luftwaffe Hauptman had been a spy for the Russians. He'd hated the salute they'd exchanged as much as Levi had.

If it hadn't been for the decision of the Führer to send him here, he might have gone there for a meal and maybe joined their network. He could be facing arrest and torture and death. Did Erik know, he wondered? He'd be devastated. He was a torchbearer for the Reich and all it stood for. The betrayal by his friend would cut deep, but not as deep as the truth about Levi would cut.

Yet again he wondered what would happen at the end of the war. It was like a loop that tormented him during the long. dark hours and went nowhere. Would he live like this forever? Or would his British handlers allow him to return to London? But what if Germany won the war and London was occupied? Where would he go then?

He let his imagination take him to the prison cell that the Hauptmann now probably inhabited. They would be torturing him to gain more names, hitting him with axe handles and truncheons. Would he stand up to it? Somehow Levi believed he would. And what about his wife? Erik had said she was forever flirting with both friends and Nazi officials and always partying, but he'd also confided that he thought she was quite fragile mentally. They had a maid, half Italian he thought Erik had said, and she'd had a baby and Erik suspected the father was his friend the Hauptmann. No doubt they'd been arrested as well. His heart ached for all of them.

He tried to ring Erik at his desk in Himmler's office. They didn't know where he was. So he tried the apartment in the Prenzlauer Berg, but there was no answer. Where was he? At the back of Levi's brain, he began to worry. Erik was a creature of habit, and if he was out during the day his office always knew where he was going and when he'd be back. Perhaps he'd gone home for a few days. That was a possibility. Levi didn't have the telephone number for the Munich home of Erik's parents, so he would just have to decide that's where Erik was and leave it at that. He'd make contact when he could.

He was sitting under one of the coloured umbrellas on the terrace, reading, when Eva Braun stepped out of the doorway, accompanied by her two dogs. They ran happily to Levi.

'Hello there,' he said, as he patted them. They barked enthusiastically.

'They like you,' she said. 'They think you're going to play with them.' One of the dogs leapt up onto his knee and he scratched its ears.

'Tell me, Hauptmann, did you say you had a friend who was the nephew of Count von Engel?' she asked lightly. She wasn't looking at him, she was surveying the panorama of the snow-capped mountains. Levi felt a stab of dread.

'Yes, Erik von Engel. He's an SS-Hauptsturmführer in Himmler's office. I met him when I had Christmas with the Count and Countess at their home in Wannsee.'

She nodded slowly. 'Have you heard from him lately?' she asked.

'No, I had a letter about a month ago.'

'Do you keep his letters?'

It was beginning to sound like an interrogation. He hesitated.

'I can see in your face that you do,' she said, turning her bright blue eyes upon him. 'Take a word of advice from a friend who cares about you, Hauptmann, and burn all your letters from your friend immediately. If anyone else asks you if you know him, deny it. I will say nothing.'

Levi swallowed. 'May I know why?' he asked quietly.

'SS-Hauptsturmführer von Engel was arrested two days ago and is in prison. He will be sent to the camp at Dachau.'

'Why?' Levi tried to keep the shock from his voice but he knew he was unsuccessful. 'He's a faithful party member, I assure you, and devoted to Himmler and the Führer,' he added.

'Very possibly. But he is a degenerate, a homosexual. He was caught in bed with a fellow officer by the Gestapo and arrested immediately.'

This was worse that if she'd told him Erik was a spy. Much worse.

'Did he display such behaviour in your presence?' she asked, her voice neutral but her eyes watching him closely.

'No! He was a friend I went drinking with in a group. He seemed just like the rest of us. This is shocking news indeed.'

Would they torture Erik? Would they try to find out who else he had slept with? Was there a danger he would give up Levi's cover name under duress? Or would they simply strip him of his rank and send him to the camp? These questions whirled alongside something Levi recognised as grief. His Erik. His beautiful, proud, loyal Erik. If Levi had secretly held a dream of them being together after the war, this was now dashed onto the rocks of reality. He'd heard enough about Dachau to know that Erik's chances of survival were slim, and that he would suffer. What exactly would he suffer? Levi couldn't bear the thought of it, so he shut it off. There was nothing he could do to help, Erik was another casualty of war. For several days he could think of nothing else until he heard, via

Eva, that Erik had been shipped south to Dachau and wasn't expected to be heard from again. It felt as if he could let out his breath for the first time in ages. Yet another close escape. And no one to tell.

The peaceful atmosphere was broken by the arrival of the Führer. The whole household rose into a different gear and the staff moved at an increased pace. Levi could feel the change even before the plane landed, and knew his tranquil and reflective time was over. He'd have to be on guard again, noting every word and action and ever-watchful of his own reactions.

The notes were his friends, and he felt them speaking to him in a language only he understood. When he played, whether by himself or for others, the emotions stored deep inside rose up, burst out and streamed from his fingers onto the keys. But he alone could see them. Sometimes they were black for his grief, or purple for the anger at his situation, or clear like the tears he could not shed. The piano allowed him to express his pain, and that searing agony took his technical ability and elevated it to the level of a spectacular musician.

He was playing the first movement from Bach's *Italian Concerto in F Major*, and the group at the other end of the room were listening in rapt silence. The Führer sat facing him, and on either side were Himmler, Goering, Bormann and Eva Braun. It was a delicate piece with some lively runs and his fingers raced over the keys with precision. At its conclusion he went straight into Brahms' *Variations on a Theme of Paganini Opus 35*, with even more thrilling trills.

Four minutes in he was pounding the notes fiercely and his entire body moved in time to the music. Here he was no one, neither Levi nor Werner, Jew nor Lutheran, prisoner nor gaoler, he was just the pianist, the catalyst between the brilliance of the composer and the superb instrument.

As the music ended he thrust his head back, exhausted but also strangely exhilarated. As always, the group stood and applauded, led by the actions of the Führer. Levi rose, bowed and waited to be excused.

Hitler beckoned to him. 'Magnificent. Come here, Hauptmann.'

The reality of his situation hit Levi like a punch in the solar plexus, and he breathed in sharply as he crossed the large room.

Hitler pointed to a chair in the corner. 'Join us, you've earned it. Bring that chair. Would you like a glass of champagne?' he asked.

Levi took the chair and put it beside Eva, as far away from the Führer as he could get. Himmler and Goering exchanged glances of surprise and disapproval.

'Thank you, Mein Führer,' said Levi quietly.

Eva took a glass from the tray on the table and poured from an open bottle of champagne. She gave him a warm smile as he accepted it from her.

'Thank you, Fraulein.'

Hitler scowled at Goering. 'I am still thinking about Africa,' he said.

Goering coughed and moved uncomfortably in his chair. 'Don't worry so much, General FieldMarshall Rommel is a capable and battle-hardened soldier.'

'More than I can say for you,' Hitler said, still looking at Goering. 'I used to say that in a time of crisis my Reichsmarschall was ice-cold, a brutal man with no scruples, but look at you now. All you do is tell me what a hero Rommel is.'

Himmler nodded. 'But he is, Mein Führer, as the Hauptmann will tell you, the darling of even the enemy's news agencies.'

Hitler turned his eyes on Levi.

'Is that true, Hauptmann? Do you read about our Rommel in the English newspapers?' he asked.

Levi nodded. 'Yes, Mein Führer. I believe they admire him because he beat them and they are surprised to see such brilliance in the desert.'

Hitler nodded. 'Well, we are sending him the supplies he has requested so urgently from the Italians. He better make good use of them.'

There was an awkward silence.

'So,' Hitler stirred, 'you don't know what to say to me, do you? We don't mention the Soviet war because that goes badly, and we have failed to gain supremacy in the air.'

Again he gave Goering a long hard stare. 'There are spies in our own capital city and the resistance continues to blow up railways and disrupt the output in our factories. Someone, give me some good news,' he continued.

Himmler put his hand to his chin and stroked it. 'The Final Solution is achieving its goals. Over three hundred thousand Jews have been transported in freight trains from the ghettos in Warsaw to Treblinka. And the killings by my death squads in the Soviet territories that we occupy continues at a tremendous rate, in Latvia, Lithuania, Belarus, the Ukraine, hundreds of thousands have been exterminated.'

Hitler gave him a slow smile. 'All I ever need to do is threaten to hand my enemies over to Himmler … So, you are more successful at killing unarmed vermin than my generals are at killing trained soldiers in combat. What do you want, a medal to hang around your neck?'

Levi studied his shoes and tried to make sense of what he was hearing. He wished he could report back, but that avenue was closed for the moment. The only way would be if he asked to go back to Berlin for a short time, and he had no reason to do that.

'Tell me, Hauptmann, what do the English papers say about the war? Are they afraid of Germany?' Hitler asked suddenly.

Levi looked up. There was almost a plea for something to crow about in the clear blue eyes gazing at him.

'Much of London was badly damaged by the bombing and the fires, many were killed,' he said. 'The people are suffering shortages. Our U-boats attack their supply ships and sink the food and fuel they need. And the airfields suffered, too; many planes were destroyed and runways blown up.'

Hitler nodded. Goering smiled his approval at Levi.

'And what do they say about the hopelessly Jew-ridden and Negrified Americans?' Hitler asked, the bitterness in his voice plain to hear.

Levi hesitated. 'The war in the Pacific is turning, the Allies believe they will beat the Japanese. The British are relieved to have the Americans in the European war, they bring much-needed resources —'

'Enough!'

It was a roar of anger. The Führer rose to his feet and faced them all. 'It is all I hear. Good news for the enemy and how much our forces are struggling. I will not have it! Germany will triumph. The Third Reich will reign for a thousand years, and if anyone doubts this they might as well take their pistol and shoot themselves now. You are all idiots! Rommel is a vain fool. Why am I surrounded by such people?'

The rant was conducted at such a pitch and with such ferocity that Levi shrunk back in his chair.

'I will not stay in your treacherous company a moment longer!' Hitler shouted as he stalked from the room and slammed the door behind him.

Himmler turned to Levi. 'Never tell the Führer that our enemies are relieved about anything,' he said, and the coldness in his voice felt like a knife slicing Levi's throat.

Goering glared at Levi. 'Stick to playing the piano, Hauptmann, you have much to learn,' he said.

Levi rose. 'May I be excused, please?' he asked.

Eva nodded without looking at him. 'Of course. Don't worry, it will all be fine in the morning,' she said.

CHAPTER TWELVE

The Berghof

July 1943

Levi's nightmares had progressed from running between bloodied corpses with the death mask of Rolf to watching a naked Erik swing by a noose, his hands clutching at the rope and his eyes bulging, and then facing a raving mad Hitler who kept yelling at him that he a degenerate and a Jew and must die, die, die!

He awoke sweating and gasping for air, his heart racing and his palms clammy. It took him a few moments of deep breathing to banish the images and still his chaotic thoughts. It was just a bad dream, he was safe in his bed and all those around him thought him to be Werner, a loyal Hauptmann and pianist. As long as he kept his head and watched his tongue he would continue to be trusted.

His fear was not helped by the growing knowledge that Hitler was clearly insane. As the war turned ever so slowly in the Allies' favour and defeat piled upon defeat, Hitler spent more time away from Berlin than he did in it. He frequently interrupted Levi's playing to rant about the bombing of German cities by the English at night and the Americans during the day. The bombers, while concentrating on the military installations, and the petroleum, oil and lubricant plants in the north, had also wreaked havoc on the civilian population. When the Führer heard about the bombing of Hamburg and the firestorm it had caused, nearly destroying all of the city, he was enraged and rained his fury down on Goering because the Luftwaffe had been unable to shoot down enough of the nimble fighters escorting the bombers, or the great cumbersome planes themselves. July also brought the beginning of the battle of Kursk in the East, Operation Zitedalle.

'This victory will reassert German strength.' Hitler seemed to be assuring himself more than talking to Levi. 'It will show all my lily-livered allies that we will not tolerate desertion. And the Soviet scum we capture can be put to work in the armament factories.'

Levi sat at the piano and listened. He knew that Hitler was still smarting over the defeat at Stalingrad after months of hard-fought battle. Twenty-two generals had surrendered, including General FieldMarshall Paulus, the highest-ranking German officer to have ever surrendered. The battle for Kursk gave Hitler a reason to believe all was not lost in the East. Levi was careful not to comment on the war for fear of infuriating the Führer.

He noticed that Himmler and Bormann visited only when summoned, and Eva and Gretl kept to themselves. Goering was conspicuous by his absence, and Levi listened to the gossip about him in the staff quarters, which said Goering spent his time at his country homes, hunting and admiring his collection of looted art. His long-term morphine addiction meant he took over thirty codeine tablets a day, and it seemed his interest in waging war had waned, much to the rage of the Führer. There was an ominous atmosphere at the Berghof, and Levi wondered what would become of them all if the war ended badly.

Sometimes he imagined the Allied troops swarming up the mountainside like vicious, furious ants and overwhelming the German soldiers. He could picture the way the staff and officers would be handled, and wondered how much time he'd have before the accusations flew, followed by the fists, boots and then the bullets. If some GI pushed him up against a wall, a gun to his head, what would he say?

'No! You don't understand. I'm not really one of them. I'm one of you. Check with British Intelligence. I'm a spy.'

Would they laugh at him and shoot him anyway? Or maybe he'd be dragged back to Berlin at gunpoint to stand trial. It would be gratifying to see those smug bastards pleading for their lives, Goering and Himmler and Goebbels. But there was no guarantee anyone would bother to follow up on his claims of being a British spy. A guillotine, a hangman's noose or rotting in a jail as a Nazi collaborator, none of these alternatives seemed fair — and yet any one of them was a real possibility if the war continued to go unfavourably for the Third Reich.

Levi let his fingers lift from the keys. He'd played a Beethoven sonata that the Führer loved, but Hitler seemed lost in sombre contemplation. Levi was about to start another when the Führer suddenly stirred and looked over at him.

'Tell me, Hauptmann,' he said softly, 'do you believe we will win this war?'

Levi was always on his guard for such questions, a wrong answer could have terrible consequences. 'Of course, Mein Führer, it is a war of attrition and Germany has by far the stronger resolve.'

Hitler nodded. 'You are a true patriot. You should be in charge of some of my armies.'

Levi smiled. 'I'm afraid I'm not qualified for such an honour.'

Hitler snorted. 'My dog could do a better job than some of the generals I have promoted,' he said.

There was a moment's silence. 'Already some of my most senior advisers are talking of what to do if the war goes badly. Can you believe that? They come to me with plans for a secret escape route, to Denmark and then Spain by air, and then by U-boat to Argentina so that we can regroup and launch the Fourth Reich.'

Once again Hitler seemed to be murmuring to himself. Levi sat very still. Every fibre registered that this was important. He should make note of this conversation.

'Franco is a silent ally and he opens Barcelona to fleeing Germans. They think I don't know. Low-ranking officials make some excuse to visit Spain and they stay there, instead of returning home to serve the Fatherland. It is disgraceful. Bormann and Muller tell me I should have a strategy in place to ensure that the top of the Nazi party lives on to fight again. This is monstrous! We will stand and fight in Berlin. We are Germans. We do not run away.'

'Yes, Mein Führer.'

Hitler looked over and seemed surprised to see Levi at the piano. He gave a deep sigh. 'Play me some Wagner,

Hauptmann — he knew what it meant to be patriotic. No first come, join me here.'

As he spoke the Führer stood and walked to the window. Levi got up and went to stand beside him. Hitler extended his arm towards the mountains.

'Is this not a spectacular view? Look at the way that ridge overlaps the one behind it. I feel I could capture that with my watercolours. Snow is hard to paint, the reflection from a summer sun ... I wanted to be an artist, you know. I applied to art school.'

Levi nodded. 'You are an artist, Mein Führer. I feel very lucky to have two of your works on my bedroom wall —'

He was interrupted by a knock at the main door.

'Come.' Hitler barked the order without looking over his shoulder. It was one of his aides, pale with trepidation.

'What is it?' Hitler asked when the man didn't speak.

'Mein Führer, GeneralMajor Alex von Halem is here. He has a special report on Operation Zitadelle from General Model. He insists he must see you at once.'

Hitler waved in the direction of his aide. 'Bring him, without delay.'

Hitler turned to Levi. 'He will bring good news. I knew when I woke this morning that today would bring news of victory.'

The door opened again and a tall, broad-shouldered man in military uniform strode in. All Levi saw was a mountain of white, silver hair, very pale skin, flashing buttons, a hand moving from a trouser pocket. Everything seemed to slow to a crawl. The man cried out. 'Death to the traitor! Germany without Nazis!'

He drew a pistol and aimed it at Hitler. Levi saw the barrel of the gun while it was still climbing to a firing position and reacted without thinking. He threw himself in front of the Führer as a loud explosion filled the massive room. A searing pain tore through his right arm and blood spurted out through his uniform. As he hit the floor, he passed out.

'Werner, can you hear me?'

The voice came from far away.

'Werner.'

Someone shook him gently and he heard the noise more clearly.

'Good. He's coming round.'

It was voice he didn't know. His arm ached — not strong pain, he'd obviously been given some medication, more of a steady throb. He winced and opened his eyes.

'Hello, Hauptmann.' The man was smiling down at him. He had glasses and friendly grey eyes, a moustache.

'How are you feeling, son?' he asked.

Levi opened his lips, but they felt dry and his tongue stuck to the roof of his mouth so he coughed.

'Sore.' It was barely above a whisper.

'You're a hero, young man, you took a bullet for the Führer.'

Levi tried to remember. He could see the mountains, the Führer standing beside him, a loud noise, and then nothing.

'I did?' he asked.

'I am Dr Fridsburg and we have taken a bullet from your arm. You need to rest now, sleep. Your arm will mend.'

* * *

He looked over his shoulder. The rows of chairs behind him were full of emaciated men and women scowling furiously. Some shook their fists at him. All wore a yellow star on their clothing. In front of him was a high wooden bench. His father sat behind it, his head shaven and his sunken eyes glowing with hatred.

'Levi Micah Horowitz, you are charged before this people's court that you did take a bullet for that most evil of men, Adolf Hitler. How do you plead?' his father intoned.

Levi tried to speak but his voice was non-existent. A large weight seemed to be pressing on his chest. He glanced down and saw that a bullet had ripped him open and blood was streaming out. He could see his heart beating.

'How could you?'

He raised his eyes and there was Erik standing in front of him, a rope around his neck. Erik's eyes were glassy and protruding and his bloated face was full of rage and pain. Levi reached out but couldn't grasp him. Slowly he felt the life running out of him in time with the blood that pumped from the cavity in his own chest.

'You will stand before our G-d condemned by your actions,' his father bellowed at him. 'You are no son of mine!'

That was the question he couldn't answer. How could he? Why had he? What would it mean to the world that the Führer was still alive? All he would have had to do was stay completely still and that bullet would have hit Hitler. Maybe it would have killed him, maybe it would have wounded him. No one would have blamed Werner for not reacting with split-second precision, he wasn't supposed to be a trained commando. And yet, he had. Without even thinking about it he'd reacted. Did that mean he'd betrayed all his fellow Jews, his family, everyone who suffered because of this lunatic's policies? Or had he done what he'd been trained to do? The questions haunted him as he lay in bed, his arm strapped and throbbing and a gentle fever raising a sheen of sweat on his forehead.

When he felt strong enough, Levi went to see the Führer. Hitler embraced him lightly, then indicated he was to stand in front of him. Hitler took a box from the table and opened it.

'This is the Knight's Cross with Oak Leaves and Swords. It is awarded for outstanding bravery,' he said. Before Levi had time to gather his thoughts he was bowing his head so the Führer could tie the medal at the back of his neck. Then Hitler took a step back and saluted.

Levi returned the salute. 'Thank you, Mein Führer, I am overcome with gratitude.'

Hitler shook his head. 'The gratitude is mine, Hauptmann, you may well have saved my life. How is your arm feeling?' he asked. Levi could hear real concern in his voice.

'A little sore, Mein Führer, but it will heal.'

'Fridsburg says you were lucky, it nicked the bone but missed the major artery. But it will be a while before you can play the piano again.'

Levi nodded. 'Yes, I'm afraid so. I'm sorry about that, Mein Führer.'

Hitler shook his head. 'It can't be helped. We might have lost you all together. Or if you had not been so fast, it might have killed me. You were very brave, Hauptmann, and I shall not forget that.'

Levi didn't know what to say, so he just gave a little nod.

'I spoke with Reich Minister Goebbels last night and he suggested that since you can't play the piano, maybe you would like to go back to Berlin and work at your job in the propaganda ministry while you recover?'

Back to Berlin? It was an opportunity he couldn't let slip.

'Yes, Mein Führer, I would like that very much if that is acceptable to you.'

Hitler nodded. 'So be it. You can fly back tomorrow.'

Berlin, July 1943

When Levi walked into the propaganda office in Berlin everyone was waiting to say hello to him. They applauded as one, which he found extremely unnerving. Throughout the day his workmates kept stopping by to shake his hand and tell him how much they appreciated his action.

When he got home to his apartment building, the same thing happened. Fellow officers wanted to shake his hand. He wondered how many felt the need to be seen to be doing this, and if any of them secretly wished the assassination attempt had succeeded, but their faces betrayed nothing.

He'd been home a week when he got a call from Erik's father, Karl von Engel.

'Hauptmann Schneider, how are you? How's the arm?'

Levi was surprised to hear from him. 'Healing nicely, thank you, sir,' he said.

'Good to hear. My wife and I wondered if you'd like to come and visit us for a few days. Have some good Munich rest.'

Levi hesitated. Were they disgraced by the actions of their son? What would Reich Minister Goebbels have to say about the idea?

'That's very kind of you. I'll have to ask permission. Can I call you back?' he answered.

'Of course.'

Still the nightmare persisted. He became afraid of sleep. He was judged and found guilty every time he fell from fitful wakefulness into uncomfortable sleep. How could he have done that? What part of his training had kicked in and allowed him to react with such instinct? No matter how hard he tried to rationalise the act by reminding himself that he had stayed true to his assumed identity, he couldn't get past the fact that he had saved the life of that loathsome creature.

When he felt safe enough in his environment he wrote out a long report on his time at the Berghof, the conversations he'd overheard and been part of, and set off for the club. There was some bomb damage to buildings in the area but he was relieved to see that the club was still intact.

The smoky atmosphere, with women sitting at the bar and officers seated at tables playing cards and listening to the band, reminded him of nights spent here with Erik. That thought pulled him up. He often wondered if his friend was still alive, and, if he was, what his living conditions were like. Even those secret thoughts felt dangerous, and he tried to dismiss them. But still Erik's fate nagged at him, an anxiety, a grief he couldn't admit to, a pain he tried to bury but which surfaced all the same. He shook his head, as if to banish the flood of memories, and went to the bar where he was immediately confronted by a new barman.

'Where's Paul?' he asked.

The man shrugged. 'No idea. They needed a new barman and I applied. About two months ago. What's your poison?'

He'd turned away and was pouring a drink for the customer beside Levi.

'I'll have a whisky on the rocks, with five pieces of ice,' Levi said.

The barman stopped what he was doing for a second and looked at him closely. 'Are you Hauptmann Schneider by any chance?' he asked quietly.

Levi smiled at him. 'Yes, I am.'

The barman put the drink down in front of the other patron.

'Glad to see you back, Hauptmann Schneider, we've been expecting you. The drink is on the house for a hero.'

Levi nodded. 'Thanks.'

He nursed his drink for exactly twenty minutes then went to the men's room. The stall at the end was occupied so he left and returned five minutes later to find it empty. The brick was still loose but he had to wiggle it hard to get it to pop out. He left his roll of paper behind it, made sure the brick was firmly in place, flushed the toilet and stepped out to wash his hands.

'Hauptmann Schneider?' The voice behind him echoed in the tiled room. Levi felt a sudden jolt of fear but turned and smiled. It was a man in a black leather coat and jackboots. Gestapo.

'Yes,' he said as calmly as he could.

The man extended his arm. 'How are you? My name is Stabsmusikmeister Wilhelm Weber. I just wanted to tell you how much I appreciate what you did. You are quite famous.'

Levi shook the hand. 'Thank you. Tell me, what rank is a Stabsmusikmeister?' he asked, curiosity getting the better of his fear.

'It's a special rank created by the Führer. I am one of the music experts in charge of the instruments we commandeer from the conquered peoples and the Jews.'

Levi was nodding when a thought struck him. Was it a man such as this who had looted his parents' house? Did he know what had happened to the family, and the violins? If so, Levi couldn't ask him directly. But maybe the man had an ego.

'I would love to hear about some of your finds. I am a pianist,' he said.

The man gave a small bow. 'And I would love to tell you, but my group is about to leave so it will have to be another time. I wanted to express my appreciation of your bravery in the face of danger to our Führer.'

With that he turned and left. Levi wanted to slump against the wall. His heart was thudding so fast he couldn't catch his breath. He felt like he was back sprinting over the moors and he sensed a sudden nauseous tug from the depths of his stomach. He couldn't follow the man and ask him what he knew without blowing his cover and, probably, losing his life. The sense of helplessness was almost overwhelming.

* * *

Three days later he received a telephone call at his desk.

'Is that Hauptmann Schneider?' an unfamiliar, yet somehow recognisable, voice asked.

'Yes, I am Werner Schneider,' he answered cautiously.

'My name is Wilhelm Weber; we met the other night. I was wondering if you would like to see something. I've been looking through a shipment from Paris and I have something I think would interest you very much.'

Levi's instinct was finely honed. If he could engage Weber's interest and ask about stringed instruments, who knows what he might find out?

'If it's musical, I'm always interested,' he said.

'Excellent. I will send a staff car for you tomorrow at noon.'

The car took him to a warehouse on the Oranienburger Strasse. Weber met him outside and ushered him in and up a flight of stairs.

'This is the headquarters of the Sonderstab Musik,' he explained. The door opened onto a large area full of half-unpacked crates. Harpsichords, spinel's, zithers, violas, violins, cellos, flutes and many other instruments lay exposed to the air. His eyes came to rest on a Flemish double virginal, with two keyboards and magnificently decorated panels. He recognised it instantly; it had stood in the corner of the music room of his house where the golden engraving could sparkle in the setting sun. Now it was covered in dust.

His heart beat so loud he was afraid the men in the room would hear it. They'd stopped what they were doing and were saluting Weber. He ignored them. Levi felt numb, no training had prepared him for this moment. He wanted to launch himself at the weasel standing beside him and shove him up against the wall. To do what? Demand to know where the rest of their property was? Weber was urging him over to one corner.

'These are some of the crates from occupied countries. In crate number fifty-six, from a villa on the outskirts of Paris owned by Wanda Landowska, we found this!'

Weber pulled a blanket off an upright piano made of rippled mahogany. There was a row of lattice inlay above the keyboard and beading around the keys. It was obviously old.

'Landowska?' Levi asked.

Weber nodded.

'Half-Polish, half-French harpsichordist —'

'I know who she is.'

'Come, sit, play,' Weber insisted.

The piano was out of tune and the sound was shallow and sharp. Levi looked up at Weber, an unspoken question on his lips. Weber beamed.

'Chopin! In 1838 he and Sand, his lover, went to Majorca to escape the cold of Paris and he wrote the *Preludes* on this piano. When they went to the monastery at Valldemossa in the hills behind Padua, he took this piano with him. It was made by Juan Pauza, one of the most famous piano-makers in history — his name is on it — but we don't know exactly when.'

Levi sat down and let him hands move over the keys. 'I can tell you a story about *Prelude Number Fifteen*,' he said, 'Chopin said that he imagined himself dead, but floating on water, and the notes came like drops of rain falling on him.'

'We will get it tuned and then you can play it for the Führer,' Weber said.

Levi frowned. 'Beautiful though it is, I think the Steinway will always have a better sound. What happened to Madame Landowska?' he asked.

'I don't know.' Weber sounded uninterested.

'I've seen a photograph of her, at this piano, taken in Berlin in 1913. She is also a well-known pianist,' Levi added. He glanced around the room and shook his head. 'What an amazing collection! Where do they all come from?'

Weber's chest seemed to swell with pride. 'Some from Poland and some from France and some from here in Germany, the property of people who should not own such things. Now they are the property of the Third Reich. I'm sure the Führer has told you about his plan to open a music museum in Linz in Austria after the Great Victory. Perhaps you are part of his plan. I haven't heard you play, but I am told you are quite talented.'

Levi stood up. 'I have a brother who plays the violin, he's still young but he is very keen. I would love to be able to write to him and tell him about some of the violins I've seen,' he said.

Weber nodded. 'I'll bear that in mind, Hauptmann. We have had instruments made by Nicola and Andrea Amati and Antonio Stradivarius, Pietro Guarneri and Giuseppe Guadagnini through here. Next time we seize a masterpiece I will let you know.'

That same week Levi received an invitation to play at the von Engels' home in Wannsee. He was surprised to note that none of the Nazi top brass were there; in fact, it was a small gathering of only twelve friends.

'I'm afraid we are out of favour', the countess said, as she watched him practise on the Steinway. He looked up at her. The light seemed to have gone out of her brilliant blue eyes, and he could see strain lines on her face.

'Why would you say that, Countess?' he asked.

She smiled at him. 'Dear Hauptmann, one of the reasons I like you so much is because you seem so guileless. I know you were a friend of my nephew. You may not be aware ... We, we don't speak of him. Himmler was deeply offended by his crime and does not socialise with us anymore. My husband also promoted the sons of two of our friends to the Führer. They were given units to command at Stalingrad, but their men were starving and they both ended up surrendering to the Soviets. Adolf was furious and decided to blame my husband.'

She looked over through the open doors, at the group assembling, ready to go in to dinner. 'It doesn't pay to take sides in Berlin, Hauptmann — remember that. It is so easy to choose badly and the consequences can be disastrous. I remember the time when we laughed and listened to your music and believed we would rule the world.'

She turned back to him and he couldn't read her expression.

'The days when we were all sane,' she said.

London, 1945

Levi looked into the camera.

'At this point I want to break from my story and make a comment or two. I will never forget that day, and I am still convinced that Weber had seen, or even still has, our violins. He was the kind of person who would keep something that valuable as a personal insurance policy against Germany losing the war. Then he would need a way to escape from Berlin to another life, and a precious instrument could fund that. Seeing that double virginal made me more determined to survive than anything else that had happened. I hold the desire to reclaim our property close to my heart, and I pray that the day will come when I can do that.

'Secondly, I was at the Berghof when Germany lost the battle for Stalingrad, and I watched Hitler frame the propaganda around that with Reich Minister Goebbels. Surprisingly to me, they made no attempt to hide how great a disaster it was. They compared Stalingrad to great cities and battles from the worlds of Ancient Greece and Rome, and used words that made it sound like a patriotic, heroic struggle.

'Over three hundred thousand German men died in that siege, and Hitler and Goebbels turned it into some giant sacrifice to save the Western World from communism. I can see now that the emotion they stirred up distracted the attention of the people from the fact that Germany was slowly losing the war on all fronts. They used the radio, the newspapers and films to persuade the public that they had to make sacrifices like the VI Army had in Stalingrad. I listened to the birth of this idea of "total war" without realising what suffering it meant to my countrymen. I was enveloped by the ravings of mad men.'

CHAPTER THIRTEEN

Munich

July 1943

Levi couldn't fly to Munich. It took him two days by train because of the detours caused by the bombing of the rail lines. When he arrived, it was dark and he was exhausted and thirsty. The von Engels were as pleased to see him as he was to see them.

'You poor boy,' Elsa said as she took his case from his left hand, 'are you hungry?'

Levi smiled at her. 'I had a pretzel in Bamberg, but that was a long time ago,' he said.

She led him into the kitchen and sat him at the table. It reminded him of home, warm, cheerful and with a lingering smell of good cooking. After a bowl of pork-and-lentil soup, some crusty bread and a stein of beer, he felt revived.

'Have you heard anything from Erik?' he asked.

She was at the bench with her back to him. 'Karl will talk to you about Erik, but I think you need a good night's sleep first.'

The bed was soft and comfortable, and for the first time in a long time he slept without dreaming. He woke to the smell of freshly baked bread and coffee. He dressed in a shirt and trousers, happy not to have to get into uniform. His right arm was still a bit stiff but had become stronger, and he decided against the sling.

Karl looked up from his breakfast as Levi walked in. 'How did you sleep, son?' he asked.

Levi nodded as he sat down where Elsa indicated. 'Very well, thank you — it is a wonderful bed.'

'Good. When you've eaten, I have something to show you,' Karl said as he stood. 'I'll be in my study, bring him through,' he said to his wife.

Levi enjoyed the eggs, kaiserfleisch, cheese and toast.

'We have our own hens, a cow for milk, pigs, and I bake our bread,' Elsa said as she gave him second helpings, 'so the food shortages don't really worry us. We barter with friends for other meats, and we grow our vegetables. I couldn't live in the city now, not with the planes dropping bombs and the queues for food. We are much safer here.'

Levi nodded. He hadn't picked her for a country wife, but she seemed to have settled into her life with Karl. Her blonde curls were scraped back into a bun, and her beautiful features were not adorned with any makeup. Her clothes were handmade and plain. She seemed happier than many of the women he'd met in Berlin, including her sister-in-law, the countess.

'It is hard to see people scavenging for scraps of food. I want to help them, but that's not allowed. Our rations are less than they were when I first arrived in Berlin. And we have to be careful with water,' he told her.

She shook her head, and he got the feeling she was holding back what she really wanted to say.

'Well you can have a nice hot bath later if that is something you'd like. Soak for as long as you want! I'll take you through to Karl if you've finished.'

Levi wiped his mouth on the napkin, rose and followed her down the long hall and into the study.

Karl sat at his desk, papers all around him. He laid down his fountain pen as his wife opened the door and ushered Levi in.

'Ah, Werner. Come in, sit.'

Levi sat on the one chair that did not have a mountain of papers or books on it.

'Forgive my untidiness, I am not a desk man. I was trained to run a ship, and maybe, if my leg ever heals properly, I can get back to it,' Karl said.

Levi smiled. 'Your desk resembles mine, sir. I have newspapers piled all over the room,' he replied.

Karl's expression suddenly became serious, and Levi could see lights of anger flashing in his dark eyes. 'Did you hear what happened to my son?' he asked.

Levi hesitated, then gave a tight nod of his head. 'Yes, news filtered through to the Berghof, only because Fraulein Braun knew that he was a friend of mine and she knows your brother and the countess.'

Karl let his head droop for a moment, then he raised it again. 'I want to show you something, Hauptmann, but I am concerned that you will betray us to the Gestapo. Your feat at the Berghof is well known, and it is said that you are a favourite of the Führer. I want to trust you, but my brain is saying it is too dangerous.'

Levi felt a wave of pity. *If you only knew*, he thought to himself. He looked straight into the anguished eyes.

'Whatever the secret is, you can trust me. I remain very fond of your son, he was a good friend to me.'

Karl waited for a full moment, searching Levi's face, looking for the answer he craved. Finally he got to his feet and turned towards the closed French doors.

'Follow me,' he said gruffly.

Levi was surprised, but he followed the older man, who limped out the doors and across the massive yard towards a barn. Karl stopped at the entrance and whistled. Then he waited for sixty seconds and whistled again. The mound of hay at the back of the barn rustled, and a head slowly raised itself from the pile of straw.

'Erik!'

Levi rushed forward. Erik tumbled down to the ground and the two men embraced. The sudden rush of joy and relief that engulfed Levi surprised him. He realised he'd resigned himself to never seeing Erik again, and yet, here he was. The need to touch the fragile figure before him, to reinforce what his eyes were telling him by immersing himself in the sensual experience of his lover, was so strong it nearly swept him off his feet. He stroked Erik's cheek with one hand and blinked against his own tears.

'How ... why ... what did you manage?' Levi asked, directing his comment at Karl.

'We smuggled him out. I still had some friends who knew people, and my brother has some sway. It is best that you don't know the details, but he has been here a month, sleeping in the hay and eating Elsa's cooking.'

Levi stood back and looked at his friend. His head had been shaved more than once and the blond hair was starting to grow back, a spiky shadow across the skull. His blue eyes were still sunken and surrounded by circles of bruised skin. He had some colour in his cheeks, but nothing like the beautiful complexion which Levi remembered, and his body was grotesquely thin. His arms and legs had lost all their muscle, and his father's shirt hung on his emaciated frame. He had a scar at his temple from a blow that had split the skin, and was missing quite a few teeth.

'Oh my G-d, it's so good to see you, my dear friend,' Levi said and hugged him again.

'It's good to see you, too,' Erik's voice was hoarse as if he'd had some pressure on his vocal chords and the loss of teeth made his speech a little slurry.

'But why the barn?' Levi asked, again looking at Karl.

'There are still those who would have him shot or sent back if they knew he was home, so for now, it is safer for him to sleep here. He does a little work when he can —'

'But I spend most of my days reading and sleeping and regaining my strength,' Erik finished, 'and I can speak for myself, well almost.'

Karl smiled. 'You have much to catch up on. I will bring some beer and cheese and bread out to you at lunchtime.'

With that he left them. Erik led Levi to two hay bales by the barn wall and sat on one. Levi reached out and touched the stick-thin arm. He couldn't quite believe the sight in front of him, and yearned to gather the other man into his arms and comfort him. Erik smiled and grasped the hand in his.

'Sit. Tell me everything — what have you been doing, where have you been? How is Berlin? How is the war going?'

Levi drew a deep breath. 'Well now, where do I start?'

Levi told Erik as much as he could without risking blowing his cover. When he came to the part where he took a bullet for the Führer he expected Erik to be excited, but instead his friend lowered his gaze and said nothing.

'Erik?' Levi asked.

Erik kept his face blank and fiddled with a piece of hay. His eye twitched with a newly acquired tick.

'You hesitate to congratulate me.' It wasn't a question.

Finally, Erik looked up. 'I want to be happy. I want to tell you that you did a brave and noble thing, but …' His exhausted voice trailed off.

'Tell me about Dachau,' Levi said.

Erik was arrested in the quarters of a fellow Hauptmann. They were not, as Levi had heard, in bed, but the bed was unmade and they admitted to having engaged in kissing and mutual masturbation, nothing more. The law was unclear in its definition. He was imprisoned in Potsdam Prison, and the Gestapo gave his father a chance to prove his son's 'manliness', but Himmler felt personally betrayed by his aide and decided that his crime was sufficient not only for prosecution, but for him to be sent to Dachau.

'It's a living hell,' Erik said quietly, his eyes not meeting Levi's as he spoke. 'Homosexuals are considered the lowest of the low in the camp hierarchy, and believe me, there is a hierarchy. I lived in constant fear of what the guards would do to me. I saw men have their testicles boiled off them by water, I saw others have pieces of wood shoved up their arses, and many were beaten daily. It was not even the beatings from the guards that were the hardest to take, it was the beatings from other inmates. Many were so frustrated and furious, and they chose to take their feelings out on the most vulnerable.'

'Were you beaten?' Levi asked.

Erik nodded, but didn't look at him. 'Many times, and I had teeth ripped out. But I was spared some of the worst treatment, and I can only assume that that was because I had been an officer and I come from a military family.'

'The amount of weight you've lost tells me that food was scarce.'

Again he nodded. 'We were fed potato soup, and men fought over scraps of potato skin and pieces of buttered bread. We slept in bunks, but crowded together so that there were men sleeping on either side of you. Many objected to sleeping near us, so we were often pushed out into the freezing cold. But it was the attention to detail, Werner. There were times when you were punished if your feet hit the floor and you had shoes on, only barefoot or socks were allowed, or if your bunk wasn't made exactly right, if you looked the wrong way, said the wrong thing.'

He paused, and the knowledge that he was omitting the worst details of his ordeal hung between them like a curtain of misery. 'But the building over the bridge ...' Again his husky voice gave out.

'What about the building over the bridge?' Levi asked.

Eventually Erik looked up. His eyes were shimmering with unshed tears. 'It was a place from which you never returned. It was a crematoria, Werner. They took dead bodies and they burned them. They gassed prisoners and burned them. There was a wall there where they shot military prisoners of war, many of them from the East, and burned their bodies. When the wind blew towards the camp you could smell it, burning human flesh.'

Levi was stunned. He'd heard Reichsführer Himmler talking about the final solution, but it had always been abstract, something that was happening to people a thousand miles away. This camp was about 18 miles down the road from where they sat.

'And the men who wielded the batons and handed out such vicious cruelty were SS officers, no different from me.'

'How did they get you out?' Levi asked.

Erik gave a mainly toothless grin. 'There was a concert, and it was the turn of all the guards in my area of the camp. Father paid for two of the remaining ones to look the other way while I climbed into an old laundry basket, then they loaded it into a van and drove me out. It wasn't checked at the gate because the guard there was busy complaining about his wife to the driver. When I was missing at roll call the next morning they were going to say I'd tried to escape and someone shot me. That happened all the time. You could get shot for looking at a guard or eating your soup too fast.'

'I understand why you can't congratulate me on saving the Führer's life,' Levi said.

Erik gave a half sob. 'I was a Hitler Youth, I couldn't wait to enter the SS. I was not raised to be evil, but I came under the influence of older men, malevolent monsters who made me do terrible things because we were at war. They persuaded me to do criminal acts and call it patriotism. I believed their lies.'

Levi didn't know what to say. 'You know you were following orders.'

Erik shook his head violently. 'No! That is no excuse. I am a sentient being with powers of deduction. That's what my father says. He thought everything we did was for the glory of the Third Reich, but now he knows how they treat their own and he is struggling with his loyalty.'

'And Elsa?' Levi asked.

'She has never been a Nazi stalwart, that's one of the reasons Father brought her to live here. He was worried what would happen if they stayed in Berlin and she voiced her opinions. I think my treatment has been enough to tip her. I think she'd join the resistance if she knew how and if she thought Father would let her.'

Levi smiled. 'I knew I liked her.'

He hadn't meant to say it out loud, and now Erik was staring at him.

'What do you mean by that?' Erik asked.

Levi shrugged. 'Between you and me, I struggle to support the glorious Third Reich and the Führer, too,' he admitted.

Karl brought them soup, beer, cheese and bread, and they talked through the afternoon and into the night. Levi wondered if Erik would ask him to stay, to sleep with him in the barn. But he'd obviously had any fragment of desire knocked out of his system, for the moment at least, and eventually he told Levi that he must return inside. Reluctantly, Levi hugged him. Erik turned his face away when Levi went to kiss him, so he left.

Dinner was filling and generous, and Levi watched Elsa slip out to take food to Erik. They lived very simply compared to Karl's brother, and he couldn't help but wonder why there were no servants or housekeepers. He offered to help her with the dishes, and her grateful smile told him she would enjoy his company.

'It is so good to see Erik alive. He has suffered immensely,' Levi commented. 'If you hadn't managed to get him out he would have died.'

She nodded and scrubbed the tureen in the sink. 'Yes, Werner, he would have. And I can never forgive that. He's a good, kind man, and he's always served his country with pride. I didn't approve of what he did, but he never shirked his duty.'

'What do you think he'll do, when his strength returns?' Levi asked. 'Will he work here?'

For a moment she didn't answer, then she glanced at the closed door, laid down her brush and looked him in the eyes.

'Promise you won't say a word?' she asked.

He nodded. 'Of course.'

'I think he dreams of joining the resistance. He made friends with some Italian-born Jews in Dachau, and they taught him basic Italian. I found him a book among the chaos of Karl's library, from a trip he took between the wars, of Italian vocab and grammar. I think Erik wants to join the Italians and fight. The resistance there sabotages the fascists from hideouts in the mountains, and, no matter what our official radio says, the so-called enemy, the British and Americans, are making strategic gains in Italy. You know that.'

Levi nodded thoughtfully. 'Yes, I do. Thank you for sharing with me, I shall say nothing.'

* * *

That night Levi lay in his cosy bed and thought about his friend sleeping in the hay. He knew that what Erik had shared was a fraction of what he'd seen and gone through. It seemed to have changed him; his eyes had been opened. He knew what it was to be on the receiving end of brutality. What did that mean to Levi? His own joy at seeing Erik again, the strength of his reaction, had been a revelation. He wanted to hold him, comfort him, reassure him that the pain and fear were over. More than that, he wanted to wash away the shame he saw in Erik's eyes. All of society branded Erik depraved, and Levi felt an intense desire to sweep away the condemnation. To show Erik that he was still beautiful, at least to him. And Erik's change of thinking just made him more appealing. Levi felt an almost overwhelming need to protect him, be near him as he healed. Could Erik be trusted? Elsa had said he'd made friends with some Italian-born Jews. Did that mean his attitude to Jews had changed? How would he react to the truth about Levi? And what of this hair-brained scheme to join the Italian resistance? How would he get there, and how would he find a group that wouldn't shoot him on the spot for being a German? Perhaps if they contributed to the fighting together it might go some way to assuage Levi's continuing guilt over having taken that bullet for the Führer. The questions continued to crowd in until he finally fell asleep.

'Erik, what will you do? You can't go back to the SS, and I am thinking you wouldn't want to,' Levi asked. They were playing chess, the board between them on hay bales.

Erik looked up. 'I have a plan, but you'll think it wildly unrealistic.'

Levi scratched his head and moved his queen.

'Will I?' he asked, keeping his voice casual.

'You know I disapprove of the methods employed in the camps. There is far too much delight taken in the act of killing innocent people. If I told you I wanted to join the resistance, would you feel you had to report me to the Gestapo?' Erik asked.

'No,' still Levi didn't look up, 'but I would suggest I came with you.'

Erik was clearly stunned. His hand froze with the rook hovering above the board. He gazed across at Levi. 'But, but you're some kind of national hero! You took a bullet for the Führer.'

Levi smiled at him. 'And it was one of the stupidest things I've ever done. I have had nightmares about that moment. All the agony this country has been through, and perhaps all it would have taken for it to end was for me to do nothing.'

Erik also smiled. 'Are you saying the Führer is mad?' he asked, his voice barely above a whisper.

'Stark raving insane. No question. And some of the others are very frustrated by that. I suspect that if they could've had things their way, it would be so much worse for the Allies. Germany may well have won the war in the East. Some of his decisions, made from Berlin without full knowledge of the front lines, resulted in the most despairing messages back from his generals. His fury was terrifying.'

Erik's exhausted face was more animated than Levi had seen since they'd met again.

'Do you think the English and the Americans will come?' he asked. 'Some of the Jews talked about surviving until the camps were liberated. That the Allies were coming. It gave them hope.'

'Yes,' Levi said with a firm voice, 'I do think that they will come and Germany will lose the war. Remember I get to read the English papers. But it is not going to happen next week, next month or maybe even next year.'

Erik was still watching him, the chess piece spinning between his fingers. 'Do you want that to happen, Werner?' he asked.

Levi nodded. 'It pains me as a German, but yes, I do. You'll like the British, they're good people. I don't think they will be cruel in victory.'

He watched Erik's eyes as the young man took in his words and processed them, then clarity came.

'How do you know that?' Erik asked.

Levi dropped his gaze to the chess board and said nothing.

'Werner?'

Eventually he looked up. It was the biggest gamble he'd taken since he landed in Berlin, but he trusted Erik and he felt the sudden need for a friend who truly understood him. Karl, Elsa and Erik were the closest thing he had to family, and it felt as if he and Erik were alone in a hostile world, with menace breathing in the shadows and risk attached to every word. He didn't know what his feelings for Erik were, he'd never been in love — but if this was love, so be it. Erik could be a comrade in arms. Besides, he was so tired of the pretence.

'Because my name isn't Werner Schneider and I am not really a Hauptmann.'

Erik blew out his breath and waited.

'I'm a spy for the British,' Levi added quietly.

'So what is your real name?' Erik asked.

'Levi, Levi Horowitz. I'm a German Jew, and I fled Berlin in 1938 for London. I was interred on the Isle of Man and the British Secret Service recruited me, because I speak English, French and Italian and I play the piano. They wanted me to get close to Hitler and report back what I heard and I did get close, very close.'

For a second longer Erik stared, then he threw back his head and roared with laughter. Levi felt the humour rumbling up from inside himself and couldn't help but let it spill out. Their combined mirth continued until they were both wiping tears from their eyes.

'And did your spy masters tell you to intervene and save his life?' Erik asked, still barely controlling his amusement.

Levi shook his head. 'No, but I suspect they are pleased I did. I have tried to tell them what Goering and Himmler and Bormann are like.'

'How do you cope with the Wagner?' Erik asked.

'I'm trained. I'd never played it before, but they knew that if I got to play for the Führer, there would be Wagner, lots of Wagner.'

Erik gazed at him, with a sense of wonder in his exhausted eyes. 'You're a Jew?' he asked softly.

Levi nodded. 'I am.'

'All those conversations we had, that time when we found those Jews on the street and you cut his ear lock and then punched —'

'Don't remind me. It was one of hardest things I've ever had to do. But I had a cover to maintain, and that was the behaviour you expected of me.'

Tears sprang into Erik's eyes. 'Forgive me. I'm so sorry. You must have hated me!'

'No, I didn't. At times I didn't understand why, but, in spite of your words and your beliefs, I loved you. So you don't think of us, of Jews, as sub-human vermin anymore?'

Erik shook his head fiercely. 'No! God, no. I saw them, Levi. I saw them praying as they marched into the gas chambers with their heads high and courage all over their faces. I saw men who took their sons' places and gave up their own lives. I saw them singing and praying and keeping each other's spirits up. And I saw kindness. I saw a Jew tending the wounds of a man like me, a man my fellow Aryans called depraved. He was nailed to a plank and had wood shoved up his arse, and a Jewish doctor got him down and bathed his blood away.'

He dropped his head into his hands and began to sob. Levi hesitated for a second, then moved beside him and gathered Erik into his arms.

'Shhh. It's over now, you're safe,' Levi whispered as he stroked Erik's back with his hand. He felt a sudden pulse of warmth, an old and familiar sensation. Slowly the tears subsided and Erik pulled away. He rubbed his face with his hands and sat up.

'So what will you do now? Go back into the lair of the devil and wait for the war to end?' he asked. 'And when the liberating forces arrive you can put your hands in the air and say, "Don't shoot, I'm one of you!"'

Levi smiled. 'Do you have a better suggestion?' he countered.

'Yes, I do.'

Erik stretched out his hand, and Levi noticed that it was criss-crossed with narrow white lines of scarring, perhaps from healed cuts. The thin fingers closed around his. 'Run away with me. Burn your uniform behind the barn and let's go to Italy and fight the fascists, fight for freedom. For justice for your kind and ours and for humanity.'

It was a huge decision. His handlers would be furious, Goebbels would be incensed, and the Führer would be manic with rage.

'You said you loved me. Do you still?' Erik asked. Even before he nodded, Levi knew it was the right choice.

'Yes, I do. And how do you feel, knowing I'm a Jew?' he responded.

Erik smiled. 'You're the bravest Jew I know. How could I not love you?'

It was the next step in this crazy adventure, to swap the lie that was his life in Berlin for the chance to fight for liberty and against tyranny and to be himself. But more importantly, he'd found a reason to go forward, face a new challenge, in the broken man beside him. Maybe it was love, maybe it wasn't, but it was the core of Levi's being, and he knew he couldn't leave Erik again.

CHAPTER FOURTEEN

The National Archives
Kew, London

September 2017

'I can't get over how nearly his path crossed with Rachel's,' Simon said as he shook his head. He looked up at Major Stratton.

'The Italian maid he referred to was our younger sister, Rachel, a German Jew posing as an Italian Catholic and hiding in plain sight. And that man he met, Hauptmann Harro Schulze-Boysen, was the father of my sister's child, Kobi's maternal grandfather. If Levi had made it to dinner at their house, he would have found her and perhaps he could have rescued her and her baby. Her daughter, Elizabeth, was being looked after by a Lutheran couple on a farm outside Berlin.'

Major Stratton was shocked. 'The Harro Schulze-Boysen of the Red Orchestra? He's a hero in modern-day Germany,' he said.

Simon nodded, surprised by the comment. 'Obviously he and Levi never had the chance to really talk.'

'It appears that the men spying for the Russians and the Americans had no contact with those who were there for the British. That seems incomprehensible today,' Stratton added.

'And maybe the girl Levi saw on the bicycle the night he murdered Rolf was Rachel; we will never know. I've read the letters she left to her daughter, and she said that she did ride a bicycle around Berlin. Part of her role was to post anti-Nazi flyers, and she was a skilled artist so she copied and forged documents. She was arrested with the rest of them in 1942, but when the Gestapo learned that she was really a Jew, she was sent to Auschwitz. My mother died there, too. I was in Dachau from 1939 to 1945 and I played the violin. In August 1943, when Erik escaped, my father was still alive and we held regular "concerts", if you could call them that. We played for officers in their mess. Who knows? Maybe we played a part in Erik's escape, maybe not. We certainly weren't the only musicians forced to play for the Nazis.'

'When I told you all about Schulze-Boysen and what I'd discovered in Berlin about the Red Orchestra, Feter Levi said nothing,' Kobi said thoughtfully.

'He may not have remembered the name, but even if he knew he'd met the man, how could he tell us without revealing everything?' David said.

'Once we all knew that Rachel was their "Italian' maid", he must have realised that he could have saved her. That would have caused him pain, pain he didn't share,' Simon reflected, almost to himself. He sighed deeply.

Cindy squeezed his hand. 'You look tired, Poppa.'

'It's such a lot to take in. Everything is so different from the Levi I knew. Why didn't he tell me?'

The last question was directed at Major Stratton, who shrugged. 'I can't answer that, Mr Horowitz. But I can guess. Maybe he was ashamed of the fact that he had worn the uniform. Maybe he felt that you wouldn't understand why he had to kill Rolf, why he had to save Hitler. Maybe he was afraid that it would ruin your relationship, that you would disown him,' he said.

Simon shook his head. 'Never,' he muttered.

'He threw himself in front of Hitler and took a bullet and he never told us.' David was still digesting the information, and his voice reflected his conflict. 'I just can't believe my Feter did that.'

Major Stratton coughed. 'And it is that reaction he was afraid of, I think. You must consider what would have happened had Hitler been successfully assassinated before 1945, and there were numerous attempts, believe me.'

'Would the intelligence service have sent him into Germany had they known he was homosexual?' Kobi asked.

Major Stratton hesitated then shook his head. 'Possibly not, but at the time of his recruitment I think he wasn't sure what he was. He'd had one very brief encounter. But it might have placed him at an increased risk. Imagine if he'd been the officer that Erik was arrested with — so much more at stake for Levi.'

'Does he see Hitler again?' David asked.

Major Stratton shook his head. 'No. The rest of his war is fought in Italy. Hitler would have had him shot for desertion if he'd gone back to Berlin.'

'Does Erik survive? Why didn't he tell me about him? What happened to them?' There was a note of desperation creeping into Simon's voice.

Cindy rubbed his arm. 'Let's watch the rest and maybe your questions will be answered,' she said.

Stratton went to the laptop. 'Yes, some of the answers will become obvious,' he said, 'others you will have to work out for yourselves.'

He hit the button and the figure of Levi came to life on the screen again.

Munich, July 1943

Levi said nothing of their plans to Karl and Elsa. That night, as they enjoyed dinner together, he told them about his life in Berlin and his time at the Berghof. He was careful not to mention Himmler, as it was clear that both blamed him for Erik's imprisonment. Levi was impressed by Karl.

'Your visit has been a real bonus for Erik,' Karl said as he watched Levi eat.

'I can't tell you how happy I am to see him, sir.' Levi smiled as he glanced at the older man. 'I had given up all hope of seeing him again.'

Across from him he saw a shudder go through Elsa, but she kept her eyes on her plate. 'So had we,' she said quietly.

'I won't lie to you, I find his sexuality hard to understand,' said Karl.

Elsa raised her gaze in response to her husband's words. 'But it is his business, not the state's,' she said, and anger flared in her eyes.

Karl nodded and Levi could see tenderness in his expression. 'Indeed, I agree. He's my son and I love him. If I felt shame, I don't anymore.'

Levi chose his words carefully, he wanted Karl to know he was impressed by his attitude, but didn't want to give any indication of the nature of his relationship with Erik. 'He is lucky to have you as a father, sir.'

Karl shook his head. 'That's as may be. I did what I could to rescue him and I want him to be healthy and to live.'

Elsa looked up, and Levi could see unshed tears in her eyes. 'Which is more than those brutes at the camp wanted. I detest them and everything they stand for!'

Karl put his hand on her arm. 'I know how you feel, but they are not representative of the whole Reich. I don't believe that behaviour is systemic. And neither do you.'

There was a distinct warning in his tone. Levi heard it as clearly as she did. After a moment's hesitation she brushed the tears away and smiled at her husband.

'Of course not, darling, the Führer would be horrified if he knew.'

Levi wondered how Elsa had coped with the Erik he used to know in Berlin, the proud SS-Hauptsturmführer who had been part of the death squads in Poland.

'How old was Erik when you married?' Levi asked.

Elsa smiled. 'Fifteen. He was a beautiful teenager, a truly good person and had such a sweet nature. The Erik I knew then, he's back with us. Those dreadful men —'

Karl raised his hand. 'Enough, Elsa! Werner can see the change for himself.'

Elsa glanced over Levi's shoulder, and when he turned to follow her gaze he saw a framed photographic portrait of the Führer on the dining room wall. Nothing more was said, but it was enough to remind him that he needed to continue with the role of Hauptmann Werner Schneider for the time being at least.

Something in Elsa's expression told him she was wondering about his relationship with Erik. Had they been lovers in Berlin? How close were they now? How much did Levi share Erik's dream of joining the resistance? He was very tempted to confide in her, but loyalties ran deep, and he suspected that Elsa's first was to her husband, and his first might even now be to the Fatherland.

He slept badly, spending hours awake planning the next day. It was safer for him to stay in uniform, at least until they reached the Italian border. Erik could be his charge, a dumb and deaf young man, under the protection of Hauptmann Schneider. That way if, by the greatest of bad luck, they were questioned, his papers and his reputation might get them through.

The next day he put on his uniform and caught the bus into Munich. He visited the Deutsche Reichsbank. He withdrew all but a few of the reichsmarks he had been carefully squirrelling away each pay day, in thousand reichsmark notes. Then he purchased a duffel bag with strings that allowed him to carry it on his back, and two sets of clothing, including two heavy woollen coats. Erik was slightly shorter than Levi but much thinner and he knew he would need a good strong belt for Erik's trousers until his waist filled out. Lastly he bought two pairs of strong hiking boots, a map of Italy and some food, cheese, sausage and fruit. No one questioned him, but he felt it safer to explain to the shop assistants that he and a friend were planning a hiking trip during their leave from the

Luftwaffe. He knew such things went on despite the war and the government encouraged those who could spend money to do so.

He went straight from the bus to the barn, showed his loot to Erik and then hid it in the hay. As evening fell he took a bath, put on his uniform, slid his suitcase under his bed, and took the few possessions he had brought with him and slipped out of the house.

Elsa and Karl were in the parlour listening to the radio. He desperately wanted Erik to be able to say goodbye to his parents, but it was too dangerous. He'd reassured Erik that one day he'd be able to return to his life and those he loved.

Erik was waiting for him, dressed in the clothes and boots Levi had bought that day, with the food and map in the duffel bag. Levi added his clothing and two bottles of water, then Erik helped him put the bag across his shoulders.

'Is it heavy?' Erik asked.

Levi could hear the anxiety in his voice. He shook his head. 'It's fine,' he said.

'To the railway station?' Erik asked. Levi looked at him. He was still underweight, but a good deal of strength had returned to his wiry body, his face was alive and his eyes were sparkling.

'To the railway station. It's about an hour's walk,' Levi answered. They would get a train to Kufstein on the German–Austrian border. That way anyone tracing them would not know their final destination. From Kufstein they would get a train to Innsbruck.

The walk took longer than they had anticipated, so they had to sleep on a bench at the station until the first morning train to Kufstein. Levi didn't share his apprehension with Erik, but he couldn't help checking to his right and left every few moments. Erik slept but Levi kept watch, telling himself regularly that with each hour that passed they were closer to freedom. If Karl had risen early and gone out to see his son, he would have discovered him gone. Logic would tell him to try the train station first, and he would be hard to convince. During the early hours before dawn Levi rose and paced the platform, silently willing the time to pass. His relief when the train eventually arrived was palpable, and he hid it by hurrying Erik into the carriage.

Just before the border, the train was stopped and boarded by German soldiers. Levi had anticipated this and was ready when they reached the carriage where he and Erik were sitting alone. Two young soldiers thrust open the door and snapped to attention.

'Heil Hitler, Hauptmann,' they said in unison.

He reached into his pocket and withdrew his papers. 'Heil Hitler. How goes your war?'

They both hesitated. Levi outranked them and he could see they were anxious not to offend him. 'Very well, thank you, Hauptmann. I'm sorry to ask you, sir, but can we see your papers?' one asked, his nervousness revealed in his high-pitched voice.

'Of course.'

Levi handed them over, and the soldiers consulted them together.

'Thank you, sir.' The one who'd asked handed them back. 'And who is this?' He was pointing at Erik, who gave him the best toothless grin he could muster.

'This is a deaf mute. I'm delivering him to Innsbruck. He is a relative of an Austrian naval officer and I am charged to look after him.'

The soldier hesitated.

'Is there a problem, soldier?' Levi asked as he started to rise to his feet.

'No. No sir, that is all in order. Enjoy your journey.'

The men looked at each other and one pulled the door shut again. Erik let out a huge sigh, and Levi put his finger to his lips to remind Erik to say nothing. They exchanged a knowing smile, and Erik went back to his book.

In Kufstein, Levi took two rooms at a local inn and they rested until evening. At a restaurant close to the station they ate a beef broth, a rich stew and some strudel. Erik's lack of teeth slowed his progress through the stew and meant he cut the strudel into tiny pieces. The waiting staff looked upon Levi's uniform with distaste and he longed to tell them the truth, but when Levi explained that Erik was a deaf mute they made up a parcel of pancakes with cherry jam and sugar for him. He gave them his toothless beam and nodded his delight.

From Kufstein they travelled on to Innsbruck, less than an hour away. It was night, and Levi decided to press on by taking the last train of the day to the Brenner Pass. It was a small village on the border between Germany and Italy. They got off the train there, and Erik kept guard outside the deserted men's room at the station while Levi changed out of his uniform.

Just outside the village they found a field that bordered onto a wood. It was wild and overgrown and seemed to belong to the whole town. Wrapped in their heavy coats they slept in the grass until morning.

'We need wood if we're going to burn my uniform,' Levi said as they munched on sausage, cheese, bread and pancakes.

'Are you better to bury it or burn it?' Erik asked.

Levi thought about that. 'The smoke from a fire might attract attention, but I do so want to burn it!'

Erik smiled at him. 'I want to see it burn. If we stay close by and douse the fire as soon as everything is burnt, it should be fine,' he said.

So they gathered pine branches and leaves from the floor of the copse and put Levi's papers in the pocket of his uniform, before dousing it with a small bottle of methylated spirits he'd taken from the barn, and laying it on the pile. He held the lit match to a dead and withered branch, and it burst into flame.

'It's a funeral pyre for Werner Schneider!' Erik laughed as he took Levi's hand in his and they watched the blaze lick at, and then consume, the clothing. It felt cathartic on more levels than Erik could begin to understand, Levi thought to himself.

'Long live Levi Horowitz, resistance fighter!' Erik added.

Levi shook his head. 'I've been thinking about that. We need new names. Battle names. If we're taken by the enemy we have a name to give them that isn't our real name. Our accents will betray us as German, but our Italian is good enough to get by. And we need less intimidating names. You sound like German aristocracy, which is exactly what you are, and I sound Jewish, which is what I am.'

'What do you suggest?' Erik asked.

'When I was young my brother and I had nicknames for each other. I was called Wolfgang Bach and he was Amadeus Bite. So I thought I could be Wolfgang Bach and you could be Ludwig Offenbach.'

Eric roared with laughter. 'I don't remember you being so funny. So just when I'm getting used to calling you Levi, I now have to call you Wolfgang.'

Levi laughed. 'No, you call me Wolfie.'

'How appropriate, hungry like a wolf.' Erik smiled.

'We need water from that stream to put this fire out before the whole village turns out to see what's burning. Come on, move that scrawny behind of yours and help me!'

CHAPTER FIFTEEN

Northern Italy

August 1943

The next day Levi changed what was left of his reichsmarks into Italian lira and they split it between them, in case they became separated. They moved at night and slept in the fields by day, keeping out of the way of people, buying what food they needed in villages as they passed. Levi watched Erik closely, and if he felt his companion needed to rest, he called a halt and they found somewhere to sleep for the rest of the night. They saw very few German troops for the first few days and were easily able to avoid them, but suddenly, as they reached the outskirts of the town of Trento, the Germans, in panzers and trucks and on foot, were pouring in from the north.

'What shall we do?' Erik asked softly as they lay in a ditch and listened to row after row of their countrymen pass by on the road. 'It's obvious they've invaded Italy. What chance will a resistance group have now?'

Levi shook his head. 'We said we were going to find a group of partisans willing to let us join,' he answered. 'Even more reason if their country has been occupied. They'll switch from fighting the fascists to fighting the Germans. Do we stop here or do we go further south?'

'What kind of target do partisans attack? A railroad, let's find a railroad and follow it,' Erik suggested.

Levi nodded. 'We need to skirt around the town to find the railyard.'

Three nights later they were using the treeline for cover and crossing fields that bordered the railroad south. Sudden movement to his right caught Levi's eye, and he signalled to Erik to stop and drop down into the shadows.

'They're laying explosives,' he whispered.

A group of figures, barely visible in the moonlight, were crouched by the side of the track. Levi motioned to Erik and they crept closer.

When their work was, apparently, done, the group picked up their rifles and ran back towards the trees. Once they were out of sight, Levi went to the track and examined their handiwork. Simple explosives were nestled snuggly under the sleepers in six different places, with wires trailing off towards the long grass a few feet from the track. Levi picked up a wire and rubbed it between his thumb and forefinger. It was a fuse.

'Put it down,' a harsh voice said in Italian, and he felt the click of a gun near his head.

'Don't shoot, I want to join the partisans. Fight the Germans. I've been looking for you,' he said urgently.

Erik emerged out of the grass and came to stand beside Levi.

'We don't want to stop you, we want to help,' Erik said.

The man holding the gun swung it from one to the other. 'Who are you?' he asked, his voice full of suspicion.

'Who are you?' Levi countered.

'I'm the one with the gun. Start talking.'

'We're Germans, ex-officers, deserters, on the run from the Wehrmacht. If we're found we'll be shot. I'm Wolfgang Bach and he is Ludwig Offenbach.'

'Do you have papers?' the man asked.

They both shook their heads.

'No. But we can help you if you let us,' Levi said.

The man gestured towards the trees. 'I have to stay here, I have work to do when the German supply train comes through. You, head for that large tree with the fork in its trunk. Twenty yards into the forest, give one long, low whistle and someone will come. Tell them Mario sent you. They may kill you, but they may not.'

Levi didn't wait to be told a second time. He picked up the bag and started to run, Erik bent low beside him, keeping stride. They did as the man had said. When they'd paced around twenty yards in, Levi gave one whistle and they stood and waited. The first thing they heard was the click of at least three guns.

'Who are you?'

They couldn't see who had asked the question. Levi dropped the bag and raised his arms in the air. Erik followed suit.

'Two men wanting to join your resistance. Mario said to tell you he sent us.' Levi said, keeping his voice steady despite his thumping heart. Suddenly he felt the barrel of a rifle in the small of his back.

'Walk,' a voice said harshly.

* * *

About a mile into the forest the ground began to rise. Soon they left the cover of trees behind and found themselves among large moss-covered boulders. They walked on. The men were behind them, two of them with guns levelled at their backs. At one stage Levi started to turn around and was told in no uncertain terms to face forward. He glanced over at Erik. In the thin, cold light of dawn he could see his companion was tiring quickly, and he prayed it wouldn't be much further. If Erik fell over, he might well be shot.

Ten minutes later they were guided between two massive rocks and came out onto a plateau, where about thirty people were cleaning weapons or splitting wood, making soap or even cutting up the carcass of a wild boar. Behind them, caves dug into the side of a mountain, and in the middle of the plateau was a rough wooden table. The men wore trousers, shirts, with bandanas tied around their necks, the few women wore heavy skirts and shirts. They all stopped to stare at the arriving group. Before anyone could speak, there was a loud explosion and a fireball leapt into the sky from down by the railway, sending a wave of smiles and back-slapping around the circle. Levi and Erik stood silently and waited.

A man emerged from the largest cave, wiping his hands on a cloth. He was over six foot, broad-shouldered, with curly dark hair and a full beard, a swarthy complexion and very quick, intelligent eyes that surveyed the newcomers.

'Mario sent you?' he asked.

Levi nodded.

'You're German?' the man asked.

Levi nodded again.

'Do you speak any Italian?' the man asked.

'Yes, we both speak Italian,' Levi answered.

The man came closer and frowned. 'Why would you want to join us? Why should we not shoot you and drop your bodies at the gates of the occupying troops?' he asked.

'We've come from Munich to find a resistance group to fight with,' Levi said.

The man was watching Erik. 'Do you speak?' he asked.

Erik nodded. 'Yes, I do. I was a German officer in the SS and then I was arrested and sent to Dachau, a camp in southern Germany. The conditions were horrific and I was beaten, starved and abused. My father paid to have me smuggled out. I want nothing more to do with the Third Reich, other than to sabotage its plans.'

The man continued to stare at Erik. 'Why were you arrested?' he asked.

Erik flicked a glance at Levi. 'I found it impossible to support the Führer's policies. I was party to the atrocities committed in the East. Millions of innocent people are being slaughtered, others are sent to camps to be worked or starved to death. It is inhumane.'

The man nodded slowly. 'We hear rumours of this. Some of our number are Jews who have hidden from the Germans and fled into the forest and then the mountains. They have watched the rest of their family exterminated in their homeland. What's your name?' he asked.

'You can call me Ludwig. Ludwig Offenbach.'

The man smirked. 'I take it that's not your real name,' he said.

'No, it's my battle name.'

'We all have such names.'

The man turned his attention to Levi. 'And you? Why are you here?' he asked.

'I'm a German Jew, from Berlin. I was persecuted by the Nazis and I have to assume my family are dead or in a camp somewhere. I evaded capture and I want to fight with you. I am trained in armed and unarmed combat.'

The man raised his eyebrow. 'Are you? Why?' he sounded unconvinced.

Levi hesitated. He needed to select the information he wanted them to know. 'The British Army trained me. I've killed a man with a knife. I know how to take care of myself.'

'And your ridiculous name?' the man asked.

'Wolfgang Bach. I can be called Wolfie.'

'My name is Peter, and for my sins I am in charge.'

Peter signalled to another man, who was sitting beside a woman at the table, watching. He came to them. Peter put his hand on the new arrival's shoulder.

'And this is our best fighter, Sandro. Show us what you can do against him,' he said.

Levi sighed and moved away from the group. Sandro followed and they began to circle each other. Sandro's arms were tattooed, solid and muscular, and the hands he held ready at waist-height were fisted. Levi pounced, hooked his leg around one of Sandro's and kicked the other out from under him. Sandro stumbled sideward. Before he could regain his balance, Levi landed a single punch to the chin, pulled Sandro's arm out straight, twisted it up behind his body and pushed the man facedown onto the stone floor. It was over before Sandro could try a move. Levi returned to stand in front of Peter.

'I'm a little rusty, but I know how to break a neck, slit a throat, and wire an explosive, send Morse code and also some basic first aid. I speak German, French, English and Italian, and it may be completely useless here, but I also play the piano.'

Peter's face was transformed by a grin.

'And I'm an excellent shot and know about ten different ways to kill a human being,' added Erik, keen not to be left out.

Peter turned to face the watching crowd. Sandro was nursing his arm and scowling at them.

'What do you think? Shall we give these two a trial?' Peter asked.

There were several cries of 'yes', along with one solitary 'no' from Sandro.

Peter turned back to them. 'Seems you've found yourself a home. We are the Liberistas, some Catholic, some Jewish, some agnostic, some atheist. All of us hate the fascists and the Germans. Are you hungry?' he asked. They looked at each other.

'Yes,' Levi admitted, 'it's been a few hours since we last ate. Bread and cheese has been our staple diet.'

'Well, we're given food by sympathetic villagers and townspeople from two settlements nearby. We shoot rabbits and there are fish in a stream about a mile away,' Peter said. 'Come this way.'

He led them into a huge cave, with a high ceiling and a cooking fire encircled by stones. A sizeable blackened pot hung over the fire. Peter grabbed two bowls and filled them.

176 of Julie Thomas

'Rabbit stew, with pasta and vegetables. Good nourishing food, but not kosher,' he said, as he gave them the bowls and a spoon each.

'Thank you very much. I haven't eaten kosher for a very long time,' Levi said.

'I grew up fishing the streams and lakes around my home in Munich. If there are fish nearby, I'll catch them,' added Erik.

Peter nodded his satisfaction. 'And when you've eaten, take a rug from the pile in the next cave and find somewhere in there to sleep for a few hours. It's dry and warm, not soft, but you can't have everything.'

And so began their time with the Liberistas. Their first assignment was to string a wire at head-height across a road outside the nearest village. When four German soldiers, who'd been drinking in the taverna, rode back towards their temporary compound on motorcycles, the wire brought them crashing to the ground. Levi shot one and Erik another, and the other two were dispatched by Sandro in quick succession. They stripped the bodies of guns, ammunition and cigarettes, then rolled them into the roadside ditch.

Upon their return, Peter broke open a bottle of Chianti and Levi and Erik enjoyed a glass each. Perhaps it was the liquor or the adrenalin that loosened Levi's tongue, but as they sat beside the fire, alone together, and watched the dawn creep into the cave, he broached a topic he'd been ignoring. Between the two of them they spoke German, but stuck to their new names.

'Tell me, do you think you'll ever want to sleep with anyone ever again?' Levi asked quietly.

Erik didn't answer. He was using a stick to draw a pattern on the dirt floor.

'I know it's been a long —'

'Why do you ask?' Erik said, his voice almost accusatory.

Levi shrugged. 'I just wondered. We sleep side by side, we spend twenty-four hours a day together, and yet you never show me any physical sign. There was a time …'

Finally, Erik looked up at him and shook his head. 'Not here, not now. It might get us killed. But one day.'

'Are you sure it's not because I'm a Jew?' Levi asked quietly.

Erik's face registered his shock. 'How could you ask such a thing? Have I shown *any* prejudice against the Jews in this camp?'

Levi shook his head. 'No.'

'I don't know what to say to you. But I promise you the problem is mine, it's not because I think you are at all inferior. I've never seen you that way.'

'You have images in your head. Horrible images, real things, you saw and felt them. I understand that. And you can't get rid of them.'

Erik shrugged. 'And the more Germans I kill, the fainter those images become. Was it wrong of me to want to kill those men tonight? They were young soldiers, like we were, or at least like I was. Doing their duty for their country, and yet I felt such rage when I saw them,' he said.

'It's not them you're angry at. We can't get to the men who give the orders, so we wage war against those we can reach.'

'What have we become?' Erik asked suddenly. Levi wanted to touch him, squeeze his arm, cover his hand with his own, but he knew Erik didn't want such gestures.

'Soldiers,' he said, 'fighting to survive.'

Levi was running, stumbling, trying to catch up, to escape. Guards in greatcoats, with ferocious dogs on short chains, were chasing him. The air was full of noise and flashes of light like huge fireworks. Relentlessly they pursued him, through the gates of the camp and towards the bridge. He could see smoke belching from the brick chimney, and the air was full of a sweet stench that clung to his clothes and filled his nostrils. Inside the building he could see ovens, huge cavernous holes with fire leaping. The air was dry and hot. He fought the hands as they ripped at him, tearing the uniform from his body.

'You saved the Führer! You must die!' voices screamed.

Levi shook his head from side to side. 'NO! No! I didn't,' he shouted back at them. He writhed, trying to escape the thin sharp nails that scratched his skin.

'Wolfie!'

The sound echoed at the back of his brain. He fought against the arms that were holding him.

'Shhh, Wolfie. You're having a nightmare. Just a bad dream.'

Hands soothed and caressed him. The visions subsided and he woke. His body was covered in sweat, he was trembling and his breathing was ragged. He could feel Erik's arms around him, clasping him tightly.

'It's just a bad dream,' Erik repeated.

Levi ran his fingers through his wet hair and blinked. 'It was so real,' he said, his voice hoarse.

Erik held a bowl out to him. 'Here, have some water,' he said as he let Levi go.

Still his heart pounded, and he felt caught in that strange place between terrible image and dark reality.

'What were you dreaming about? What didn't you do?' Erik asked.

Levi drank from the bowl. The water was cold and sweet. 'I was being chased and they were accusing me of saving the Führer. That I must die for that. They were trying to push me into an oven.'

For a moment Erik let him sit there and drink, recover.

'It's your subconscious mind,' Erik said at last, 'it blames you for taking that bullet. You need to reconcile yourself to what you did. Logically you know that if you'd done nothing and Hitler had died, someone even worse might have taken his place. You've told me what they were like, the others, and I have first-hand knowledge of Himmler myself. The man is a freak, an ogre. But your emotional self blames you for what was an automatic reaction.'

Levi shook his head to clear the fog that clung stubbornly to his thinking. 'What are you telling me?' he whispered.

'Goering and Gobbles. These men, along with others like Bormann, they would have taken the reins of power and they're at least as mad as, if not worse than, the Führer.'

Levi looked at him. He could see the general outline of Erik's face in the glow of the fire, but not his features.

'What can I do? To stop the nightmares?'

Erik raised hand and touchèd his cheek. 'I'm not sure I know. You just have to keep telling yourself that it was not a wrong thing to do. Keep forgiving yourself in your conscious thoughts.'

'Have you forgiven me?' he asked.

'You don't need my forgiveness,' Erik said simply.

'Yes, I do. When I think of what they did to you. The despicable regime that could create a place like that. The brutality. The cruelty. He's responsible for it. Men like Himmler and Goebbels, they get away with what they do because he encourages it. Allows it. I could have stopped all that.'

'You have no way of knowing it would have stopped. Maybe it would be even worse with someone else in charge. He didn't order what happened to me. I was a victim of an efficient and judgmental system.'

Levi took a deep breath and nodded. 'It will all end, Erik; we have to believe that. One day they will all be called to account.'

Peter ran a very strict organisation. They knew who the sympathetic farmers were, and they tried not to be too demanding. If people were short of food themselves, they were not asked to contribute.

On their fourth day they were put on food-collection duty with Sandro and some of the other men. The farm seemed deserted when they left the cover of the trees and ran across the open ground. The house was empty and the dogs were barking in the yard. They were about to leave when Sandro checked the barn and let out an involuntary yell. They sprinted to join him. Four bodies, two adult, two children, swung from the rafters. They had tight nooses around their necks and one wore a placard in German that said, 'Collaborator with the partisans.'

'Damn the Germans!' Sandro swore as he dragged a wooden bench towards the bodies. 'Help me get them down. The least we can do is bury them.'

Levi could see his own reaction mirrored in Erik's pale expression and grief-stricken eyes.

'They know the risks, all of them,' Sandro said as he handed Levi a shovel, 'and they choose to help us anyway.'

Everyone had a job to do, and they all did it willingly. Women cooked, repaired clothing and learned to strip, clean and fire weapons, as if the camp was discovered and overrun by the enemy, all must know how to defend themselves. Older women went on scouting missions, because they could move more freely without attracting suspicion, and if they were caught they might be able to convince the Germans that they were housewives going about their normal lives. Both men and women took it in turns to guard the camp, stationed on the rocks, twenty-four hours a day.

When winter set in it became harder to find food, and the villagers had less to give. The Germans confiscated stores of wheat flour stockpiled for pasta-making, and vegetables didn't grow in the frozen soil. Animals that had been kept for milk or eggs, or fattened for bacon, were taken by the Germans for food.

Hunger was an ever-present sensation, something new to Levi but not to Erik.

'Here, try this,' Erik said as he sat down beside Levi.

"What is it?' Levi asked, looking at the brown lump inside the metal cup.

"It's snow with a little coffee poured over it. If you suck it slowly, it will give you water and the taste helps to keep the hunger pangs at bay. We did it when we could get some coffee in the camp.'

Levi took the mug and smiled at Erik. 'Thanks.'

They talked endlessly about the parties at the count and countess's house in Wannsee, and the bountiful food they remembered.

On a particularly cold night Erik found an old coat and tore it into strips of felt.

'What are you doing?' Levi watched as the firelight leapt off Erik's figure, bent over his work.

'Here,' Erik picked up a bundle and came to sit at Levi's feet. 'This is another trick I learned in the camp. It will help you to stay warm.' He pulled the boots from Levi's feet and started to bind the strips around his toes. Levi said nothing, and just watched the bony fingers go about their work. It pulled at his heart to see Erik replicating a skill that had kept frostbite at bay in that terrible place.

As the Germans began to round up the local Jews for deportation to concentration camps, many fled into the forest and found their way behind the rocks. The men would gather in small groups, reading the Torah and praying, and the women would do their best to keep Shabbat. Levi watched them, realising he had all but forgotten these rituals. When some Orthodox men with ear locks arrived, it made him wonder if Erik remembered the group they had abused on the streets of Berlin. It played on his conscience, but he didn't mention it and neither did Erik. One day Levi sought out a rabbi who had been with them only a few days.

'I've had to break so many laws I hardly feel Jewish anymore,' he said, as they sat together and ate.

'Do you still believe in G-d?' the rabbi asked.

Levi hesitated a second too long.

'It is hard to find G-d in the midst of all this suffering. How well do you know the Book of Job?' the rabbi asked.

'I know he suffered and kept praising G-d,' Levi said.

The rabbi nodded. 'That's right. He loses his oxen, his sheep, his camels and his children, and he reacts by saying that when G-d sends us something good we welcome it, so how can we complain when he sends us trouble?'

'But he curses eventually and questions G-d,' Levi said hesitantly.

'As we all do, son, when we see such anguish and feel our own pain. Never forget that Job answers the Lord and is ashamed and repents, and G-d blesses him. I believe G-d will bless you, too, one day. The last part of your life will be blessing upon blessing, and you will live, as Job did, to a very great age.'

The rabbi's words haunted him. Such a future seemed so unlikely, and he doubted it was what he deserved.

One day a group of Jews followed one of the food-gathering patrols back to the mountains.

Peter slapped Sandro on the back. 'I send you out for food and you bring back more people!'

Sandro shrugged. 'What was I supposed to do? They were huddled at the base of a tree and the snow was beginning to cover them. I told them to go down to the town, but they followed us. Every time we turned around, there they were. They don't speak.'

'Where are they from?' Peter asked.

Sandro shrugged again. 'I don't know, like I said, they won't speak.'

Peter motioned to Levi to join him. He pointed to the group, two men and two women, one girl and a young boy. They were watching the men and women of the camp. They wrapped their coats around themselves, but still shook with fear. The large dark eyes were wary, and yet there was a sense of determination there as well.

'They followed Sandro. See if you can talk to them.'

Levi nodded and walked over to the group. 'Hello,' he said in French. They shrank back and said nothing.

'Hello,' he tried in German. Understanding blossomed on all six faces. 'Do you speak German?' he asked.

One of the men stepped forward. 'We understand and speak German. We are originally from Poland, from Warsaw.'

'And you have evaded capture all this time?' Levi asked.

The man nodded. 'I am Marcin, and this is my wife, Maria, and our children, Freyderyk our son and Roza our daughter. This is my brother, Pawel, and his wife, Sofia. My parents were with us, but they died and so did Pawel and Sofia's twins.'

Levi smiled at them all and indicated the fire inside the cave. 'My name is Wolfie and I am from Berlin. Are you Jews?'

Marcin hesitated, then nodded.

'Come and sit by the fire, you must be very cold,' Levi said, as he guided them into the cave. The children had shawls drawn around them and were shivering. He gathered up a pile of blankets and distributed them around the group.

'We don't have much food, but there is some soup and bread,' he said, as he dished out bowls for them from the pot.

The names they'd given Levi were battle names. Peter was impressed by that and by their resilience, and he invited them to stay. Marcin was a shoemaker. He mended all the holes in the partisans' boots with solid pieces of wood wrapped in wool then covered in animal fat, creating watertight footwear. Maria was a teacher, and she took over from the elderly woman who had been telling the few children stories about life before the war. Pawel was young and fast and joined the raiding parties, and Sofia had been a nurse, so she looked after the minor cuts, bruises and bumps of everyday life.

Roza was nearly twenty, elfin with a cap of dark hair, sharp features, serious brown eyes and olive skin. She reminded Levi of his sister, Rachel, and he didn't mind that she became his shadow. There was a fierceness about her that he liked, she wanted to be every bit as useful as the men.

'Tell me about Berlin,' she said, as he sat by the fire, cleaning his rifle.

'What about Berlin?' he asked.

'Your family. How many siblings do you have?'

'I have two brothers and a sister. My youngest brother and my sister are twins.'

'My cousins were twins. They got sick with fever and died last winter,' she said, and he could hear the pain in her voice.

'I'm sorry. You must miss them.'

'The middle brother, the one younger than you, how old would he be now?' she asked.

Levi hesitated. Somehow he still thought of Simon as a child but he would be twenty-two. 'A little older than you, twenty-two.'

'What's his name?' she asked.

'I'm Wolfie Bach and he is Amadeus Bite.'

She laughed. 'Why such silly names?' she asked.

He smiled. 'We both loved music, we both *do* love music. I play the piano and he plays the violin. The composers were his friends; I think he liked them better than real people — especially the Gentiles in the city where we lived! He had pictures of them on the walls of his bedroom. So it seemed natural, when we were young, to call ourselves Wolfgang and Amadeus and Bach and, so, Bite.'

She laughed again. 'You're quite mad, but I like it. I haven't laughed for so long, and to speak in German with someone other than my family, that is a treat, too.'

'How long have you been away from home?' he asked.

The laughter trailed away. She looked down at her hands, they were rough, calloused and the nails were broken. She was a pretty girl, small and bird-like, so like Rachel.

'It seems such a long time. None of the rest of our family would come, and they were all rounded up. I think they must have moved into the ghetto. Papa spent all his money on train tickets.

'We were going to cross Germany to Switzerland and then to London, but we were warned that they were rounding up Jews at the next checkpoint. So when the train stopped we leaped off onto the grass and ran into the trees. Since then we have been walking and sleeping, stealing food where we could, and avoiding the Germans.'

Levi shook his head. He felt a sense of awe at the spirit such families displayed in the face of sheer brutality. 'You are all very brave. You father is a remarkable man. I'm glad you found your way here.'

She looked up at him. 'So am I. Tell me about your war, Wolfie. Why are you here?' she asked.

Alarm bells sounded in his head. How much could, or should, he tell her? If he told her the truth it would endanger her life. If she was taken by the Germans and interrogated, he would be at risk.

'I ... my family were turned out of their house and I think all our possessions were confiscated. I escaped and I wanted to fight. So I came here, with my friend Ludwig. He has been in a concentration camp and he hates the Nazis as much as I do. He's not Jewish, but he has a strong sense of justice.'

'So you don't know what has happened to Amadeus?' she asked solemnly.

He shook his head. 'No. But I'm sure he'll be fine and we will meet up again after the war. You can't kill music.'

One miserable day, as snow fell in swirling blasts, Erik went out on a routine food-gathering mission in the forest. Levi stayed behind to help Mario to mend some broken rifles. Two gunshots rang out from the direction the mission had taken, and the guards on the rock signalled for the camp to be on alert. Levi fought against a rising tide of fear as he helped the women and children into the caves and grabbed the rifles with the other men, ready to mount a defence if the camp was breached. The need for action kept panic at bay, but he still said a silent prayer for Erik.

Ten minutes later the group hobbled through the heavy snow at the gap in the stone entrance. Half their number were gone, and Erik was supported by two young men.

'Ludwig!' Levi ran to him and took his arm from Pawel's shoulders. 'What happened?' he demanded.

'A patrol. They surprised us before we could take cover. He's been hit in the leg,' Pawel said.

It was a long, deep gash, with a broken thigh bone and no exit hole. Sofia came running to examine Erik by the light of the fire in the main cave. Erik was lying on a pile of blankets, his face ashen and his eyes closed.

'We need to try to set the bone, then get the bullet out or the leg will become infected,' she said.

'Can you do it?' Levi asked anxiously.

'I can try. It depends how deep it is and how close it is to the main artery. He's lost a lot of blood and shock has set in.'

Sofia rinsed the knives and tweezers in alcohol and held them over the fire. Levi held Erik's shoulders from behind his head. He hadn't regained consciousness and didn't move at all. Peter sat on the other side of Erik, holding a lantern so she could see.

'I'll do my best,' Sofia said, looking at Levi, the knife poised above Erik's bloodied thigh.

Levi nodded. 'I know you will.'

The bullet was lodged deep in the muscle and she had to move some of the splintered bone to reach it. The makeshift tourniquet above the wound stopped some of the bleeding, but it was still hard to see. Rag after blood-soaked rag was tossed aside. Then Sofia tried to realign the bones in place. When she'd finished and sewn up the wound and splintered his leg, she sat back. Her dark eyes were full of concern.

'It's up to him now, he's lost a lot of blood,' she said.

Twenty hours later, Erik was wracked by fever. His lips were cracked and dry, his skin was sallow, and his eyes more sunken than when Levi had first seen him in the barn.

'Come on,' Levi murmured as he sat beside Erik and prayed. 'You can't leave me now. We still have too much to do.'

He looked at the black stain spreading over the crude bandage and knew that it would take a miracle for Erik to survive. In his delirium, Erik called out Levi's real name, tossed and turned and burned. Levi wiped him with a cold cloth.

'I didn't tell you, you were so broken by that terrible place.' He stroked the hand that lay on top of the blanket. 'You didn't want to hear. Listen to me now, my love, my Erik,' he said softly. 'I love you.' He leaned down and kissed the parched lips gently.

The hours passed. Finally, Levi lay down beside the patient. Exhaustion tugged at his brain and he felt himself slipping towards sleep. Much as he longed to keep vigil, to stay awake until the fever broke, he was spent. He'd close his eyes, just for a few moments, and his renewed strength would help Erik to fight.

'Wolfie.'

It was a light, carefree voice. He could feel the sun on his face. They lay, he and Erik, side by side on a rug in a field. He could hear Erik's laughter, such an infectious sound. It wasn't the Erik he'd first known, misguided, arrogant, charismatic and brainwashed; no, it was the Erik he'd become. A kind, gentle man who had had the scales of prejudice peeled away and felt a fierce need for justice. Suddenly Erik kissed him on the lips and he felt a swelling of happiness and joy —

'Wolfie.'

The voice was more insistent this time. The dream broke like a shattered mirror and he opened his eyes. He was in the cave. It was daylight. He sat up.

'How is he?' he asked.

He felt the absence before his brain registered it. The body wasn't there anymore.

'Where is he?' he demanded.

Sofia sat beside him. He couldn't read her expression.

'I'm so sorry, Wolfie. He died peacefully while you were asleep. Peter wants to take him down to the forest and bury him with the others, and I knew you'd want to go.'

Dead? Erik? It was so unfair. How was he supposed to tell Karl and Elsa? He'd promised Erik that he'd go home one day. And they had a pact. They were going to grow old together. It was understood. Unspoken. They were going to find a place where they could be true to each other, in no fear of judgment. He shook his head, hoping this too was a dream.

'I'm sorry, Wolfie, I know he meant a lot to you,' Peter said.

Levi climbed to his feet. His legs felt heavy, reluctant to follow the small party down to the stream that ran below the caves but high up on the forest line. Levi helped to carry

Erik, who had been wrapped in a piece of sugar sack. He was cold and weighed far more than Levi could have believed. They'd already dug a hole and fashioned a crude cross from two sticks. Other crosses, and sticks with crude Stars of David drawn on them for the Jewish dead, commemorated members of their band who'd given their lives for the cause, sticking out of the snow like stark mute reminders that they had lived at all.

Levi made a silent promise to bring Erik's parents there one day, and then said his goodbye. His mind felt numb, as chilled as the air around him. There was no time for tears, and as he turned away he felt a door bang shut on this part of his heart, never to be opened again.

CHAPTER SIXTEEN

The National Archives
Kew, London

September 2017

'Roza.'

The single word sat in the silence. Major Stratton froze the image on the screen and waited for someone else to speak. Finally Cindy sighed. 'Well at least we have a name to put to her now, even if we know it wasn't her real name,' she said.

Major Stratton coughed and walked to the centre of the room in front of the screen. 'A name to who? If you don't mind me asking,' he said tentatively.

David stirred. 'I'm sorry, Major. When my Feter died and Papa was sitting Shiva for him a woman visited the house, the home he had shared with Feter Levi for so many years. She was old and very small, spoke with a faint accent, we thought perhaps Eastern European. She told Papa that if Wolfie had died and he was his brother, then he must be Amadeus Bite. She promised to return and tell us about his war. She said —'

'She said I would be amazed and that I should know he had had a full life,' Simon interrupted.

'And you haven't seen her since?' Stratton asked.

David shook his head. 'No. We didn't know her name or where she came from.'

'When she saw that Levi Horowitz had died in Vermont, how did she know that he was Wolfie? When did he share his real name?' Daniel asked

Stratton frowned. 'You'll find that out later in the story, and she must have remembered all those years. There are organisations for people who fought in partisan groups and they keep records. We know she was Polish, born in Warsaw around 1924, and she shares her real name with Levi. It might be enough. I'll see what we can find.'

'We would be very grateful if you could find her. It was three years ago, she might be dead,' David said.

Simon looked over at him. 'And she might not! I'm still alive,' he said. They all laughed, and Simon gave a shrug. 'Ancient, but still alive.'

'But you're invincible, Poppa,' Daniel said.

'They must have shared something, to make her revisit that part of her life so many years later and come to pay her respects,' Cindy said thoughtfully. 'Feter Levi must have meant a great deal to her. And he never said a word to us about her.'

David Horowitz wondered how many secrets one family could hold. He was mulling over all this new information and thinking about his childhood. He'd been born in New York to a German Holocaust survivor and an American mother. But they weren't a typical post-war nuclear family, because Feter Levi lived with them. He'd never questioned the fact that he had a dad and an uncle, and when his dad was hospitalised, which happened often because of the digestive problems the years of starvation had left him with, his uncle took over fathering him. They were very different men. His father wanted to be 'American' with a passion that had taken David years to understand. They'd gone to baseball games and celebrated Fourth of July barbecues. Simon insisted that his son could recite all the American presidents in order of office, and explained just how lucky they were to live in a country that was free and where the police were kind and didn't hurt the people. He kept the pantry well stocked and gathered armfuls of wood in the winter to keep them warm. While no food was ever wasted, he went to great lengths to ensure his family were fed and warm. There were nightmares that frightened a little boy listening in the next room, and periods of silence, a withdrawing to a place of anger and fear, which David now realised were common to Holocaust survivors.

But in contrast there was his artistic, gentle Feter Levi, who read to him and helped him to paint pictures. Levi was the one he copied, the one he studied. He held his head the same way and practised his uncle's long-legged stride. From an early age he noticed how Feter Levi treated people, his genuine smile and his quiet care. David's school friends loved his uncle because he cooked them treats and took them out on Halloween, read them stories and played them music on the piano.

Only once had he seen a different man beneath the quiet exterior. His mother had taken him to the new amusement park on Coney Island and Feter Levi had come with them.

It was a magical place of hotdogs, rollercoasters and rides. A group of men had heard Levi's accent and accused him of being a Nazi. He'd tried to defuse the situation by walking away, putting himself between the aggressors and his sister-in-law and nephew. But the thugs had smelt fear and they'd persisted. David's mother had scooped him up and tried to hide his face in her shoulder, but he'd seen enough of the flashing fists and feet, and the way his Feter Levi had left five fully grown men lying on the pavement, groaning and spitting blood and teeth. His mother told him never to mention it, especially to his father. Now he knew how and why his Feter had learned those skills.

When he was in his twenties, she'd told him she had a secret to share with him. She'd planned to take it with her to her grave, but had reconsidered after viewing a television programme about people who needed bone marrow from a relative.

'If that ever happens, you need to know who your closest living relative is,' she said quietly.

David frowned at her. 'Don't worry yourself about things that may never happen. We will still have Poppa, and Daniel has Cindy and me.'

She shook her head. 'I know you love Simon with all your heart and he's your father, no doubt about that. But we tried for years to conceive a child and I finally realised it wasn't going to happen. Your biological father is your Feter Levi. He's every bit as much your family, and you look so like him, so like the grandmother neither you nor I ever met.'

He hadn't spoken to Feter Levi about this revelation, and then suddenly, when his uncle had died of a heart attack, it had been too late. He couldn't share his secret with anyone in his family while Simon was still alive; he knew that the family, and especially Daniel, were his father's proudest achievements. But oh how he longed to have his Feter back now! Why had he kept so much from them all? It wasn't because he didn't love them. He had been more fiercely protective than David had ever realised. It must have been because he loved them so much that he felt the need to keep the truth from them.

Kobi Voight excused himself from dinner at the kosher restaurant they'd discovered close to the hotel. He wanted time to be alone and think about his great-uncle. Had he wondered why Feter Levi didn't marry? Had he spared a moment to ponder whether the elderly man had had a love of his life? He hadn't known Levi as anything other than a man in his nineties, quiet, thoughtful and watchful. Kobi's cousin, David, and the other members of the family had memories of him as a younger man, possibly athletic and a bit of a daredevil. He'd always been creative, an artist, a potter, an interior decorator. Kobi, as an artist and an art history professor, shared those traits. Levi was the one who had spent hours with him, studying every inch of the Albrecht Dürer painting that Kobi had persuaded the family to allow to go on public display. Levi had died before he'd seen that happen, but Kobi knew that he would have been greatly pleased by the way it was received. No one else looked at the painting the way Feter Levi had. Feter Simon was obsessed with the Guarneri violin and listening to his grandson, Daniel, play it, but Feter Levi had adored that painting since childhood.

No one in the family had known his other secret. If Levi had been honest about his sexuality, then maybe Kobi could have been honest about his.

Kobi had felt confused by his feelings at school. He had waited to meet a girl he wanted as a girlfriend, like his friends seemed to be doing. It hadn't happened. His one sexual encounter with a woman, at a party when he was at art school, was an absolute disaster. Then he'd lost his heart to an older man and had a brief gay affair. When the object of his infatuation left town without telling him, he was devastated and decided against pursuing love of any kind.

In 2014 he'd gone to Berlin on sabbatical, taking some letters his mother had given him. He'd had them translated, and subsequently discovered that his mother was a Horowitz by birth. The letters were written by his grandmother, Rachel, Levi and Simon's younger sister, to his mother, Elizabeth, before the Red Orchestra network was broken. If Levi had found Rachel and rescued her and her daughter before they were betrayed in 1942, what would that have meant? Elizabeth had grown up with German, Lutheran parents who'd immigrated to Australia in 1950, and she'd married and had three children, including Kobi. How different things could have been didn't bear thinking about.

Elizabeth hadn't discovered the truth about her heritage until 2014. She'd met her uncles, and had been there when Feter Levi died. And now he had still more to tell her. How would his mother react to all that had happened since, all the new revelations?

While in Berlin he'd met George Ross and they'd ... What? They'd done nothing. A little flirting, some museum visiting together, some shared dinners. George was on his own pilgrimage, finding his Jewish Polish roots. They'd split up before Kobi had discovered his own Jewish family. How ironic would George have thought it — they shared the same kind of background, the same tragedy and stories of survival.

And now here Kobi was, in London, in a hotel room reflecting about George, his mother and his Feter Levi and life and lost opportunities. Almost without thinking he rolled off the bed and opened a drawer. Empty. What hotel stocked a phone directory in 2017, he scolded himself, as he opened his laptop. Within five minutes he had a telephone number written down on the bedside pad. The phone rang several times and he nearly hung up.

'Hello?' a voice said.

He hesitated.

'Hello? George Ross speaking,' the voice said. He could hear the irritation.

'George. You probably won't remember me, my name is Kobi Voight. We met in Berlin,' he said, wincing at how insecure he sounded.

'Kobi!'

It was so loud he had to take the phone away from his ear. He grinned.

'Yes, Kobi.'

'Where are you?' George asked.

'In London, long story. I wondered if you'd like to go for a drink?'

There was no hesitation at all. 'Hell yeah! Where are you staying?'

'Near Leicester Square,' Kobi answered.

'Bar Soho. Old Compton Street, you should be in walking distance. I'll meet you there in thirty minutes.'

It was a gay bar, as Kobi knew it would be. It shimmered with class; wooden floors, plush sofas, heavy red curtains and a bar lined with old books. George was there when he walked through the door. He looked much the same, short dark hair, olive skin, designer stubble and tawny eyes behind rimless glasses. Kobi wondered in passing what Feter Levi would have thought of him. He still had a lean, muscular body underneath the Amani suit and a handsome face, but he looked a little more thoughtful, as if life had knocked some of the sheen off him.

Kobi extended his hand and George shook it. 'Good to see you, Kobi,' he said. 'What would you like to drink?'

Kobi was about to ask for a beer, but changed his mind at the last minute.

'I'll have a cosmopolitan, please,' he said.

George grinned. 'Excellent choice.'

He took the steps to the bar two at a time and eventually returned with a drink in each hand. A cosmopolitan for Kobi and an espresso martini for himself. Kobi had sat down on one of the red sofas and George joined him.

Kobi accepted the glass with a nod. 'Thanks. Imagine being able to find you so easily in a city this big,' he said.

George shrugged. 'I don't think anyone can stay hidden nowadays, not with social media. What brings you to London?'

'Family. We were contacted by the military archive at Kew. They'd found a recording made by my great-uncle when he came back from the war. They wanted us to see it. My Feter

Simon and his family were coming over, so I said I'd meet them here. I still live in Melbourne.'

'Feter?' George was looking at him with a frown of confusion. 'They're Jewish?'

Kobi nodded.

'You didn't tell me.' There was a slightly accusatory note in George's voice.

'I didn't know. It was through the letters I had with me, In Berlin. The author was my maternal grandmother. Feter Simon is a Dachau survivor.'

'Good Lord, how amazing! My family were Polish, also Jewish. I often wondered what happened to you,' George said. He sipped his cocktail.

'Feter Levi told his family that he stayed in England during the war, but it appears that wasn't the case. He was sent back to Germany, in uniform, as a spy, and he ended up in Italy with the partisans.'

George was staring at him. 'And you're finding this out now?' he asked.

Kobi nodded again. 'It's quite a story. He played the piano for Hitler and he took a bullet for him. And we've discovered something even more enlightening.'

'It sounds like a movie script,' George said.

'He was gay.'

For a moment they looked at each other. Kobi felt a connection running back in time to his great-uncle, the feelings he'd hidden and the love he'd lost when Erik died. It surged forward and seemed to engulf him. He smiled at George over the rim of his glass.

'And so am I,' he said quietly.

CHAPTER SEVENTEEN

Northern Italy

January 1944

To Levi, it was almost as if someone somewhere had had a hand in what happened next. Three days after Erik's death, a Jewish doctor from Rome arrived on his way north. He told the group about Assisi, where the men of the Catholic Church were involved in an underground organisation hiding and smuggling Jews, procuring false papers that allowed them to travel or to live openly in the town. He didn't know much, but he knew it was G-d's work and it was a beacon of hope. As he listened, Levi felt a wave of calm wash over him. He had to make his way to Assisi, he had to help.

He went to Peter and explained to him that he wanted to leave and travel south. He asked to take nothing more than a pistol and some ammunition and a small amount of food.

Peter embraced him warmly. 'We are so sorry to see you go, Wolfie, but we understand. You need a change, you need to be somewhere new, somewhere without memories of Ludwig. Our love and all our prayers and our thanks go with you.'

'Tell Roza I will pray for her family,' Levi said.

He slipped away that night when most of the group had gone to sleep. If he was honest with himself, he feared that Roza or Sandro might persuade him to stay. He and Sandro hadn't gotten off to the best of starts, but they had become firm friends. The Italian was a man of few words, but his heart was fierce and genuine and he admired strength and commitment in others. He knew that when Wolfie was beside him, his back would be covered, and no matter what happened the German-turned-Italian wouldn't miss. Now he wore Erik's warm coat — it was a tight fit, but it kept out the chill.

And little raven-haired Roza was a source of confusion to Levi. Since Erik's death she'd wanted to sleep cuddled up to him so that his body heat would keep her warm, but he'd insisted that she continued to sleep between her mother and her aunt, safe from any instinctive reactions on his part. Her eyes sparkled when she laughed and she was good company. He knew she was fonder of him than she should be and she would miss him.

It felt good to be on the move again, but in the still moments of solitude Levi grieved his companion with an ache that threatened to knock him sideways. He carried Erik with him in his heart, but it didn't compensate for not having him there. His mind was flooded with words he'd wanted to say and hadn't, because he'd assumed that they would have time. Now that that opportunity was lost he couldn't help but curse his reticence.

Once again he planned to travel at night and find hiding places to sleep during the day. However, twenty-four hours into his journey he recognised a car and flagged down a businessman from Trento who ran an armament factory vital to the German war effort, and who secretly supported the Liberista by giving them food and bullets. He was travelling to Rome on sanctioned business, and he hid Levi in the boot of his vehicle and took him all the way to Assisi.

Assisi was a medieval city set among the rolling hills of Umbria, on the southern flank of Mount Subasio. As the birthplace of St Francis, one of the most important saints in the Catholic Church, it held abbeys, convents and basilicas. Some were open for people to pray, learn and be healed, but some were cloistered, which meant their occupants led secluded lives of silence and prayer, and the Germans, most conveniently for the resistance, left them alone.

His first stop was a house called 'Casa Papa Giovanni'. The door was answered by a young Italian woman.

'Can I help you?' she asked.

Levi took a piece of paper from his pocket. 'I am looking for ... one moment ... yes, Monseigneur Don Aldo Brunacci,' he said.

She smiled at him. 'Are you Jewish?'

The question was so simple and yet, under the circumstances, weighted with such significance. His shock must have registered on his face.

'What's your name?' she asked.

Again he didn't know what to say. Which name should he give her?

'I have heard that there is an organisation here that hides Jews,' was all he could think of. She looked up the empty street, both ways, and then motioned for him to follow her inside.

'Would you like a glass of water?' she asked.

He smiled gratefully. 'Yes, please.'

She pointed to a bare kitchen table. 'Please take a seat. Don Aldo is out, but he will be home soon.'

She gave him a glass of water then left him in the room by himself. *Who are these people? What am I going to say to this man? Have I made a terrible mistake?* He turned the glass in his hand and stared miserably at the grain in the wood of the table. Suddenly he felt very alone.

About twenty minutes later a man in a simple brown Franciscan habit, with a white rope belt at his waist, opened the front door. He was in his thirties, sturdy and strong, with glasses and an open, smiling face. He spoke briefly to the woman who'd welcomed Levi, then came into the kitchen. Levi stood up.

'Hello, are you Father Brunacci?' he asked in Italian.

The man extended a large hand. 'I am. What can I do for you?'

'I'm German and I've been fighting with the partisans in the north. I heard that you are helping Jews to hide and to escape, and I want to help with that work.'

The priest sat and indicated for Levi to do the same. 'What's your name?' he asked.

'Levi, Levi Horowitz.'

'So you are Jewish?'

Levi nodded. 'We lived in Berlin before the war. My father was a banker and I had three younger siblings. I was sent to London at the end of 1938, after the Kristallnacht. I haven't heard from any of my family since then. I was interred on the Isle of Man, and then in late 1940 the British Special

Operations Executive sent me back to Berlin in uniform and I spied for them. But I decided to flee to Italy and fight with the partisans ... and here I am.'

It felt so good to tell the truth.

The Father nodded. 'You have certainly played your part against the enemy. We can hide you and provide you with false papers if you want to travel. We use Southern Italian names because the south is in the hands of the Allies now, and the Germans find it almost impossible to check records from the south.'

Levi frowned. 'I don't want to travel, at least not yet. I want to stay here and help. I can speak and write English, French, German and Italian, and I'm used to danger. I want to help Jews until this war is over and we are all free.'

Father Brunacci studied him for a long moment. 'Do you believe in God, the God of the Old Testament?' he asked.

'Absolutely, but I find it harder to pray now. I have committed more sins in my need to stay alive than I ever thought possible. And I haven't been able to obey the laws of my people for years.'

The priest smiled at him. 'God will forgive — He can see your heart and your motives — and we can undoubtedly use you. For now you need to rest. I'm going to dress you as a Capuchin friar and take you to the monastery of Santa Croce, a little way into the hills. First you must learn to act as a pious Christian until we can get you false papers, and then you can live in Assisi.'

That evening Levi donned his third disguise since 1938. It was a brown woollen habit, tied at the waist with a white cord, with a pair of leather sandals on his feet. He walked with the Father to the monastery, where he was greeted by other friars, men of all age groups. Some he discovered were genuine Catholic men of G-d, and some were Jews in hiding. He ate a meal of pasta and vegetable sauce with bread, then retired to a tiny cell to sleep. It contained a bed and a chair and had a cross on the white-washed wall. He wasn't sure whether he felt safe or a little uneasy lying underneath the crucifix, but discovered that sleep came quickly.

He was woken when it was still dark and told that it was time for the first of eight cycles of daily prayer in the chapel. He followed the other monks, keeping his silence and walking in step with them. The small chapel was brick, unadorned apart from a rectangular painting of the cross with two women at the foot, behind a plain altar. He had told Father Brunacci that his name would be Father Erik and he would say very little, speaking only when he absolutely had to.

The chapel was freezing cold, and he shivered as he followed the actions of the others, kneeling when they knelt and prostrating himself on the stone floor when they did so. The Latin sounded foreign and unintelligible, and he did as Father Brunacci had suggested and said nothing. Silently he prayed for his family, for Teyve Liebermann, for Peter Dickenson, for Erik's soul, for Karl and Elsa, for Roza and the rest of the partisans, and took comfort in the knowledge that all the men there were praying to the same G-d.

After breakfast Father Brunacci arrived with two bicycles. Levi had ridden a bicycle as a child and it didn't take him long to recover the skill.

'Just remember that where your eyes go, the wheels will follow. If you look at the ditch you will end up in the ditch, so keep your eyes on the track ahead,' Father Brunacci said as he watched Levi weaving around the courtyard. Together they rode slowly down tracks in the melting snow until they reached the city itself.

'I am taking you to meet the most important person in our town, Bishop Giuseppe Placido Nicolini. Without him our work would be impossible. You will like him, I think; most people do.' Levi said nothing, but hunched down against the bitterly cold wind. Nicolini lived in the Bishop's Palace close to the cathedral. They leant their bicycles against the stone wall. Father Don Aldo rang the bell and the door was opened by a friar in a black habit.

'Don Aldo! Good morning. Please, come in.'

They were ushered into a book-lined study.

'His Grace will be with you shortly. Would you like coffee?' the friar asked.

Don Aldo looked at Levi, who nodded enthusiastically.

'Yes please, brother,' Don Aldo said. A fire spluttered in the grate, and Don Aldo heaped more wood onto it. 'It is hard to keep the wood dry in this weather, so a good fire is one of our daily miracles,' he said cheerfully.

The door opened and the friar returned with a tray, a coffee pot, a milk jug and three cups on saucers. He was followed into the room by a man in a black robe, half-covered by a white lace overlay to his knees, which was, in turn, covered by a black cape. Around his neck hung a heavy cross on a chain.

He was in his late sixties, with short silver hair and a small cap on the back of his head. He had a presence about him, a sense of charisma that gave him dignity and authority. Levi couldn't help thinking that even in trousers and a shirt he would have been able to command the room. The bishop held out his hand towards Don Aldo, who knelt and kissed the ring on his finger, then stood and shook the hand.

'Your Grace, this is Levi Horowitz. He is hiding at Santa Croce as Friar Erik. He's Jewish, from Berlin.'

Bishop Nicolini turned his dark eyes on Levi and scrutinised him. The bishop had a powerful face, strong yet calm and serene, his smooth skin remarkably unlined. Levi moved forward and kissed the outstretched hand.

'It is an honour to meet you, Your Grace. I want to help with the work you do here.'

The bishop smiled. 'You are welcome, my son. I can't help but feel that God has sent you. Please, have some coffee and tell me about yourself.'

Levi told them more than he had intended. He kept to himself the murder of Rolf, the nature of his relationship with Erik and why Erik was sent to Dachau, but everything else came spilling out.

CHAPTER EIGHTEEN

Assisi

February 1943

Levi's false papers declared that he was Friar Erik Bartolli, Italian-born, but to German parents who took him back to Germany to raise him, which accounted for his German-accented Italian. After five nights at Santa Croce he said goodbye to the brothers and moved into a back bedroom in Don Aldo's house. It was plain but comfortable and warm, and he attended one set of prayers daily, instead of eight.

One of his main jobs was to share the load of the creation and distribution of false ID cards. Once a refugee had an ID card they could acquire a ration card and get food, live in a hotel or private home, or travel. Many chose to stay in the convents and monasteries as they felt safer there, away from the public gaze, but if German soldiers stopped them on the streets of the city they had a valid card, with a new Italian name, and came from a southern Italian town.

Everything was rationed, bread, sugar, oil, wheat, rice, meat. The religious communities grew their own vegetables and had house cows and chickens, some had vineyards and made their own wine. Herbs could be gathered from the side of the road, and mushrooms flourished in the fields. Italian cuisine meant that with a little flour and salt and maybe an egg, some vegetables, or wild herbs and olive oil, you could create a hearty and filling meal. The more ration cards a religious community had, the better they all ate.

Levi rode his bicycle to the City Office in Perugia to meet Mrs Paladin. She was a local woman who risked her life every time she gave him a parcel of blank ID cards. They had a system for the handover.

'Morning, Mrs Paladin,' he said, handing her a basket of goodies from the bishop's garden and kitchen.

'Morning, Father, what have you got for me today?'

'Some egg pasta and some brassicas from the garden, cauliflower and cavils nero. Eggs, milk, Father Wilhelm's cheese and some of Monica's chocolate cookies.'

She clapped her hands together with delight. 'You spoil me! Wait here a moment,' she said.

She took the basket into a back room, and when she returned it was filled to the brim with books. They both knew that hidden underneath, in the false bottom, was the bundle of ID cards.

'Some more books for the bishop,' she said, as she handed it over to him. Levi took his leave, balancing the basket expertly in the cane carrier on the front of his bicycle.

Several times a month, as he was leaving the city, he spied a German patrol checking all cyclists and pedestrians. Instead of risking a confrontation, he turned down a side street and made his way to the church of Santa Susanna. It appeared empty, but he knocked firmly on the side door. A coded message.

'Who is it?' came a voice from inside.

'Father Erik,' he said quietly, 'from Assisi.'

The door swung opened and he was welcomed inside. A group of young Jewish men were hiding inside, and they were always delighted to see him. Some of Monica's chocolate cookies had already made their way to the supper table, along with bread, wine and cheese. He sat with the men and talked about the war, about their homes, the things they missed, until it was time to lie down in the straw in the loft and sleep. In the morning he thanked them for their hospitality and made his way out into the cold dawn.

He took the blanks to Luigi Brizzi in his print shop in Assisi. Brizzi would create the ID cards using his skill and his massive printing press, and the finishing touches added by artistic Jews in hiding. Sometimes Levi had to cycle to Foligno to see a friend of Don Aldo's who would add a stamp to make them look official.

Delivering the ID cards was always the best part of his job. These simple acts of kindness seemed like something Erik would approve of, almost as if this duty of care pierced through the grief and warmed Levi's heart. If there were children in the family, he wrangled some amaretto sweets from Monica's tin in the bishop's kitchen, and the joy on their faces brightened his day. Treats were such a long-forgotten cause for happiness, and small things brought so much delight and helped to build trust. Once a villager gave him a football, left behind by a child long grown-up, and he took it to a family with three sons, hiding in a convent. The boys were thin and weak, but they were determined to kick that ball around, much to the consternation of the nuns. At night he often sat by the fire and fashioned dolls from corn stalks and scraps of material, for little girls who'd lost every toy they'd ever owned. Large eyes, full of fear, shone with sudden wonder when he handed out these treasures.

But the risks posed by the package buried in the basket, as he cycled through the cobbled streets, never left him. He thought often of the dark-haired girl he'd seen in Berlin the night he'd killed Rolf. Was she just putting up propaganda posters or was she delivering false papers and much-needed food? Doing what he did, but doing it on the treacherous streets of Berlin. Risking everything for others. Did she know, as he did, the terror in their eyes, the trust in their trembling hands, and the tears of gratitude?

The fascists were more dangerous than the German soldiers, who left the townspeople alone as long as their papers appeared in order. When the soldiers saw him they merely called out a greeting, which he answered with a wave of his hand. The fascists followed Don Aldo and the other friars around and took photos of them. They seemed convinced that something illegal was going on. Levi joined in the game that Don Aldo played with them, smiling and waving for the camera as he rode past on his bicycle. The knowledge that they were frustrated brought him deep satisfaction and was something he was sure he should take to confession, if he were truly a Catholic priest.

'Hello, Father. Get off your bicycle.'

It was two fascist fighters, rifles slung over their shoulders, both smoking cigarettes. As Levi dismounted he thought about his partisan friends, who knew what real danger was. They didn't have to pose and pretend to be important like these two.

'Certainly gentlemen, what can I do for you?' he asked mildly.

'What's in your basket?' one snarled, peering into it. Levi wanted to say something sarcastic, but knew it wasn't worth the trouble that would cause.

'Books, for His Grace, the bishop.'

'Empty them out.'

Levi felt a pang of fear. He could only hope the false bottom of the basket would hold up to any scrutiny. Impassively and slowly he took the books out one at a time, hoping they would grow tired of waiting and move on. One of the fascists kicked at the pile on the ground.

'Hurry up!'

A flash of anger surged through Levi and he straightened. He was considerably taller than both of them. 'Those are holy books and I'll thank you to treat them with respect. You do our Catholic faith a disservice.'

They stepped back a pace, and Levi could see a frown of concern. He took the last of the books out and turned the bicycle so they could see.

'Nothing more,' he said.

One moved over and ran his hand over the cane sides of the basket.

'Frisk him. He's hiding something, I know he is,' the other ordered.

His companion turned towards him. 'You frisk him, if you're so sure. I'm not frisking a priest!'

The leader stood very close to Levi and looked up at him. Their eyes met. Levi held his gaze.

'What are you hiding, Father? Why do you cycle to Perugia to pick up books?'

Levi smiled, but it didn't reach his eyes. 'The bishop has read all the books in his own library.'

The man remained where he was for another minute, then dropped his stare and turned away. 'On your bicycle. But remember, we're watching you.'

Levi waved to them as he stacked the books. 'Very good, gentlemen.'

Only the bishop and Don Aldo knew Levi's real name and identity, to everyone else he was Father Erik. The noise pulled him from a deep sleep. He lay on his back in the dark and listened. Voices, multiple voices. And the sound of movement. He sat up and pulled his woollen habit over his bony frame.

Don Aldo stood in the centre of the kitchen. At the table sat a man, a woman and three children, two boys and a small girl. Snow flecked their clothes and their faces were flushed and wet. The eyes were all dark, sombre and exhausted.

'Hello,' Levi said cheerfully as he stepped into the room. They all shrank back slightly.

'This is Father Erik, he will help me to help you,' Don Aldo said gently. 'Perhaps some coffee, Father Erik?'

'Of course.'

Levi crossed to the stove and checked the kettle, filled it with water at the sink and put it on the flat element.

'And who do we have here?' he asked.

Don Aldo pointed to each in turn. 'This is Mario and Catherina and these are their children, Pietro, Tony and little Maria. They're Jews and fled from Milan before they could be rounded up by the Germans. They've walked a very long way.'

Levi reached for the terracotta biscuit barrel on the windowsill. 'Who is hungry and would like a biscuit?' he asked.

All three of the children shot their hands up into the air.

He took a plate from the cupboard and poured the biscuits onto it. He could see the gleam in their eyes. Hunger was familiar to him, and he knew that it would take more than a few biscuits to make up for what they lacked.

'Mario is a dentist,' Don Aldo said, as he took the kettle and poured cups of steaming coffee.

Levi grinned at the man. 'That is good news indeed. I know of at least three in hiding who need their teeth attended to. They are in great pain.'

Don Aldo nodded. 'That thought had occurred to me, too. I'm sure we can find, or borrow, the tools he needs, and he can set up a clinic in the convent. God's blessing, indeed. How does that sound to you, Mario?'

The man nodded. 'I would be pleased to help in any way I can,' he said through a mouthful of biscuit.

'Excellent! I am going to take you to Sister Francesca and she will look after you until we can get you false papers. She will have beds for you and a hearty breakfast in the morning.'

Catherina seized Don Aldo's hand and kissed the back of it. 'Thank you so much, Father. We knew if could just make here that G-d would look after us.'

'Good morning,' Don Aldo looked up from his newspaper as Levi came into the kitchen.

'Good morning, Father Don Aldo,' Levi answered as he sat down at the table.

'There's a pot of coffee on the stove.' Don Aldo smiled at him and returned to his paper. 'Our new family will need papers as quickly as we can get them. Can you ride over to the palace and tell the bishop about them? I'll go see Luigi and we'll create new identities for them.'

When he arrived at the bishop's palace there was a large black car, a German staff car, parked outside. The sight of it sent tremors up his spine, and he nearly turned around and headed for home. But Monica, the bishop's cook, saw him from the side garden and came to welcome him.

'Who does the car belong to?' he asked.

'The new commander of the city, Colonel Valentin Müller. Come and meet him, the bishop will want you to.'

Reluctantly he followed her into the house, fiddling with his habit as he walked. The two men sat facing each other in the library. Müller was in uniform. They both rose to greet Levi. He couldn't help it, the uniform made his stomach heave.

'This is one of our hardest-working friars, Father Erik,' the bishop said.

The man's handshake was dry and firm. His eyes behind his glasses were reflective, wary but unusually kind for a Nazi. 'Pleased to meet you, Father Erik,' he said. It was a southern German accent.

'You are from ... Bavaria, I think?' Levi asked.

The colonel smiled. 'Very good. I was born in Zeilitzheim. You?'

Levi hesitated. 'Berlin,' he said softly.

'Colonel Müller is a doctor, with hospital experience, and he is also a Catholic. I was just telling him that it is not the Third Reich that has sent him here, but God,' the bishop said.

The colonel gave him a small nod. 'I believe you're right, Your Grace. I will attend mass every morning at the tomb of St Francis, 7 am sharp.'

He turned and looked at Levi. 'Were you a member of the Hitler Youth?' he asked.

Levi shook his head. 'No, Colonel, I have never been a member of the Nazi party.'

Müller smiled at him, and Levi was surprised to see the warmth in his eyes. 'Neither have I, Father Erik, but please don't tell my superiors that. I think Berlin will be too busy with other problems, they will leave me to run Assisi as a hospital city.'

Over the next two months it became clear that they were indeed blessed to have Valentin Müller as the commander of their city. He set up his headquarters at the Hotel Subasio and his phone number, 210, became the most well-known number in the city. He made house calls, even visiting some of Don Aldo's hidden Jews when they needed him, and he established six small hospital sites in the city. It was never stated, but his distaste for the government of his homeland and its policies was evident in his actions.

When two German soldiers confiscated bicycles from locals and rode away, he took the staff car, chased them down and made them return the bicycles. When women and children were bullied by German soldiers, Müller was quick to stop the behaviour and made it clear that such conduct would not be tolerated. These people were the true inhabitants of the city and they would be treated with respect. In return, the locals began to call him 'Il Colonelo' an affectionate term he was proud of.

'I need your help with something,' the bishop said. Levi sat waiting for him to finish writing a note that Levi was to take to Sister Francesca.

'Anything, Your Grace, you know that,' Levi said.

'Usually I would use Father Don Aldo, but he is not well today, so I am going to trust you with this special task. Come with me.'

The bishop put down his pen, pulled out a drawer and removed a small bundle wrapped in a piece of linen.

'Bring the candle,' he said.

Levi picked up the candle, lit it from one burning in the candelabra on the sideboard, and followed him into the entrance chamber.

'This way.' The bishop held open a heavy door. 'You go first and cast light back on the steps.'

They descended into the palace cellar. The bishop led the way over to a wall with two pick-axes leaning against it.

'I hide things in here for people who cannot keep them safe', the bishop explained as he unwrapped the cloth. Inside was a silver mezuzah, a miniature menorah and some scraps of parchment, as well as three sets of papers.

'You hold the candle while I make a hole in the wall, in that corner. Not too deep ... Hold it up higher.'

Levi did as he was told. The bishop used a pick-axe to make a small square hole, then he hid the items, safely wrapped in their cloth.

'Now, we take some soil from over there and fill the hole, then I can plaster it shut. Did you know I was once a bricklayer?' the Bishop asked.

'No, Your Grace!' Levi knew he sounded shocked, but also a touch amused.

'Ah, son, the Lord uses the skills we have when he needs them. I live by "or et labora", the Benedictine motto. It means "pray and work". This way I can keep these treasures safe for our guests until they are ready to move on. We can't keep records, it is too dangerous, and so I remember where I put each set of belongings.'

As he lit the steps for the bishop to climb back into the palace, Levi marvelled yet again at these humble men of G-d who risked their lives every day for strangers. He was acutely aware that not all who professed themselves to be Christians were so kind or so brave. He'd come across many in Berlin and since who would have said they believed in God, but who abused their fellow men, Jews, homosexuals, gypsies among them, without a second thought. The men of Assisi put their faith into action and followed commandments, and Levi could see the difference around him.

CHAPTER NINETEEN

Assisi

May 1944

Winter gave way to spring and the fields around Assisi burst back into life. When he had time, Levi took a packed lunch and biked up into the low-lying mountain meadows. He knew that Erik would have loved this part of Italy, and often found himself talking to him about the work he was doing and the people he had met.

New arrivals brought news of bitter fighting further north, and that the English were pushing up rapidly in the south. They would reach, and liberate, Rome in a few weeks. For the first time Levi allowed himself to believe that Germany really would lose the war. He missed his newspapers. How were things going in the East with the Soviets, and on the Western Front? How much of Germany was being bombed, how were the Americans faring against the Japanese? Who would liberate Berlin? What would they do with Hitler? And Himmler, Goering, Goebbels, Bormann, the other men he had listened to. There must be war trials, they must be held accountable for the souls of the dead. The beliefs of his childhood told him that the men who had ordered such mass killing must die. They had sinned against G-d and his chosen people.

And yet the faith he pretended to follow told him that all men were redeemable and it was his duty to forgive the sins of his fellow man as G-d forgave him. He had no idea what the numbers of dead would be, but something chilling in the pit of his stomach told him it would be in the millions.

He remembered the conversations, or the rantings, of Hitler. The plans for retreat that the Führer had railed against. Levi had carefully noted all of that and sent it back to his handlers when he'd returned to Berlin from the Berghof.

Where would the ordinary people go? How would they find their families and friends again? Where would they live if their homes and livelihoods had been destroyed?

The practice of the Christian religion was second nature to him now. He knew all the Saints' days and the prayer he repeated as he counted the rosary beads. He felt the bread and wine on his tongue, a wafer and red wine, which was, to those of his assumed faith, the real body and blood of Jesus. He'd read the Gospels and recognised much of it as the beliefs of his ancestors. He liked this man, Jesus, a Jew, who had opened his heart and his mind to the weak, the sinful, and the outcasts. That kind of social conscience sat well with Levi. But could he accept Jesus as the Messiah, the Son of G-d his people had waited so long for? Jesus hadn't delivered the Jews from Roman servitude, and now his G-d was not delivering the Jews from the oppression of the Nazis. And yet, it was wrong to say he wasn't, because he was. There were rescued Jews all around Levi, and he didn't doubt that others were doing the same elsewhere. Was this the work of G-d?

So what would he be left with? After all his different disguises, who was he, a Jew who'd posed as a Lutheran and then a Catholic? What did he believe in? The Old Testament G-d of his heritage, a judging but loyal G-d, or the compassionate father of the New Testament, who taught him to love and forgive his fellow man? Who was he supposed to forgive? Hitler? The patrol solider who shot Erik? The officer who now lived in his house? The people who had tortured Erik in Dachau and left him a broken husk? How was he supposed to do that? The questions rolled around in his head as he cycled through the summer fields. Perhaps all he could pray for was clarity.

On the morning of 15 May he was leaving church with Father Don Aldo when they were stopped at the Don's front door by the local police.

'Father Don Aldo Brunacci?' the officer asked.

Don Aldo smiled and shook his head. 'You know who I am, Otto. What do you want?'

The officer looked uncomfortable. 'We have orders to arrest you, Father. You are to come with us,' he said avoiding the priest's eyes.

'Why? What have I done?' Don Aldo asked.

'I can't answer that. We just have orders to collect you and take you to the station in Perugia.'

Don Aldo threw a quick glance at Levi. There was a Jewish university professor and his wife sleeping in the study. They hadn't felt safe in the church where they'd been put, and had asked to stay with Don Aldo until their papers came through. If the police searched the house they would be found, arrested and deported to a concentration camp. The door was open, but Don Aldo pulled it shut.

'I will come as I am, I have nothing to gather from inside. Father Erik, would you be so kind as to let the bishop know,' he said.

Levi swallowed hard to get his jangling nerves under control. If Don Aldo could be calm, then so could he. 'Of course, Father. God be with you,' he said.

As soon as he could, Levi biked over to the bishop's palace. When darkness fell they transferred the family there. The bishop was as gracious and welcoming as always, although every room in the palace was full of refugees awaiting papers.

'I will sleep in my study and you may have my bedroom,' he told them.

Word reached them that Don Aldo had been sent to a concentration camp in central Italy. The bishop appealed to the Archbishop of Perugia to intercede on his behalf. It wasn't the Germans who wanted Don Aldo incarcerated, it was the neo-fascists. By the time the Archbishop's plea reached the commander of the guard in the camp, Don Aldo had escaped and made his way to Rome. His absence was felt deeply in Assisi; Levi did his best to reassure the families, but they had come to rely so heavily on Don Aldo and there were frightening times ahead.

'I want to tell you what I've done,' Valentin Müller said as he sat at his desk. Across from him the bishop and Father Erik watched him impassively.

'I have sent a letter to General FieldMarshall Kesselring. He's the commander of the Mediterranean theatre and therefore responsible for all of Italy. I've officially requested that Assisi be declared a hospital city. This means the Allies will be notified and it will not be bombed.'

The bishop nodded thoughtfully and steepled his fingers.

'That is a worthy action, Valentin. We all, obviously, approve, and God will be well pleased. So much history, so much of St Francis and St Clare is in these precious buildings, and once they're gone the heart of the Church in this area goes with them.'

'The US Fifth Army and the British Eighth Army are making progress, and it seems inevitable that they will liberate Assisi in the days ahead. The German SS is on the retreat from Rome and looking to destroy as much as they can,' Müller said. 'It is my aim to make the conflict here as bloodless as possible. I have substantial medical supplies, over ten million lira's worth, which I will leave behind for the treatment of the injured and the sick.'

'What can we do about the SS?' the bishop asked. 'If they enter the city the Allies will bomb it.'

Müller frowned. 'I've set up a twenty-four hour guard around the perimeter of the city gate. Any SS officer who tries to pass through, they will be repelled, by lethal force if necessary.'

A week later Colonel Müller asked to meet with them again. He was troubled, pacing the room briskly when Levi entered.

'Morning, Your Grace,' Levi said.

'Morning, Father Erik.'

The bishop sat and gazed at the German officer who turned and smiled at Levi.

'Ah, Father Erik, good morning,' Müller extended his hand.

'Good morning. What is it, Il Colonelo? You look distressed,' Levi asked.

Yet again it struck him how fond he had become of this man, how different Müller was from almost all the German officers he had met.

'I've haven't heard from Berlin, so I've decided to take my own action. It's too important to leave it to chance. I want you both to bear witness to the fact that I have drafted a letter, in German, declaring Assisi a hospital city, an open city, not to be bombed, and I have signed it with Kesselring's signature. If it is uncovered as a forgery and falls into the wrong hands it will be considered an act of treason and I shall be shot. Are we clear?'

There was silence as all three digested the implications.

'Yes, Il Colonelo,' the bishop said quietly. 'God be with you as you do His work first and foremost.'

'Good. I suggest you round up all your "special guests", the ones I am not supposed to know about, and be ready to hand their details over to the Allied troops.'

Without Don Aldo, Levi's days were frantically busy. He visited all the families, those who had been there for months and those who had just arrived, and prepared them for the chaos after the liberation. He was still picking up blank ID cards and taking them to Luigi to be printed. The danger for the families would come not only from the retreating SS officers, but from the neo-fascists who would try to fill any power void.

A night of intense fighting took place on 16 June. SS Officers set fire to grain silos and barns and blew up bridges outside of Assisi. Rapid gunfire in the hills could be heard for miles, and the smell of cordite hung over the city. As tall pillars of flame licked at the night sky, terrified citizens joined with the bishop, Father Erik and the other clergy to pray the rosary at the Tomb of St Francis. No one knew what would happen in the hours ahead. As he knelt on the cold stone floor, Levi prayed with all his heart.

'If these are to be our last few hours, at least we will die knowing that God's grace and His forgiveness shelters us,' the bishop said, his melodic voice bringing a sense of calm and resolve.

After midnight Levi rode his bicycle to the St Francis city gate and watched the Germans leave by car and on foot. The bishop was already there. Müller leapt from his car and stood on the wall overlooking his departing troops. He cocked his pistol and trained it on the Germans.

'If anyone attempts to harm a civilian, or loot anything from this beautiful city, he will be shot!' he yelled at the top of his voice. 'We leave in peace.'

'We may find we miss that man,' the bishop muttered to Levi, 'he is truly a man of God.'

The next morning Levi was woken by thunderous banging on the front door. Two neo-fascist fighters stood on the step, rifles over their backs and wooden truncheons in their hands.

'Good morning, gentlemen,' he said cautiously.

'The Germans are gone and we're in charge now!' one of them barked out.

'By whose authority?' Levi asked.

The man went to swing his truncheon, but his companion stopped him.

'We can't have no law and order, so we have filled the gap. If you don't submit to our authority you will be tortured and imprisoned.'

'And how, exactly, are we supposed to submit to your authority?'

The more violent of the two raised his weapon but didn't point it at Levi.

'We'll have no more lip from you, Father. This town belongs to us and we'll run it as we see fit. Twelve o'clock in the town square. We want everyone who can come to be there. And make sure the bishop is there, too.'

Before he could react, they strode off. He was certain that the Americans would arrive within hours. The important thing was to make sure nothing happened to the families in hiding before liberation came. He shut the front door behind him and jumped on his bicycle. There were people everywhere, not knowing what to do. Several of them stopped him and asked for his advice.

'Go home, close your doors and wait,' he said. 'This next chapter won't last long, but we don't want anyone hurt.'

The bishop was in his study. He appeared relieved to see Levi.

'Come in, Father. I have been praying for our town and the families we have in hiding.'

'Do we go to the town square, Your Grace?' Levi asked.

The bishop nodded. 'Yes, I think it would be wise to avoid confrontation for the moment. The Americans should be here soon.'

So they went, along with hundreds of others. The neo-fascist soldiers fired bullets into the air and were about to read out their requirements when the first American tanks rumbled through the St Clare gate. At first it looked as if the neo-fascists would stand and fight, but the superior American fire power was obvious within minutes and they fled through the back alleys and into the hills. As news spread, more and more people poured out onto the streets to shake the hands of their liberators, while music played in the cafés.

'So what are you going to do?' the American asked. The question was addressed to Levi, who sat beside the bishop and across from the commander at Colonel Müller's old desk.

'Some of our families want to go south, to Rome,' Levi answered.

'The church will find safe places for them until the war in northern Europe is over and they can go home. Some come from Italy, but many are from Poland, France, Hungry, Belorussia and Germany. It won't be safe for them to return north for months, maybe years,' said the bishop.

'How many have you hidden?' the American asked.

The bishop shrugged. 'It has always been too dangerous to keep records, but at least three hundred souls,' he said.

The American nodded and looked at Levi. 'And you want to go with them?' asked the American. 'To Rome?'

'Yes, I want to see Don Aldo. Then I'll go north, back to the partisans. They're fighting with the British, liberating town by town.'

The American frowned. 'You could hand yourself over to our high command in Rome, they would organise for you to go to England by ship. Germany will be too dangerous for you for a long time.'

Levi shook his head. 'Not yet. My war is not over. If I could I would join the liberating army and march all the way to Berlin, but I'm not a soldier. I have my reasons for wanting to go back to Trento.'

'Very well. When you're ready to go north, ask for safe conduct as far as the army can take you.'

Two days later Levi said goodbye to the bishop, Luigi, Monica and all the people who had sheltered him and allowed him to help others. It was a hard farewell and he blinked back tears.

'God will go with you, my son; He knows the good you have done here. We will miss you,' the bishop said as he used his thumb to make the sign of the cross on Levi's forehead. 'I know you don't believe in this, but your G-d is my God and He will keep you safe.'

'Thank you, Your Grace, I shall never forget you,' Levi replied. Then he climbed aboard the nearest army truck. His bicycle was strapped to the rear of the vehicle. There were children and adults in his truck, and one little boy went to sleep leaning against Father Erik's side, encircled by an arm. The going was slow as the drivers had to be on the lookout for buried German bombs. When they came to what looked like a minefield, the trucks stopped and specialist soldiers picked their way over the rubble strewn roads and detonated the explosives.

CHAPTER TWENTY

Rome

June 1944

Rome had been bombed from the air. As the truck rolled through the suburbs and into the central core it became obvious that sections of the city lay in ruins. Jagged walls stood stark against the darkening sky, whole apartment buildings with their fronts or sides blown off, and children in rags played among piles of bricks and chunks of concrete. When they flagged down the vehicles the soldiers broke open their rations, but most of all the children wanted to clamber up and shake their hands. Scores of people, some carrying American flags, stopped any military convoy to exchange smiles, waves and words of gratitude.

Don Aldo was in the relief office at the Vatican. He embraced Levi in a giant bear hug.

'I'm so grateful to see you alive, Father Erik, and to know our people are safe,' he said.

'I am equally overjoyed to see you, Father. We prayed unceasingly for you, and when we heard you'd escaped there was much amusement. It was such a typical Don Aldo outcome.'

The large man laughed heartily. 'It's a good story, I'll grant you that. When we have time I'll tell you all about it.'

Then he led Levi to a window. 'Look at the people,' he said. 'Day after day, still it goes on.'

Hundreds of people were dancing, laughing, drinking, and exchanging hugs and kisses. 'This is what freedom from oppression looks like. May we never forget it,' Don Aldo said.

Having said his goodbyes to Don Aldo, it was time to head north again. Levi continued to wear his habit, but he carried his old clothes in his duffle bag. When the American Jeep dropped him behind the front-line, he exchanged farewells with his liberators and biked off down the road. A priest on a bicycle was a common sight in Italy, and if he was stopped he had papers to prove he was Father Erik Bartolli.

Once again he moved mainly by night, sleeping by day. The sound of gunfire was ever present, and he occasionally heard planes overhead and the reverberation of bombs exploding. When he ventured out during daylight hours he was passed by exhausted women and old men, some on foot and some riding donkeys, the women often with bundles balanced on their heads, slowly making their way south to reclaim their devastated homes.

He chose farmhouses out in the countryside, and watched them to make sure there were no Germans in the area. When he knocked on the door and told the inhabitants he was making his way north to fight with the partisans, they gave him a hot meal and a place to rest in the barn. Only once did he hear the rumble of German tanks down the road ahead. Gathering his possessions, he fled into the nearby forest.

Partisan camp, September 1944

Eventually Levi came to the outskirts of Trento, not far from the camp. He changed out of the habit and buried it, his belt, papers, sandals and the bicycle in a ditch. His first stop was the gravesite beside the stream in the top reaches of the forest line. The cross made from two wooden sticks was still there, barely discernible in the grass and leaves. He cleared the area around it and sat down beside the grave.

'I'm back, my love,' he said softly. 'I told you I would come back and I have kept my promise. Remember how we talked about the end of the war? Whether the Americans and the British would come? Well, they're here, my love. And they're going to win. One day our Germany will be free again, and I'll make sure your parents know what happened and where you are.'

He stopped and looked around him. It was a quiet place, just the sound of birdsong and of the stream running over the rocks.

'This is a lovely place to be. I know you like it here. It reminds me of the meadows around your house.'

Swamped by the memory of a tentative kiss, he gave a loud sigh. It was the first time he'd been alone with Erik, no one watching, no one there to judge. For a moment he felt as if something was going to rise from a long shut-off compartment in his gut. A keen, a moan, a sob of grief, something that yearned to see the light of day. He sensed an almost tsunami-like wall of black rage and anguish starting to gather momentum. But it was not the place nor the time, so he slammed the door shut.

'I'd better go and see if I can find the camp. Maybe it's gone, who knows? Goodbye, sweet friend.'

He hauled himself to his feet and walked away without a backward glance. Just inside the forest he let out a long low whistle and waited.

'Wolfie!'

He couldn't see anyone, but the word was whispered close to his ear.

'Yes, Wolfie. Who's this?'

Marcin swung down from the branch of a tree, a rifle over his shoulder. He was more muscular than Levi remembered, his face was lined and stained with camouflage mud, and he'd grown a beard. The two men embraced.

'You've come back to us,' Marcin said.

Levi nodded. 'I heard you were fighting beside the British and I thought you might need a hand.'

Marcin laughed. 'Come, everyone will be so pleased to see you.'

The group was larger. Peter was still in charge, Sandro had died in a raiding party not long after Levi had left, Roza looked much same, but her younger brother, Freyderyk, had grown taller and stronger. Maria was as lovely as ever. Marcin's brother, Pawel, had taken Sandro's place as Peter's lieutenant, and Sofia, Pawel's wife, was pregnant.

They all wanted to embrace him, eager to hear what he'd done. He ate a bowl of pasta and a hunk of bread, sitting beside the fire, the others all in a circle, listening to his every word.

'A Catholic priest!' Peter threw back his big head and roared with laughter.

Levi told them about Don Aldo and the bishop and Colonel Müller and the wall in the cellar with the Jewish treasures hidden it and the dancing in the square in Rome. Those who didn't know him hung back and watched with amazement.

'So,' he said finally, 'what I want to know is what you are doing.'

'Sabotage,' Peter said.

Levi grinned at him. 'Making it hard for the Germans to fight the English.' It wasn't a question, but Peter nodded.

'The Allies drop explosives and we blow up bridges, Jeeps and tanks, and we steal guns and ammunition where we can. Sometimes we get into firefights with the Germans. We have machine guns, and we can force them to retreat.'

Roza was sitting a little way off, cleaning her stripped-down rifle. She stopped and looked at them. 'We women still go out first, we lead the way because we can move around much more easily than men. We don't draw attention to ourselves.' Levi looked over at her with astonishment. Her face wasn't the soft, fresh innocence he remembered.

'That's very brave,' he said.

Roza looked at Peter, who gave her a slight nod. Recognition, Levi thought, or permission to continue. 'If the way is clear we whistle, and that tells the group they can commence their operations. Sometimes I lead an expedition and I have learned how to set a bomb,' she said.

'But for now,' Peter said, 'you rest. Tomorrow you join the fight.'

There was no moon. The darkness was all-enveloping. Levi crouched beside Marcin, a rifle in his hands and an ammunition belt slung over his shoulder. His faced was blackened with mud, and he wore black clothes. The man in front of him held a slim torch which gave off a dim light. He couldn't see the rest of the party behind him, but he could sense their presence. A low-toned, soft whistle rose and fell. Peter raised a bent arm in the air, palm facing forward, and let it fall. The signal to proceed with care was passed along the line by touch. In formation they crept along the track, zig-zagging down the side of the mountain. At the foot of the track a line of German Jeeps sat empty in the middle of the road.

A few yards away sat a circle of enemy soldiers, smoking, laughing and talking. They were boasting about a farmhouse they'd raided that day, the women and girls they'd raped and the crops they'd burned. He felt the cold anger rising inside. Marcin, like Levi, understood the German language, and uttered an oath under his breath.

When the group reached the end of the track, Peter raised his fist, signalling them to stop. The minutes ticked by and the soldiers in the circle didn't move. Very slowly Peter extended his arm, then let it drop. One by one the partisans ran to a Jeep and rolled underneath it. The road was rough and hard. Levi opened his pocket, took out the explosive and stuck it to the cold metal above him. It adhered with a satisfying clunk and the timer began to tick. He held his breath. The chattering from the Germans continued.

Levi gathered himself and rolled away from the Jeep, sprang to his feet and sprinted for the track. They withdrew to a safe distance and waited. When the explosions happened, ten seconds apart, they ripped the night air with noise and flame, Jeep after Jeep. The Germans were blown over by the blasts. Before they could recover, the partisans with machine guns broke cover and mowed them down.

As the group ran up the track in tight formation, Marcin slapped Levi on the back.

'They'll never hurt another Italian woman,' he said.

The next night they blew up a bridge. It took careful placement, and Levi's job was to keep watch. He didn't have the expertise needed to plant the explosives, so he kept his rifle trained on the road leading north to the structure, ready to fire at the slightest sign of the enemy.

'Did Peter tell you that our names are battle names?' Roza asked. Levi nodded.

'No one seems to go by their real name anymore,' he said between mouthfuls of pasta.

Levi glanced at her. Sometimes she seemed so vulnerable, and he wondered what her life would have been like if Hitler had not invaded her homeland.

'It won't happen as long as you stay here. When the war is over you can go back to your real name,' he said.

'Will you?' she asked.

'I expect so.'

Then she glanced around. There was no one near them.

'You miss Amadeus, don't you?

He nodded. 'Of course I do.'

'Tell me about your family, what do you remember most?'

He'd spent so long trying to forget, it took him a moment or two to know what to say.

'My papa used to say to me, "You're the eldest, you must set a good example." We used to have music nights, Papa and Amadeus played our violins, and I played our beautiful Steinway piano. All through my teenaged years I had to practise pieces when I wanted to be doing something else.'

She grinned. 'Like what?'

'Oh, I don't know, playing soccer with my friends or going ice-skating or going to the movies. There was a group of us, and we used to go to cafés and drink coffee. We thought were so sophisticated.' There was a note of bitterness in his voice.

'And then the Nazis came to power,' she said softly.

He nodded. 'And our lives changed. Every week there seemed to be new things that we weren't allowed to do, or own, or be. I wanted to go to university but I wasn't allowed to, so I went to work in my father's bank and it was so boring! And I learned who my true friends were. They didn't treat me any differently because I was a Jew. When they invited me out and Papa wouldn't let me go because he thought it was too dangerous, I climbed out my window and down a tree and went anyway. I got into so much trouble when I got home!'

She laughed. 'Did he spank you?' she asked.

He laughed as well. 'He was shorter than me and he wasn't the spanking kind. But he could certainly show me that he was disappointed, and that made me feel so guilty I didn't do it again — until the next time someone invited me out!'

'Did you have a girlfriend?' she asked.

He hesitated. Memories of Rolf started to push their way up and he swallowed against them, forcing them back. It was over, done, no point in tearing away a scab just to feel the pain again.

'No. I had a group of friends and some of them were girls. But no one special.'

'I've never had a boyfriend.'

He wasn't sure what to say in reply to that. She wasn't looking at him, she was watching the flames in the fire.

'There will be plenty of time for that, after the war,' he said finally.

She shook her head. 'But what if I died tomorrow? I've never been properly kissed, and if I was shot tomorrow I'd never know what it felt like.'

The words hung between them.

'If you kiss me, Wolfie, I'll tell you my biggest secret.'

He had no idea what to do. She turned towards him, her dark eyes pleading. He could see that she desperately didn't want to be rejected. They were alone, in the middle of a war, with a higher than average chance of not being alive by the end of the week. He leaned over and kissed her lightly on the lips. When he pulled back, he looked at her face. It was tired, with the strain of her life etched around her mouth and on her forehead.

'I'm Elzbieta Krawczyk. I bet you can't pronounce that.'

He whispered in her ear. 'I'm Levi, Levi Horowitz. Now forget I told you.'

She laughed and leaned against him.

He laughed too. 'You'd be right, I can't pronounce that. Now, enough secrets for one night.'

After fierce fighting between June and December, the Allied forces pushing north withdrew for the winter and to regroup. The Germans still held the northernmost part of Italy, the

Apennine Mountains. It was the job of the resistance to cause them as much grief as possible, weaken their ability to fight and pick off patrol units, using snipers in trees. They proved ruthlessly good at this form of guerrilla warfare.

Sofia gave birth to her baby boy in the depths of a December snowstorm. Pregnancy was frowned upon, because they didn't have the basic necessities to keep the adults warm and fed, let alone a baby. And the nurse who would have led the others in caring for the labouring woman was Sofia, herself. Nevertheless she was delivered of a healthy baby. They called him Mathew, as he was a precious gift after the loss of her twins.

Peter allowed the opening of a bottle of whisky to celebrate, and there was much toasting and singing in the cave. Levi listened to the Polish, Hungarian, Russian, Italian, French and German, and pondered, yet again, how this international band of brigands had become his family. As the festivities were drawing to a close, Marcin drew him aside. He could smell whisky on the Pole's breath.

'Tell me, Wolfie, do you like our Roza?' Marcin asked, his arm around Levi's shoulders.

'Of course, she's a wonderful young woman. You should be very proud of her,' Levi said.

Marcin shook his head. 'That's right, she's a young woman. And life is short. She's very fond of you.'

Levi didn't understand his meaning at first, and then realisation dawned. 'You mean … oh no, Marcin I couldn't possibly!'

'Why not? She's Jewish, you're Jewish. And you both like each other's company, I think love will grow.'

'There's a war going on. It would be irresponsible of me to consider such a thing. What if I got killed? I can't leave her a widow, not at her age,' Levi answered.

Marcin shrugged. 'What if she got killed? So be it. You would have snatched a moment of happiness. What's wrong with that?'

Levi didn't meet his eyes. How could he explain? What could he say? *I like your daughter very much, I admire her, but I don't love her, not like that.* It was vital that his compatriots didn't know his deepest secret. He thumped Marcin on the back.

'Let's wait till the summer. The weather will be better and the war may well be close to over.'

Marcin shook his head sadly. 'Don't blame me if she finds another in the meantime.'

Roza kept her distance from Levi for the next few days. He wondered if her father had said anything to her, and silently cursed Marcin. The last thing he wanted was to hurt Roza, but it couldn't be helped. He was haunted by one of Peter's rules: no bad feelings, no argument left unresolved, you never knew if you'd have the opportunity to put things right.

It was time for yet another operation. The group's mission was to raid a warehouse and steal German supplies, handguns, ammunition, explosives and petrol. The men were waiting for the all clear signal from Roza and two other women, Enyo and Bellona. On this night the whistle never came. Peter waited an extra twenty minutes to be sure and then the men retreated to the camp. The women knew that if they had to make a run for it they were to lay low in the forest and not sneak back into camp until it was obvious they weren't being followed. The last thing they must do is lead a German patrol back to the base. Peter, Marcin and Levi stayed awake all night, but the three scouts didn't return.

'They've been taken,' Peter said grimly.

'So what do we do now?' Marcin knew the answer, but he needed his leader to say it aloud.

'We mount a rescue and get them back!'

The women had rounded the warehouse and were about to signal the all-clear when a small German patrol charged out of the shadows and bowled them to the ground. The snow was freezing against their skin, and the shock of loud German voices and rough hands stunned them. The soldiers bound their hands behind their backs and hauled them to their feet.

'We are villagers! We are just looking for food,' Roza protested in German. One of the soldiers slapped her across the face with the back of his hand.

'How can you speak German?' he yelled at her.

'I was born there, but I live here now,' she said, her breath catching in her throat as a sob.

They were marched to a truck and pushed aboard. As the vehicle rumbled over the stony ground, the girls exchanged terrified but determined glances.

About ten miles from the town the Germans had set up a holding camp. Enemies of the Third Reich, partisans, military prisoners of war, Jews and others were marched there and imprisoned while their fate was decided. Some were trucked north into Germany, some were shot, and some were garrotted using piano wire.

The girls were unloaded and herded into one of the two long huts. The soldiers thrust them onto three wooden chairs.

'What are your names?' one of the soldiers roared at Roza. She closed her eyes and said nothing. The man hit her across the face again. His furious expression was inches from her.

'I said, what are your names?'

'Suzanna,' she said in a small, choked voice.

He turned to the next girl. 'And yours?' he yelled.

She had a defiant glare in her eyes. 'Maria,' she said. 'And yours?'

Enyo thrust her head up and looked at him with disgust.

'Carlotta,' she said.

He nodded towards the group of men who stood smiling eagerly, waiting their turn.

'See those men? One word from me and they will ravish you all until you can't walk. Now, tell me everything you know about your partisan camp.'

Roza took in a huge breath. 'We are not partisans, we are village girls and we were hunting for food.'

He smirked. 'And you happened to be looking beside one of our warehouses? Do you think I'm stupid?'

She shrugged. 'You're on the losing side of the war, you tell me who is stupid,' she said.

His face was thunderous. He turned towards the men.

'They're all yours,' he said curtly.

It was imperative the partisans got their women out of the holding camp before they were transferred or killed.

'This is a volunteer mission, the stakes are high. So who wants to join me?' Peter asked as soon as night fell.

'I do,' Marcin said immediately, took his gun and stood beside Peter.

'I do,' said Pawel, and joined his brother, gun in hand.

'I do,' said Levi, as he grabbed his rifle and stood beside Pawel.

'I do.' It was Mikel, who was sweet on Roza.

'That should be enough. The rest of you need to mount a special guard. If they've tortured our women, there is a possibility the location of the camp has been given up.'

He ignored the heads that shook in disagreement. No one wanted to believe that their women would break under torture.

The camp was a good thirty minutes' jog away. A large rectangle of snowy ground was surrounded by a high fence, topped by barbed wire. Mounted spotlights swept the darkness, highlighting the snow swirling in the icy wind. Soldiers in greatcoats, with dogs on short leashes, patrolled the area. At the centre of the enclosure were two wooden huts, long and low, with snow piled against the walls.

The men halted a few yards from the fence and waited. When the lights were sweeping the other way, Peter and Pawel sprinted to different corners of the outer fence. Peter lobbed a hand-grenade over the wire. It fell silently and then exploded. The guards rushed out of one of the huts, towards the noise. They were yelling and pointing their guns into the darkness. A few seconds later, Pawel threw his grenade high in the air and it landed only feet from the Germans. It too exploded, blowing some of men from their feet. The soldiers' attention was well and truly diverted.

Peter had started cutting the wire as soon as the first grenade went off and the lights were redirected. He peeled the wire back, and he and Marcin raced across the open ground to the second hut. A guard emerged. Marcin shot him and pushed the body out of the way. The three girls had jumped from their bunks and were almost at the door.

'This way!' Peter bellowed.

The girls followed him. Shots rang out. Levi and Mikel stood at the fence line, feet firmly planted, firing at the pursuing soldiers. Mikel had a machine gun, and he scythed through the Germans as they rushed out of the hut.

Levi held the wire open and the women scrambled through, followed by Peter, Pawel and Marcin. Pawel lobbed another two grenades into the compound to give them cover. The explosions lit the area with a burst of flame. They all shadowed Peter's large form, across the snow and into the cover of the trees. The sound of dogs barking and men yelling in German not far behind them spurred them on. This was their land and they knew all the shortcuts, the frozen streams to slide across and the mountainous trails to scale. It wasn't long before they lost the pursuing soldiers, but still Peter urged them on.

Suddenly he pulled up so abruptly he nearly fell over his own feet. The others tumbled into him. Ahead, standing still in the centre of the track, stood a large grey wolf. Its eyes were trained on Peter and it snarled.

'Gently,' Peter said softly.

'Shoot it,' Marcin said, putting himself between Maria, Roza and the wolf. 'It's food.'

'A gunshot will give away our position,' Levi said quietly.

The wolf shifted its gaze from Peter to Levi as he stepped forward and took two small strides towards it.

'Don't be a fool, Wolfie,' Peter said, 'they carry rabies and their teeth are like razors.'

Levi pulled his knife from his hip pocket. '*Canius lupis*,' he said, 'if my memory serves me correctly. Come on, boy, have a go.'

He took another step forward, hands out, palms facing the wolf, the knife nestled between thumb and forefinger. The animal swung back on its haunches, growling, a deep guttural noise that rose in volume as the wolf launched forward. Levi had his arms in the air before the wolf got to him, and the knife glinted in the moonlight reflecting off the snow. The slice was clean, across the throat, and then as the animal fell he plunged the knife into its heart. Death was instantaneous.

'Someone else can carry it,' he said, wiping the knife on the snow.

Peter slapped him on the back. 'I don't know whether to call you insane or insanely brave,' he said.

Many of the partisans teased Levi for the next few days, saying his name, Wolfie, was justified by his slaying of the grey wolf. He was embarrassed by the attention and withdrew whenever possible. One evening when he was reading in the cave he heard a commotion outside. It was twilight and nearly time to eat. Peter came looking for him.

'We have visitors. They want to see you,' he said.

'Why?' Levi asked.

Peter shrugged. 'How should I know, but I think they're speaking English.'

Levi put his book down and followed his leader outside. Four of the partisans were pointing their rifles at two British officers in uniform. One officer held a photo in his hand. He looked at it and handed it to his companion.

'It's him,' he said in English.

Levi walked towards them. His instinct was telling him he needed to get rid of these men as soon as possible for the safety of the camp, not to mention the safety of the officers themselves.

'What can I do for you?' he asked in English.

They both saluted him. He tentatively returned the salute.

'Sir, we know who you are. British Intelligence sent us some photos of men and women they're looking for. They haven't heard from you for a long time. Our orders are to take you with us back behind the front line and escort you to Florence.'

Levi frowned. 'Why?' he asked.

'They want you to take a steamer back to London and to be debriefed. If, after that, you want to return to partisan activity, they will parachute you in. But the war is coming to an end, possibly only another six months.'

'And if I refuse to come?' Levi asked.

'They are orders sir, you would be best to obey them.'

Levi turned to Peter. 'They want to take me to Florence and ship me back to London,' he said in Italian.

'How did they find us?' Peter asked.

Levi turned back to the soldiers. 'How did you find the camp?' he asked in English.

'We've been airdropping supplies to these partisans for months. Reconnaissance followed the trail to the mountains, and we did the rest on the ground,' the officer said.

Levi shrugged and looked at Peter. 'Airdrops, reconnaissance and they seemed to have scrambled around in the mountains until they found us,' he said in Italian.

'It's not a hardship, sir. We're offering you a hot bath, good food and a ticket home,' the officer said.

Levi smiled. 'Well, I'm certainly prepared to go as far as Florence and sleep in a real bed.'

Both men looked intensively relieved.

Levi extended his hand to Peter. 'I'm going to go with them,' he said in Italian, 'at least as far as Florence. I'll find out what they plan for the spring and summer. If I can, I'll come back.'

Out of the corner of his eye, Levi saw movement. Before he could brace himself for the impact Roza threw herself at him. He caught her.

'You can't leave!' she cried out in German.

He held her at arm's length. 'I'll come back,' he promised.

She shook her head and tried to fling her fists against his chest.

'No, you won't. You say that now, but once you get to Florence you'll forget all about us.'

He let go of one of her arms and ran a hand over her hair.

'What makes you think I'll forget you, Meine Geliebten?'

She looked up at him, desperation on her face. One eye was blackened and nearly closed and she had a red mark on her cheek where she'd been slapped hard.

'Please, Wolfie, just come into the cave and talk to me. It won't take long,' she pleaded.

'Of course.'

He followed her into the sleeping cave. Two men were resting there and she shooed them out.

'What is it, Roza?' he asked.

She balled her hands into fists and pressed them to her eyes. 'They ... they hurt me.'

Her voice was small and full of pain.

'Who hurt you?'

'Those German soldiers.'

He gathered her into his arms. She was shaking.

'What did they do to you?' he asked gently, stroking her hair.

'I wasn't going to say anything — Papa will be so angry and I'm afraid of what he'll want to do. Most of them were killed anyway.'

She gave a huge sob and seemed to gulp air into her lungs. Then she looked at him. 'But I thought, if I'm pregnant I'd ask you to marry me. So you can't go away.'

He wiped the tears from her cheeks with his thumb. 'Did they rape you?' he asked gently.

Her head dropped down and she nodded. Her body was wracked by a low moaning sound, grief and pain and fear. He held her until she was spent, then he lifted her away from him.

'Sweet Roza. I'm not the marrying kind. But Mikel, he thinks the world of you and if you —'

'I don't love Mikel, I love you!' She was half-pleading and half-angry at him for even suggesting it.

'I have to go. I have no choice. For the safety of everyone I have to go with them. But if you do find yourself pregnant, you make sure I hear about it. Tell your mama, Roza, she will take care of you.'

She pulled away and stood up. 'Well go then, see if I care,' she said not looking at him. He hesitated.

'Please, Wolfie, just go!'

He stood up and walked out of the cave. She stood with her back to him, her arms wrapped around her slight body.

CHAPTER TWENTY-ONE

Florence

March 1945

The only bridge the retreating Germans had left standing over the Arno River was the Ponte Vecchio. The historic centre of Florence had been badly hit, but stonemasons had removed the remaining blocks and numbered them so that buildings could be reconstructed in the years ahead. As they passed the Uffizi gallery, Levi could see parts of it open to the sky, parts covered by a makeshift roof and corridors stripped of art works.

The officers took Levi straight to the Eighth Army offices. He sat in an empty room and sipped a cup of tea while he waited for his superiors to interrogate him. His mind wandered back over the past six years, the flight from home, the relative safety of England, the peril of life in Berlin, Erik, the partisans, Assisi and the heroics of the Italian clerics, and now this. What would be next? he wondered. Where were his family? Were any of them still alive?

'Mr Horowitz.' The door had opened and shut so quietly that it hadn't disturbed his reverie. The officer held out his hand and Levi shook it. He was about Levi's age, shorter, balding, with lines of exhaustion at the corners of his blue eyes. It felt strangely comforting to be addressed by his real name.

'Yes, sir.'

'We've been looking for you for quite a while. My name is Major Harrison. Please take a seat.'

Harrison sat behind the desk, while Levi sat opposite him.

'I know. I wanted to tell you where I was, but it was simply too dangerous. I went on holiday to see the parents of a friend of mine and left from Munich for Italy.'

'Why Italy?' Harrison asked.

Levi hesitated. 'It was a chance to fight. Berlin was becoming more treacherous as the madness of impending defeat seemed to be descending, I wanted to help the partisans.'

Harrison nodded. 'No one can accuse you of shirking your duty. The government thinks it's time you went back to England. Had a breather for a few months and then made some decisions.'

'About what?' Levi asked.

'We have a unit in the Eighth Army called the Jewish Brigade, made up of men such as yourself. There will be a fight for liberation in British Palestine soon. Once the war is over there will be hundreds of thousands of people who will need help to find their way home, or to a new home, all over Europe. There will be Nazis who may escape legal justice, and Jewish groups who want to make sure they don't escape moral justice. Whatever you choose, your skills will be much in demand. You will be able to make better decisions about what to do next from London. And you deserve a rest.'

Levi didn't answer for a long moment. 'Major Harrison, what can you tell me about the campaign in Northern Italy?' he asked.

'The rain and mud are slowing us down. The mountain ranges sit horizontally across the country with a river between each range. The Germans appear to have heavy artillery guarding the ridges, with panzers and pillar-box artillery behind it. We bombard the first defence, then swim the swollen rivers under cover of night, split into two flanks and circle around to take out the tanks and pillar-boxes. Then we finish them off with grenades and flame-throwers. It is slow, difficult fighting, but we are making progress. In the summer we will break through and join up with the partisans.'

Levi nodded. 'Can I take some time to consider my options?' he asked.

'Of course. There's a train for Rome on Monday, and from there you'd go to Bari and by truck down to Taranto. The steamer leaves from there for Southampton.'

Levi was in no doubt that the suggestion that he had a choice was an illusion. If he told them he'd rather return to the partisans, the gloves would come off and he would experience the resolve of the British Army. If he'd gone outside for a cigarette and melted into the populace of the city, with the intention of making his way north, he would be rounded up before he had the chance to leave Florence. He wondered how Roza was and if she felt abandoned. He hoped she'd taken his advice and told her mother what had happened while she was in the German transit camp. She was yet another victim he'd encountered and left behind as the war progressed. He wished he had the opportunity to tell Peter what Major Harrison had told him about the plans for the summer campaign in the north. Still, if it was time to follow orders, so be it.

London, December 1945

Levi shifted uncomfortably on the seat and gestured towards the officer off-screen.

'Can I have another cigarette, please?' he asked.

'Of course, sir.'

The hand leaned in and gave him a cigarette and then proffered the lighter. Levi took a deep drag and closed his eyes.

'Please continue when you feel ready, sir.'

He looked at the camera, scratched the back of his neck and frowned.

'By the time I'd gone to Rome, seen Don Aldo, some of our families and the bishop, who was there to see the Pope, taken a train to across the country to Bari and then caught a truck to Taranto it was late April. The trucks were full of Italian women, war brides. They'd married their army and air force sweethearts in Florence, travelled with them to Bari and then said their goodbyes. For some it would be months before their new husbands were sent home. Any who found themselves in a truck with me, a man both able to speak Italian and to tell them what England was like, didn't stop asking me questions all the way south.'

'How long did it take you to get to England?' the voice off-camera asked.

'About five weeks. We sailed around the bottom of Sicily, along the coast of North Africa, through the Straits of Gibraltar and out into the Atlantic. At times the sea was very rough and everyone suffered with sickness; other times it was calm and sunny and we played deck tennis and spent hours in the sunshine reading books.'

'Did you know that Germany had surrendered?'

He nodded. 'Yes, the news came through in May. Hitler was dead and the war in Europe was over. Everyone celebrated. I took myself off to the quietest corner I could find and said some silent prayers for my parents, my siblings, Erik, Eva, Sandro and all the others who had died.'

'Did you take Erik's parents to see his grave?'

Levi hesitated, then nodded. 'It wasn't easy, but the chaos in Europe helped. I flew to Paris and then got an army transport, by Jeep, to Munich. They were surprised and delighted to see me. But their grief was intense and raw. Herr von Engel used his brother's influence to get us permission to travel to northern Italy. It was late summer and still warm. With an army escort I took them up to the treeline and found the site beside the river. They stayed at the grave for some time. Herr von Engel said they would organise for him to be dug up and brought back to Munich for burial near them. I assume they have done that, or will when transportation is easier.'

'That was a huge thing for you to do.'

'It was a promise I made. You don't break promises to the people you love.'

There was a moment's silence.

'What have you been doing since your return?'

'I couldn't be officially discharged from the army as I never enlisted, but they gave me a letter thanking me for my service and offering me the George Cross for my bravery.'

There was an awkward pause. Levi looked at the ground.

'And, for the record, what was your response?'

'I turned it down.'

'Why?'

'Because the British government is acting like a bully. Other refugees who have given just as much as I have are being repatriated to their country of birth, even though they had official refugee status. They are being made to go back to countries like Poland or Hungry, even though they have been liberated by the Soviets.'

As he said the word 'liberated' he made the sign of quotation marks with his fingers.

'And others are being sent back to live among the ruins of Germany. I have a trade that is deemed essential to the restoration of the British economy, I'm a banker, so I am allowed to stay.'

'So you have returned to your job at Mr Dickenson's bank?'

Levi nodded. 'I was considering selling one of my diamonds and funding my own travel to the British Mandate of Palestine. There is a lot of work to be done there to establish the Jewish state and they need the talents I have. But just recently I have received news that has changed my mind.'

'Would you like to share that news with us?'

For the first time, Levi smiled directly at the camera. His eyes glistened for a moment with what looked like unshed tears, and then he blinked and they were gone.

'I received an official letter from the Red Cross. My younger brother, Simon, is in a displaced persons camp in Germany. He was interred in Dachau. He must have been there at the same time as Erik. He has nowhere to go so they will send him to London to be with me. I need to be here when he arrives. I remember the state that Erik was in when he was smuggled out of that place, and Simon will have been there a lot longer than Erik was. He'll have suffered, and I must take care of him.

'When he is strong enough I am hopeful we will go to America to live with our Uncle Avrum. He is our father's eldest brother and he immigrated to America in 1925. He works in banking too.'

'You must be delighted to know that another of your family has survived.'

Levi said nothing, and then he shrugged. 'So much death and so much loss. "Delighted" is not a word I would use. It doesn't explain how it feels. It is too frivolous. "Lucky" is a better word. So many families have been completely destroyed because of the beliefs and actions of men I saw and listened to and tried to understand. Monsters like the Führer and Himmler and Goebbels.

'Families that lived and worked and owned property and contributed magnificently to the world for hundreds of years, and in one short period they have been totally obliterated. The fact that we don't share their fate is more good fortune than something we deserve. That is all I have to report. The war of Levi Horowitz is consigned to history.'

CHAPTER TWENTY-TWO

The National Archives
Kew, London

September 2017

'At least you know he was pleased to find out you had survived. Look at his eyes, he's more deeply moved than he wants us to know.'

It was Cindy who spoke first. Simon gave her a gentle smile.

'He's right when he says "lucky" was the correct word. I have always felt it was some kind of karma. Good people died, bad people lived and vice versa. Levi understood that,' he said.

'Do you remember your reunion?' Daniel asked.

'Oh, yes. I was in a displaced persons camp near Munich. Conditions were still harsh, there was little food and they had to impose restrictions on us because there were so many to house and feed.'

'What was the camp like?' David asked. 'I've always wanted to know, but you've never talked about it.'

Simon sighed. 'I remember we used to say we were liberated but not free. Most of the people were sick, malnourished and exhausted, some were dying. The hardest thing was to find the energy to do anything.

'But we formed an orchestra and started a newspaper, and I spent hours with the children, teaching them basic Hebrew and telling them stories about the great prophets of our people. Most of them under seven had no memory or concept of what it meant to be Jewish.'

'How did they find Feter Levi?' Daniel asked.

'We had to fill out registration cards, and the Red Cross started to collate the hundreds of thousands of people who had been forcibly moved and were still alive. On my card I listed my family, and they traced Levi in London.

'It was winter when they put me on a train to Marseilles. I had the clothes I stood up in, which were too large for me, and my violin in a case, the one Kurt had given me to play in Dachau. I remember I was terrified of authority figures. When someone in uniform spoke to me I automatically looked at the ground and pulled the non-existent cap from my bald head.

'The boat was crowded, the sea was rough and we were in bunks, kept below deck for days on end. Eventually people began to yell that land was in sight. We would soon be docking in Southampton.'

He stopped and looked around the room. Every pair of eyes was looking at him, every person was holding their breath.

'There were so many people that at first I couldn't find him. I was lost in a mass of people hugging and crying and calling out names in so many languages. I thought I was going to be trampled underfoot. Then a lady from the Red Cross took me to a room and there he was, wearing a suit, shiny shoes and a hat. He looked very dapper and I felt so dirty and scruffy. We couldn't speak. He hugged me so tightly I thought he'd crush the air from my lungs. The first thing he said to me was "It will be all right now" in Hebrew. I just nodded.'

A tear ran down Cindy's cheek, and Simon reached out and brushed it away.

'He took me to a hotel and I had a hot shower. He'd bought me a set of clothes, and they were too big, but they fitted better than the ones the camp had given me. Then he took me to a tea house and we had toast and lemon curd and coffee. The weather was cold and the coffee was bitter, but I was too happy to notice.'

For a moment no one spoke.

'So that was the winter of 1945–46?' David asked.

Simon nodded. 'It was January 1946 when I arrived,' he said.

'What did he tell you he'd been doing since 1938?' Major Stratton asked.

Simon frowned and seemed to be searching his memory. 'From the very beginning he was reluctant to talk about it. He told me about being stopped at the border and the Gestapo agent and the gun jamming. But then he just said he'd made his way to London. I'm sure he said he'd gone via Switzerland, or maybe I just assumed that. He said he was in an internment camp but not where.'

Simon scratched his head.

'But nothing about going back to Europe?' the major prompted.

'No. He said he'd worked on the land, for a farming family in Somerset who had sons in the RAF. He used to say he had a very easy war.'

'That's probably what he was told to say. The spy forces weren't keen on people talking about what they'd done.'

'But ... me. I would've thought he would have told me,' Simon said softly, almost to himself.

Major Stratton shook his head. 'I suspect he was told that if he admitted the truth to one, it would become harder to keep it hidden. And he was concerned about how you would react, given what you'd been through.'

They all sat, assimilating the idea that Feter Levi was able to keep such an enormous truth from them.

'What would it have done to Levi psychologically to be trained like that and then to bury those experiences and go back to normal life? Do you think he suffered from PTSD?' Kobi asked.

'Possibly, although I think the training that allowed him to become Werner also allowed him to bury those five years, to become disassociated from them,' Stratton said.

'So eventually it would feel like they'd happened to someone else?' Cindy asked.

'Precisely. His sole focus was Simon and making up for the fact that Simon had been the one to be interred and survive.'

Simon sighed. 'I was very dependent on him for a long time. The world had changed, and I found trusting people almost impossible. I spoke no English at first, and the currency was confusing — first English pounds and then American dollars. Levi was my compass for my every decision until I met Ruth, my wife. Even then I couldn't contemplate him not living with us. He understood me. He was the one of the few people around us who I could speak German with, and he shared my memories of Mama and Papa, Rachel and David. Life before the war, home, the music, I was afraid I wouldn't live to be an old man, and I needed to know that Levi would be there for Ruth, and then Ruth and David. I never thought of it as being selfish.'

'What else would he have done?' David asked.

No one answered immediately.

'Don't forget you were a successful banker and that allowed him to be what he wanted to be,' Cindy said at last. 'When he left banking and started his own business, your income allowed him to do that.'

Simon nodded. 'True. It was like an unspoken reward for how well he'd taken care of me.'

'And in those years it was a difficult time to be gay in conservative America. If he'd pursued an openly gay lifestyle, he'd have been ostracised,' David added.

'So he chose nothing and I never questioned him,' Simon said.

Major Stratton waited for someone else to comment, but no one did. Eventually he rose and walked to the space between the blank screen and the sofa. 'I think that's enough for today. Can I ask you to come back tomorrow? We want to talk to you about the recording and whether we can use it.'

David looked at the other members of his family. They all looked tired and stressed, but they all nodded.

'Of course,' he said.

A digestive episode, caused by the strain of the past few days, kept Simon in his hotel room for the next week. David, Cindy and Daniel took the opportunity to do some sightseeing. Kobi spent the days writing his book about Raffaello Sanzio da Urbino, the Renaissance artist known as Raphael, and the nights with George Ross.

When Simon felt up to it, David rang Major Stratton and told him they would be back the next day. The major asked if they could meet him at the front desk of the National Archives at 10 am.

'I wonder why he was so specific,' Cindy commented as the car drew up outside the building.

'For goodness' sake, Mom, you're suspicious of everyone,' Daniel said with a laugh in his voice. 'It's not as if he suggested a graveyard at midnight. I think 10 am at the front desk is a perfectly reasonable request.'

Cindy frowned at him. 'There's a plan, you mark my words — I can sense these things.'

Daniel shook his head and helped his grandfather out of the car. With his stick in one hand and leaning on Daniel with his other, Simon made his way towards the door. The major was waiting for them by the front desk. He looked ever so slightly as if he was controlling excitement.

'How are you, Mr Horowitz?' he asked.

Simon looked up at him and smiled. 'Better. At my age, better is an achievement.'

The major had a wheelchair waiting, and Simon sank into it. 'Thank you, that's very thoughtful of you,' he said.

'Now, this way,' the major led them to the lift, up to a corridor and along to a conference room. There was a large table with several chairs on either side of it.

'Please take a seat, I'll be with you shortly. There are refreshments over on that table.' They sat down and Daniel and Cindy served everyone coffee and tea. Ten minutes later the major returned. He held the door open. Outside stood a small, stooped woman, her weight on the cane she held in her hand.

'I have someone here you might want to meet. Horowitz family, this is Mrs Elzbieta Liswski, or Roza.'

She waited for a moment in the doorway and surveyed them, Wolfie's family. It was time for them to hear the truth, and her job to relay it. Simon rose, went to her and clasped her hand. 'Hello, Elzbieta, it is a privilege to meet you again,' he said.

She drew herself up and looked at him. 'Amadeus,' she said.

Simon returned to the table, and the major showed Elzbieta to a chair.

'When you call me that it takes me back over seventy years to the music room in our house,' Simon said, smiling at her.

She returned the smile. 'I heard about that room, the wallpaper, the piano, the mural on the ceiling, the violins in glass cases,' she said.

'Where do you live?' David asked.

'New York for the last twenty years; before that, Israel.'

The major coughed. 'I have shown Elzbieta the parts of Levi's tape that pertain to her. So she knows what you know. She would like to tell you her side of the story,' he said.

'We would be very grateful for that,' David said. 'Would you like a cup of coffee or tea or a glass of water?'

She looked over at the side table. 'I would like an herbal tea, if there is such a thing there.'

Daniel got up and went to the table. 'There's a green tea or a ginger, honey and lemon,' he said, showing her the boxes.

'Ginger, honey and lemon would be lovely,' she said.

When she was settled, with her tea in front of her, she looked at each one of them.

'It fills my heart with joy to know that he had a brother to go home to and an extended family to be proud of. Since I knew about you I have followed your career, Daniel, and I like to imagine how much Wolfie loved to sit and watch you play. He used to tell me about Amadeus playing his violin when they were children. He never played the piano for me, but he talked about music, and it seemed to be the cornerstone that kept him sane.'

Daniel blushed slightly. His mother looked at him with obvious pride.

Wolfie's nephew, David, looked so like him, older than she remembered Wolfie, but with the same coloured hair and eyes and freckles on the bridge of his nose. The same straight back and long fingers. She closed her eyes. Where to start?

'We came from Poland. Warsaw. My papa could see what was happening and that if we stayed there eventually the soldiers would come for us. He tried to persuade more of our family to go, but they were stupid or scared. He cashed in all our savings and so did our Uncle Pawel and Aunt Sofia and my grandparents. We bought train tickets west, for Switzerland, and we packed one suitcase for each family. Mama promised us that when we reached our new home we could buy new possessions.

'Papa gave us all new names, and we thought that they were very strange. My brother and I made up silly songs so we would remember our new names. I can still hear him singing "Roza, Roza ..."

'We were in Germany when a man came into our carriage. He was very scared. He told us that they were stopping all the trains and searching for Jews fleeing from the East. Some of them had decided to pull an emergency brake and make an escape while the train was stationary. Papa gathered us all together, and when the train suddenly braked he pushed us out onto the grass. Then we started walking. So much walking!

'First, Grandma got sick and we stopped for a couple of days while Aunt Sofia tried to take care of her. But her coughing was terrible and we had no medicine. Then Grandpa got it too. Papa and Pawel looked for a place where we could leave them to rest, but there was nowhere. They died on the same day, and we held a small funeral for them and buried them together.

'We walked over the border into Italy and it was starting to get colder. Pawel and Sofia's twins, my cousins, were only four years old and they were always very tired. Papa carried one and Pawel carried the other. They cried a lot because we didn't have much food and we were always hungry.'

She stopped and looked around the table.

'I felt angry at them. I was hungry too but I wasn't allowed to cry. Anyway, the twins died just before we found the party of partisans out in the snow. No one else knew I'd been angry, but I remember the guilt as if it happened yesterday. We were all very scared and exhausted, and I think my aunt was so grief-stricken she had decided she couldn't go on any further. Then all of a sudden there was this huge man in a fur coat standing on the path. He looked so ferocious. Papa told us to follow him, so we did. He turned around and tried to shoo us away, but we just kept following him. I don't think we would have cared much if he'd shot us all by that point.

'When we got to this campsite, they were yelling at us in a language we didn't understand but that we knew was Italian. Then this tall, thin man with a gentle smile came up to us and said hello in German. My papa spoke to him and told him who we were, using our battle names. That was Wolfie. He took us into a cave, and we sat beside a fire. He gave us blankets to get warm and some food. All of a sudden we wanted to live.'

There was silence while she studied her fingers.

'We know you became a very skilled partisan, and we know you became very fond of Wolfie,' David said.

She smiled at him. 'Yes I did. He taught me to shoot and to strip down and clean my rifle. And he and I used to sit by the fire and talk, about our homes and our families. I remember vividly me asking him if he would kiss me because I could die tomorrow and I'd never been properly kissed.'

'Did you know your father had spoken to him about marrying you?' David asked.

She shook her head. 'No. He thought I was avoiding him, but I didn't know. More than anyone, I knew how close he was to Erik. They shared a special bond, sometimes they didn't need words, just a look would suffice. I think I knew instinctively that Wolfie didn't love me the way I loved him.'

'So tell us, what happened to you after he left?' Simon asked.

For a moment she said nothing, and then she sighed. 'As you know, I was raped by the German soldiers when they captured us, and for a few weeks I was afraid I might be pregnant. But thank G-d I wasn't. Papa wanted me to marry Mikel, because he wanted to know someone would look after me if he was killed, and Mikel was a good man, a kind man. I didn't love Mikel, but I agreed. Mikel was killed a week before we were due to be married, shot by a German patrol. Uncle Pawel was killed that same night. We buried them beside Erik, and everyone mourned them a great deal.

'In the summer the English broke through and captured all the towns in the north. The Germans had mined the roads and blown up what bridges were left. We eventually surrendered to the British Army, and they put Mama, Papa, my brother, Aunt Sofia and little Mathew and me on a truck north. We were handed over to the Red Cross, and they sent us to a displaced persons camp in Poland. I married Asher, a survivor of Auschwitz who I met in the camp. He was a lovely man, and he understood about loss and suffering. He'd lost his whole family in the Holocaust. We applied to go to Palestine and were accepted.'

Simon had been looking at the table, and at the mention of Palestine he glanced up at her.

'Levi nearly went there. If he hadn't heard about me and decided he needed to take me to America, I think he would have. He wanted to fight for freedom in Palestine.'

She nodded. 'Asher was a freedom-fighter in those first years. He despised the British. He was in jail when our first son, Micah, was born.'

'How many children do you have?' David asked.

'Three. Two sons and a daughter. When Asher died in 1996, two of my children were living in New York and they persuaded me to move there.'

'What about your brother and your parents?' Cindy asked.

'They stayed in Warsaw. My brother married and lived not far from my parents. Mama and Papa lived under Soviet rule the rest of their lives, but after the collapse of communism my brother came to Israel to see us in 1992 and then to New York several times. He died two years ago and left four children and fourteen grandchildren.'

'How did you know Levi had died?' Simon asked.

She smiled. 'I have a friend who lives in Vermont. Sarah Cohen —'

'I know Sarah! She's a member of our Shul congregation. She lives about a mile from me,' Simon exclaimed.

'I know that now. Sarah knows I love music and she told me about Daniel and how she goes to the same Shul as his poppa, and his great-uncle had just died. When she said "Horowitz" it rang a little bell. I asked her the name of the poppa and the great-uncle, and she told me. Instantly I was back beside the campsite fire where we whispered our real names to each other. The connection to the music was too much — it had to be my Wolfie. So I came to see you. I know I told you I'd be back, but I lost my courage. I didn't know what to say. When the major rang and told me about the recording Wolfie had made and that you were all in London, I knew I had to come.'

'And I'm so glad you did,' Simon said.

'So am I.'

'Just imagine, if you'd gone to Shul with Sarah before Feter Levi died you might have seen him,' Cindy said.

Elzbieta shook her head. 'Asher was a Jew, he wanted a kosher home and a good Jewish wife, and I gave that to him.

We raised our three children, we even lived on a kibbutz for a few years. One of my grandsons is a rabbi. But when I moved to New York I had to find my own way in the world, and I realised that I didn't want to go to Shul anymore.'

Simon looked away, as if he didn't know what to say.

'Both Levi and I have had our own battles with our faith over the years. We've had to come to terms with the suffering our people went through during the Shoah. I do know many Jews who lost their faith because of their experiences and I don't condemn anyone,' he said.

Kobi shifted in his seat. 'My biological grandmother was Simon and Levi's younger sister, Rachel, and I haven't been a member of this family for very long. I was raised in Australia as a Lutheran. My sister has converted to Judaism, but my elder brother, my mother and I remain Lutheran. No one in this family will judge you for anything.'

CHAPTER TWENTY-THREE

London

September 2017

'When are you going to tell your family about me?' George asked. He was sitting up in bed, watching Kobi pull on his clothes.

'Every night you creep back to your hotel so you can go down to breakfast as if you've slept there all night. It's deceitful, Kobi — are you ashamed of me?'

Kobi stopped what he was doing and looked at his lover.

'No! You know I'm not. There are so many people I need to explain —'

'You mean come out to,' George interrupted.

Kobi sat down on the bed, his shirt in his hands. 'I guess so. My mum, my brother and sister. I just feel I ought to tell them before this side of the family find out. I love the Horowitzs dearly but they've only been part of my life for three years.'

'Do you wish you could tell Feter Levi?'

Kobi nodded. 'Him most of all. I promise you I will Skype with Lisle tomorrow and ask her to organise for Mum and Andrew to be there the day after so I can tell all three.'

George patted the bed beside him. 'And I don't suppose I can persuade you to come back here in the meantime?'

Kobi grinned. 'Be patient.'

'You know that is my least apparent quality,' George said, smiling back.

Major Stratton studied the six faces around the table. Simon, David, Cindy and Daniel Horowitz, Kobi Voight and Elzbieta Liswski. They held the key to what he wanted to do and he had no idea how they would react to the request.

'Thank you for gathering here once again,' he started. They all acknowledged his words, either with a smile or a nod.

'We brought you here and showed you this film because we wanted you to know the truth about what your brother, uncle, great-uncle and friend did during the war. We believed that you should know. If some of it caused you pain, I apologise sincerely. Obviously Levi had his reasons for keeping his war a secret, and I believe that part of that was to spare you, particularly you Simon, some of the grief these revelations have brought.

'But now that you do know, I have something to ask. This is a different age for the military. But we still need our heroes and we still need to remember the sacrifices of the past. Our technical department works with an outside production company to create recruitment and training films. And we would like to make a programme about Levi, using some of his debrief, and filming some interviews with you, Simon and you, Elzbieta. The piece would be scripted and you would be able to vet that and your questions in advance.'

He paused.

'What would be the point of such a film? What would you use it for?' David asked, his tone neutral.

'Well, good question. It has an internal use for the army, but it would also be shown to the general public, open recruiting days, available for purchase on iTunes, maybe even shown by the BBC.

'We find that some of our recruits today have limited knowledge of last century and the risks taken to keep this country free. Levi's story is one that is easy to relate to. He was a member of the public, and yet he showed enormous courage and initiative. And it includes some of the major figures of the Axis war effort: people we simply read about in books come alive with his descriptions.'

'Would you include the fact that he was gay?' Kobi asked quietly.

Simon turned towards him. 'Absolutely not! He didn't live the majority of his life like that, and it is a private matter.'

Simon's anger was plain to see.

Kobi shrugged. 'And yet if you want to show truthfully what his war was like, that part, his relationship with Erik, had a huge effect on him, on the decisions he made.'

'But does it honour his memory?' Cindy asked.

'Does it dishonour it?' Kobi snapped back at her.

'Who has the final say?' Simon asked the major.

Stratton hesitated. He had anticipated that this might arise. 'Theoretically the film created in 1945 belongs to us, but as he has descendants, we would, naturally, consult with you.'

'What are you trying to do with it? Recruit homosexual soldiers and show them they can be spies?' There was a bitterness in Simon's voice that hinted at much deeper feelings.

Major Stratton coughed. 'If I gave you my word we would not use anything that pertained to his sexuality, would you be happy for us to make the film?' he asked.

Kobi slammed his fist down on the table. 'But that's not being true to Feter Levi! If he didn't want the truth to be recorded, in all its personal agony, he wouldn't have mentioned it. He wasn't making it for us to see, he was making it for the army. I don't think he was ashamed of his relationships. Remember he was talking in a time when this was simply not mentioned. Had he and Erik walked down Oxford Street hand in hand in 1945 they would have been arrested. And yet he was brave enough to admit he loved the man on a debriefing film!'

There was an uncomfortable silence. Finally, David turned to his cousin. 'Why does it matter so much to you?' he asked.

Kobi shook his head. 'Oh no, you're not going to cloud the issue by bringing me into it. This is about Feter Levi and how he honoured who he truly was.'

Simon looked at Kobi. His colour was high and his eyes were bright with anger. 'I understand what you're saying, but the final decision is mine. I am the curator of Levi's legacy in this world, and I say that any public release of the film will be about his time in Berlin and his time in Italy. In the first part it will showcase his ability as a pianist and his conversations with Hitler, in the second it will tell the story of Assisi and the heroes he worked with and the partisans he fought with. His sexuality will not be mentioned. My word is final.'

Kobi slumped back in his seat and said nothing.

Major Stratton gave a brisk nod in Simon's direction. 'So be it.'

'I feel betrayed and I feel as if they have betrayed Feter Levi,' Kobi said. He took a sip of his cocktail and sighed.

'I can see why,' George commented.

'It is homophobia and it comes from my own family. Not the military, or the production company who seem keen to include the parts about Erik. My own family!'

George reached across the table and covered Kobi's hand with his own. 'I know what it's like to come out to family, you don't. Often it is the hardest thing a gay man or woman ever does. The opinion of those you love means so much more.'

'I don't feel I can tell them now. I just don't trust them.' Kobi pulled his hand away. 'I feel angry, like I want to kick something, hard!' He put his drink down and scrubbed his face. 'And I feel sad, too, ashamed of them.'

George smiled at him. Those lazy, sexy hazel eyes that made his pulse race. 'I think you might find they already know. Is there one of them you could tell, just to break the ice?'

Kobi shrugged. 'I don't know. We've had so many secrets in this family for so long, it feels wrong to burden someone with another.'

'I have a question for you,' Major Stratton asked as he watched the soundman position the microphone on Simon's jacket lapel. Simon looked up at him.

'Yes?'

'I did a digital cross-check with Levi's name to see if we had any other records anywhere and I came across a letter sent by the Red Cross in Jerusalem in 1957. The writer was asking about Levi Horowitz on behalf of a Mrs Elizabeth Bernstein. I have no idea why the Red Cross was referred to the army or who she was. A letter was written back stating that Levi Horowitz was on record as a partisan fighter, parachuted into Europe, and there was no record of him returning to England, so it was assumed he died fighting. I imagine that the clerk responsible didn't make more than a cursory check of the records, otherwise they would have discovered the recording. Does the name Elizabeth Bernstein mean anything to you?'

Simon frowned. 'No. The letter doesn't say who she was?' he asked.

'No. Just that the request for knowledge was placed on her behalf. Never mind, it was a long shot.'

'I do remember the lady who bought my aunt and uncle's house after they died stopping us once at Shul and telling us they'd had a call from a lady in Israel. They couldn't remember her name. They'd told her that Uncle Avrum and Aunt Sarah had died and had had no children. She apologised because it hadn't occurred to her at the time to tell the woman about us. Probably not the same person,' Simon mused, almost to himself.

The soundman stepped back. 'There we are, Mr Horowitz. Just one moment,' he said. He went to look at a screen over to the side of the room and fiddled with a couple of buttons. 'Could you say something for me, sir?' he asked.

'My name is Simon Horowitz and I am Jewish and German,' Simon said.

The sound man nodded. 'Excellent. If you could keep your voice around about that volume please, sir.'

A young man sat down opposite Simon. He had an iPad in his hand.

'Right, are you comfortable, Mr Horowitz?' he asked.

Simon smiled at him. 'Please, call me Simon. I am perfectly comfortable, thank you,' he said.

'Good. If you want to stop at any time, you just have to ask. We can take as many breaks as you like. I want to start by asking you about your life before the war and what you remember of Levi.'

Berlin, 1930

Simon watched the preparations for Levi's Bar Mitzvah with a keen eye. He knew that when he reached his thirteenth birthday it would be his turn, and he wanted to be ready. Levi went with Papa to the Neue Synagogue on the Oranienburger Strasse to practise. On the Sabbath closest to his birthday he would ascend the platform and read from the Torah, and then there would be a wonderful party at their home. Simon knew that his parents had bought two leather tefillin boxes for Levi. They contained parchment scrolls, and he would wear one on his head and one on his arm. When Simon had asked what he could give his elder brother as a Bar Mitzvah present, his mama had said that he could join with Rachel and David and give Levi a beautiful new fountain pen.

The day itself was hot and cloudless. The synagogue was huge and ornate, with a massive gold dome that could be seen from all over the city. It seated over three thousand people, and was the largest synagogue in Germany. He knew Levi was very nervous, and his papa was so proud Simon thought he would burst.

It went without a hitch, and all Papa's friends crowded around Levi to congratulate him and shake his hand. Then it was back to the house for a feast and much celebrating. Simon watched the men carrying Levi aloft in a chair, following traditions that were centuries old. Not for the first time he felt blessed to be Jewish, to be part of this universal culture that honoured their G-d and lived by his laws. He could see himself marrying and giving his parents grandchildren, being part of a family circle that would include Levi and Rachel and David, that would honour his parents in their old age and continue the circle forever. It never occurred to him that life could take any other path.

It was a hot summer and Simon was bored. His younger brother and sister were in the nursery with Nanny. Rachel was giving her dolls a tea party, and David was playing with his new train set. He'd tried to interest Simon in joining him with the promise that he could move the signal flags up and down and guide the trains onto their separate tracks, but Simon knew he was too old for trains.

He wandered down the staircase and into the entrance hall. The sound of music drew him through the drawing room and into the music room. This was his favourite place on earth. The painting on the ceiling was worth lying on your back and staring at. It showed the Greek god Apollo playing a lyre made of gold, cherubs blowing trumpets surrounding him on all sides. But he loved the wallpaper even more. It was covered in music notes in gold leaf, and the silk was cold to his touch. The curtains were red and made of velvet, and there was a huge sparkly crystal chandelier in the centre of the room.

The room was full of instruments, precious architects of sound that his parents had collected. A 1586 Flemish double virginal with two keyboards and beautifully decorated panels sat at one end, and a huge grand piano at the other. In between were glass cases holding a tenor recorder, a wood-and-ivory serpent, an Italian lute and two magnificent violins.

The source of the music was his elder brother, Levi, who was having a lesson on the grand piano. His teacher, Herr Fleischer, was a young man, only about ten years older than his pupil, supplementing his meagre income with teaching. He was earnest and tried far too hard at times, and Levi and Simon used to imitate him when no one else was around.

Simon slipped into the room and sat on one of the chairs against the wall. Levi lifted his hands from the keys.

'Good, but you need to be a little slower here,' Herr Fleischer said, pointing to the sheet music. Levi nodded.

'See this, this slur, it is telling you *legato*. So you need to be smooth and gentle. Try it again, from there.'

He pointed to the music again and Levi settled down and started to play.

'Good ... better ... even more *glissando*. As if it were a nocturne ... yes! That's better.'

The music was lovely, but Simon was hot and fed up with being on his own. He slid off the chair and made his way out of the room and through to the kitchen.

'Hello young Simon, how are you?' Cook asked. She was peeling apples over a bowl at the table.

'Bored. What are you doing?' he asked.

'Making strudel. Are you hot? Would you like an iced lolly?'

He grinned at her. 'Yes please,' he said.

She got up and went into the cold pantry. He reached into the bowl and took a large slice of apple. It was tart and juicy.

'I saw that! Keep your hands out of that bowl,' Cook's voice came booming out of the pantry.

Simon laughed. 'Just one,' he said.

She came back with a square of muslin and unwrapped it to display a red chunk of ice, which she gave to him.

'A strawberry iced lolly,' she said. He held it by the muslin and sucked on the ice.

'Thank you,' he said.

'Where's Master Levi? Still at the piano?' she asked.

Simon nodded. 'He's playing a piece that is so slow it'll be Christmas before he's finished,' he said.

She laughed heartily. 'Well, if it's still summer when he's free, tell him to come and have a lolly with me. He likes stirring the strudel.'

Berlin, 1935

It was one of the Horowitz music nights and the house was full of people. The Nazis had been in power for two years, and some of the restrictions were harsh. But these people were well-known and rich; they might not be able to practise as doctors, lawyers, dentists or teachers anymore, but they were creative. They loved music and theatre and cabaret and art. Among this crowd were composers, conductors, singers and instrumentalists. Their passion for classical music united them all.

Several shops refused to serve them, and some were shopkeepers who knew that their gentile customers were staying away, but the Jewish population was large enough to keep most in business. They hated Hitler and the Nazis, and knew that fully paid-up members of the National Socialist Party followed their leader's example and hated them back, but on a night such as this it didn't matter.

Cook had worked her magic with limited supplies, and the canapes were beautiful. Benjamin had opened the champagne and the cognac from his cellar. Elizabeth wore her green silk, her auburn hair swept up into a French roll and her magnificent pearls around her elegant throat. Benjamin, in his suit, was, as ever, round, jolly and companionable.

To begin the evening's entertainment, Franz Reinhardt played the Steinway and Lillian Hauptman played the Amati violin. Simon was thrilled to be allowed to stay up and watch. He was entranced by every note, and knew that he would discuss each piece in detail with his music teacher during the days to come.

But tonight was a special night. Simon had been bullied at school and on his way home, for being a Jew. His parents were horrified, and as a treat he was allowed to play the Guarneri violin for the first time. He played Debussy's 'The Girl with the Flaxen Hair'. When he finished, everyone clapped and he took his first bow. But most of all his papa and mama both hugged him, and Levi was so excited for him he was nearly in tears.

Berlin, 1938

Simon and Levi had gone through the Kristallnacht together. Levi had gone out with friends without telling his parents where he was going. When Herr Reinhardt, the pianist, had rung and told them about the rioting and suggested they came to hide in his shelter, Simon had escaped before his parents were ready, and had gone out on his own to hunt for Levi. The streets were a screaming, smoking mass of shattering glass, burning synagogues and storm troopers rounding up Jews and taking them away in black vans.

Simon had managed to avoid capture and made his way to the café where he guessed Levi would be hiding with his friends. Rolf had wanted them to stay, to be sheltered by their gentile companions, but both boys knew that their papers would give them away if the group was confronted. Their only hope was to make it home.

But they hadn't reached the haven of their front door. Instead they'd been taken in by Maria Weiss, a gentile, who'd offered them chocolate cake and chicken sandwiches and coffee. They'd discussed all the subjects they loved with her, music and art and history and literature, and she'd shown them her late husband's collection of first edition books and played them his radiogram. They'd stayed the night, and in the morning she'd cooked them breakfast. Simon had often wondered if she had any idea how much her kindness had meant, but when he saw her again in Berlin after the war he'd realised that her fate and that of the Horowitz family was interconnected from that night.

The next day Levi had left for London. It felt very strange to know that his elder brother wouldn't be there anymore. He'd watched Levi pack and watched their father strap documents around his son's chest and hang a pouch in his armpit. There was so much he suddenly wanted to tell Levi, fears, hopes and dreams. Levi had told Rachel that Simon would take care of her and she was to take care of David. It felt like a huge responsibility. The house would sound so empty without Levi's piano practice, and Simon would miss going to sleep with his brother's snoring from the room next door. But leave he must. They had waved him goodbye from the doorstep. His mother had given him her blessing.

'G-d will take care of you, my precious firstborn boy,' she had said to him. Simon would never forget the desolation on his mother's face as she watched Levi depart.

CHAPTER TWENTY-FOUR

Vermont, USA
November 2017

David enjoyed the drive north to see his father. It gave him some thinking time. All in all the trip to London had been a great success. Parts of Feter Levi's interview had been hard to see, and he'd felt for his father, learning all this new information and having to process and accept it. But Simon's brain remained as sharp as a tack, and he had reserves of personal strength and courage that his son found awe-inspiring. David very rarely let himself think about the secret he carried in his heart: that Simon was in fact his Feter and Levi had been his father. Biology meant nothing, nurturing was all that he cared about and both men had fathered him in different ways. When the family had undergone DNA testing to establish the authenticity of the Voights' claim to be related through his Aunt Rachel, David's good friend and Daniel's conductor and mentor, Rafael Gomez, had discovered the truth. David knew he could trust Gomez to keep his secret, it wasn't a hard one to hold, and in many ways David liked having something that no one else in his immediate family knew. He loved his wife dearly but she was a controlling person, and this was a fact that she didn't have access to; it belonged to David alone. He wouldn't dream of revealing a truth he knew would break Simon's heart, so he let it be.

The major had been very grateful for their co-operation. On their last day in London he had told them that the army would like to award Levi his George Cross posthumously, if Simon would be prepared to come back the following January and receive it on his brother's behalf. The news had caused much rejoicing in the family. David had wondered what Feter Levi would think of such a gesture. He was pretty certain that if Levi were alive he would have told the army where they could put their medal, but he wasn't there and Simon was adamant that his brother deserved the recognition. There was no arguing with that. It was agreed that they would all return for the medal ceremony and to see a rough cut of the documentary.

Simon had been very tired after the trip. Cindy had tried to persuade him to come and stay with them so she could look after him and he could rest. But he was a stubborn old coot, which was why he'd survived, and he'd insisted on going home. But he'd looked exhausted when they'd Skyped with him, so David had decided to fly to New York and hire a car to drive north to Vermont.

The trees were changing colour. It was worth the price of the rental car to see their magnificence as he listened to Daniel's latest CD of Paganini pieces and reflected on the past few years. Their lives had been turned upside down so many times since 2008, he wasn't sure which way was up anymore.

When Daniel was fourteen he'd refused to play the violin because his mother had forbidden him to play his beloved baseball, and that had brought Spanish conductor Rafael Gomez and Russian billionaire Sergei Valentino into their lives, which had led to the discovery of their long-lost Guarneri del Gesú violin. Maestro Gomez had contrived a situation that forced Valentino to allow Daniel to play the Guarneri for concerts and when recording, otherwise it stayed with the Russian. On his death he would will it to Daniel.

Then Kobi Voight had appeared one day with Maestro Gomez and some letters that had been written by David's aunt, Rachel. Kobi been given the letters by his mother, and while he was in Berlin he'd discovered that Rachel's biological daughter was his mother, Elizabeth Voight. That had led to the extension of David's family, adding Elizabeth and her three children, particularly her youngest son, Kobi, who had become like a brother in many ways to David. Each crisis had added something to the rich tapestry of the Horowitz family, and now he wouldn't have it any other way.

He frowned as he swung into the drive. The blinds were still down. That wasn't like Simon; he liked to let in the light as much as possible. David honked his horn once. That was usually enough to bring his dad to the front door, and in summer down the path to welcome family at the car. Nothing stirred. Maybe he was asleep.

David got out of the car and walked to the front door. It was locked. He found the key on his key ring and unlocked it. The house was dimly lit, no lights were on. A sudden flash of alarm, with more than a little fear, ran down his spine.

'Dad?' he called out as he made his way through the neatly arranged sitting room. 'It's David. Are you awake?'

There was no response. The kitchen bench was clear, dishes done and no sign of breakfast. He went to Simon's bedroom door and knocked gently.

'Dad?' he asked again. As he turned the knob something inside of him told him what he would find. His father lay in bed, on his back, his hands by his sides under the covers and his eyes closed. David crossed quickly to the bed and put his fingers to his father's throat. The skin was cold and there was no pulse.

'Oh, Dad.'

David sat down heavily. He was overcome by a rush of emotion, gratitude that Simon had died peacefully in his sleep and was now with his family, and grief at the loss of his much-loved father.

'*Baruch Dayan Ha'emet*,' he said softly. He left the room and came back with a cloth and some candles. He laid the cloth over Simon's face, lit the candles and placed them on the bedside table close to Simon's head. He knew he was supposed to lower the body to the floor but he couldn't do that by himself, so he asked for forgiveness from his father. Finally, he found Simon's prayer book and recited the Psalms, Psalm 23, verse 17 of Psalm 90, and Psalm 91 in Hebrew. Only then did he call 911 and then Cindy on his phone.

They all gathered in Vermont. They got permission to delay the funeral long enough for Kobi to bring his mother, Elizabeth, and his sister, Lisle, from Melbourne. Elzbieta came from New York, Rafael from Washington, and Sergei from London. Friends who had known and loved Simon since he moved to the USA came as well.

They gathered at the local Shul for a simple service that reflected Simon's life-long commitment to his Judaism. David, Cindy and Daniel tore the clothing over their hearts to express their pain and sorrow, and then the local rabbi gave a moving eulogy.

'Simon was one of those rare people who understood how precious life is. After his experience in Dachau he made a commitment to his G-d to live every moment he had left on this earth, so to honour the memory of those of his family who had perished. He was a learned, kind and wise man who loved to share his knowledge with the young people of our community. And he had a keen sense of humour — he often pointed out to me the error of my ways.'

They walked behind the coffin to the graveside and buried him beside his brother. After they had shovelled the earth on top of the coffin, Cindy pointed out the wonderful view.

'He'll be happy here, David — look at the trees!' she said.

'I'll miss him so much,' Daniel said through his tears.

'I know you will, but his spirit lives on in you. Every time you play he'll be with you,' David said.

Daniel nodded and wiped his face with the handkerchief his mother supplied.

They sat Shiva for seven days at Simon's house. People came and went, brought food and comforting words. Then on the morning of the seventh day they got up from Shiva and got on with their lives.

Elizabeth Voight inherited a half-share in the Dürer painting, while David inherited the other half. As Rachel's only living heir, she was also left a share of the money Simon and

Levi had received as part of a class action against the German government over Jewish-owned banks that were unlawfully acquired by the Third Reich. It had been established that the gold and cash in Benjamin and Mordecai Horowitz's bank was transferred into a Swiss account in 1940.

'I think we should contact Major Stratton and tell him we've changed our minds,' Cindy said as she and David ate dinner in their home in Newbrick.

'About what?' David asked.

'Letting the world know about Feter Levi's sexuality. It was your father who had the objection to that. I think we should honour the fact that Feter Levi was brave enough to talk about it to camera.'

David sat back and considered her words. 'Tell him we think those bits should be included in the documentary,' he said.

She nodded. 'Yes. It's 2017. Such things are accepted nowadays, and it would mean Feter Levi had a right to be who he was.'

Slowly, David nodded at her. 'Okay, I will. I'll call him and let him know it can be included.'

London, January 2018

David took Simon's place as head of the household. It was now his responsibility to stand in for Feter Levi and receive the George Cross on his behalf.

'Are you nervous?' Cindy asked, as she brushed the shoulders of his morning suit.

'Yes,' he said, and smiled at her.

'You look wonderful. Your father and your Feter would be very proud of you. I am very proud of you.'

He kissed her on the cheek. 'Thank you.'

The room was very red. The carpet of the Ballroom at Buckingham Palace was very red. Red with traces of gold. This thought kept going through David's head as he stood in line and waited. Prince Charles, in his naval uniform, stood on a dais, a small step above the floor. David could feel the nerves clenching and unclenching in his stomach, and he wondered if this was what Daniel felt before a performance. In his peripheral vision he could see the others watching, waiting, and smiling. Cindy, Daniel, Kobi and Elizabeth. It occurred to him that he and Daniel were there because of Feter Levi. In his resistance lay their existence. And at that moment he made a decision. His thought pattern was broken by the sound of his name. He walked slowly to stand in front of Prince Charles.

It passed in something of a blur. The medal was presented to him, he exchanged a few words with the Prince about Feter Levi, shook his hand and then stepped back, bowed his head, straightened and moved on. It was a squat silver cross on a plain dark-blue ribbon. The words *For Gallantry* were inscribed around the circle where the four arms of the cross met, with a small relief sculpture of St George on a horse, slaying a dragon, in the middle of that circle.

Once outside, there were photos taken and hugs exchanged, and everyone had a look at the medal.

'What are you going to do with it?' asked Kobi.

'I'm not sure. Major Stratton suggested we loan it to the Imperial War Museum. They would make a glass-case display with photos of Feter Levi and a card detailing what he did. It could sit in the Holocaust exhibition section. If Dad was still alive he would take it home, but it feels wrong in a way for me to keep it.'

'I disagree,' Cindy said sharply, 'you are his closest living relative and you should be proud to show it off.'

David smiled at her. He knew she wanted to show it to her friends.

'We'll see,' he said, and winked at Daniel.

The next day they made the car journey to the National Archives once again. Major Stratton welcomed them and congratulated them on the George Cross, and offered his condolences on Simon's passing. He led them to his office, and they took seats in the viewing room.

The documentary was about forty minutes long. It included an establishing clip of Simon explaining how Levi came to be in London and why he was sent back to Berlin. The pieces of Levi to camera talking about Hitler, Goebbels and Himmler were very powerful. They used some stock footage of the men, and backed it with piano pieces from the repertoire Levi talked about. It was raw and real. Simon and Elzbieta spoke about their war, and Elzbieta recalled how they had come to join the partisans and her impressions of 'Wolfie'. And they included the parts to camera where Levi spoke about Pierre and Erik von Engel and his obvious love for Erik. When it came to a close, they all applauded.

'I think it is brilliant,' Cindy said, and smiled at the major.

'David?' the major asked.

David nodded. 'It's a true and honest record. I think Feter Levi would be well pleased with the way it was all handled.'

That afternoon, before they went to a party that Sergei Valentino was throwing for them at his Mayfair mansion, David asked them all to gather in his and Cindy's hotel room. Cindy, Daniel, Daniel's girlfriend Melissa, Kobi and Elizabeth Voight sat and looked at him expectantly. He'd decided not to share the fact that Maestro Gomez already knew the truth he was about to impart; that wasn't something his wife needed to know.

'I've thought long and hard about this, and if Dad was still alive I wouldn't even consider it. But I came to a decision while I was waiting to accept the George Cross. You all deserve to know the truth, especially you, Daniel.'

'The truth about what?' Cindy asked. David could see the concern in her eyes. He waited a few seconds, and then drew in a deep breath.

'When I was in my twenties Mom told me something. I promised I'd keep it to myself, and to date I have. She'd seen a programme about someone needing blood or bone marrow, something like that, from their closest family relative and in case it ever happened to us, she wanted me to know. I don't think Dad or Feter Levi knew, but I can't be sure.'

He paused and looked around the circle of faces. 'Feter Levi was my biological father.'

'I knew it!' Cindy sprang to her feet. 'I've always wondered, because you were so alike. But then you were like your grandmother, too.'

'She had tried for years to have a child, and nothing happened,' David continued. 'My father refused to accept that there could be anything wrong, and told her that if it was G-d's will for them to have children, then it would happen. But one night, when my father was in hospital because of his stomach complaints, Levi opened a bottle of wine and he and Mum drank it all. She opened a second, and eventually asked Feter Levi to dance with her. One thing led to another and she seduced him, on the sofa. When he woke up the next morning he was confused and embarrassed, but she assured him that whatever he thought had taken place was just a sweet and flattering dream of his and nothing untoward had happened. He agreed never to speak of it again.

'Six weeks later she discovered she was pregnant. Her husband had only been in hospital for a few days, and she had made sure they had sex several times over the week after his homecoming. As soon as I was born she knew whose son I was. At least that's what she told me. They didn't have the exact medical science they have nowadays, so Simon never suspected anything. If he did wonder, he never voiced it in my hearing.'

There was a silence, as if none of the others knew what to say. David looked at Daniel. He was very pale and his dark eyes were huge, but he said nothing.

'How does that make you feel, son?' David asked.

Daniel shrugged. 'Does it really matter?' he asked.

David shook his head. 'Not in the least. Poppa was your poppa and he always will be. You were the light of his life, and that will never change.'

'How about you?' Kobi asked, looking at David, 'Did it change anything for you?'

'No. I grew up living with both men, and they both fathered me in different ways. But it means that Levi left more than just the memories of his war years and his life afterwards. He left us.'

Kobi stood up. 'If we are talking about honouring Feter Levi, there's something I would like to tell you. Mum knows, but I've never said it out loud to you, my Horowitz family. I am, as Feter Levi was, gay. And proud to be so.'

David smiled at him. 'I have to say it comes as no surprise, but I'm glad you've told us,' he said.

Cindy hugged Kobi. 'That was brave, thank you for sharing,' she said.

'So, I also have someone I want you all to meet. I'm going to text him and ask him to come to the party. His name is George Ross, and I love him. I met him in Berlin in 2014, and then reconnected with him when we were here last year. I think you'll like him.'

'Oh, Kobi, that's wonderful,' Cindy said.

David gave his cousin a nod of approval, and Kobi pulled out his phone.

'I told you it would be fine,' George Ross said, as he and Kobi sat sipping wine in the rooftop hotel bar. 'They're people who know what it's like to be different, they don't judge.'

Kobi nodded. 'But you never know what will happen when it becomes personal. People can be as liberal as the day is long when it's concerning generalities, bring it back to their own family and that's a different matter.'

'True. But they said it wasn't exactly a surprise.'

Kobi stood at the window and looked out at the view. The sun was setting, and the rooftops of London were tinged with an orange glow.

'I just wish I'd told Feter Levi,' he said quietly.

'Told him what? That you were confused and couldn't accept that you could let a vital part of your identity out into the world?'

Kobi turned and looked at him. 'Maybe if I'd known about him and he'd shared with me about Erik it would have helped.'

George shrugged. 'Maybe, or maybe you just weren't ready.'

Two floors down, Daniel was doing finger exercises on his practice violin and watching his girlfriend, Melissa, get dressed. She was five months' pregnant with their first child and her bump was showing. He loved the way she stopped and touched her belly sometimes when she thought he wasn't watching. A moment between mother and unborn child. They'd been together for a year and the pregnancy wasn't planned, but they'd come to accept it as a gift.

'Come here,' he said gently and laid the violin down on the bed. She smiled and walked over to him. The dress she was wearing was a royal blue, layered and floaty, and the colour enhanced her eyes.

'Tonight's special, isn't it?' she asked.

He took her hands in his and stood up. 'It's the first time I've played in public without Poppa here. I need to do him proud.'

'You will.'

He kissed her. 'Thank you for coming to London with me, I know travelling tires —'

'No, I'm fine. But you haven't said anything about how you're feeling. What your dad said. Does it matter?'

He shook his head. 'I can't process it. So much has happened since we first got the phone call to come and see the film. Poppa will always be Poppa, but I did love Feter Levi and he understood what music means to me.'

'If the baby's a boy, do you still want to call him Simon?' she asked.

'Of course. Simon Levi Horowitz. The next generation.'

Cindy turned the medal over in her hands. David was in the bathroom. It was a beautiful thing. Shiny. Sombre. A true reflection of the bravery it represented. She understood why Feter Levi had refused it, and yet the fact that the family had been so unaware of why he'd been offered it frustrated and irritated her. She was a woman to whom prizes and honours mattered.

To think that Levi had been offered the highest award for bravery bestowed upon a civilian in the United Kingdom and he had turned it down! The years of bragging to her friends she'd been denied. Well, not anymore. As soon as they got home she would throw a huge party and show off the medal. Daniel could play for her guests, and she'd get the best catering firm in town to do the food. She smiled.

Across town, Maestro Rafael Gomez was also preparing for the party. He was a sixty-two-year-old Spaniard who had been at the top of his game in the realm of classical music for over thirty years. He'd spotted Daniel Horowitz when the boy had won an international violin competition at the age of fourteen and had mentored him ever since.

'How does it feel, knowing Simon won't be there?'

The question was posed by his wife, Magdalena Montoya, who sat at the mirror in the bathroom and finished her makeup.

'I know it in my head, but it won't be real until we are all watching Dan play,' he replied.

'I imagine they are still reeling from the revelations about Levi,' she said. He turned and looked at her.

'It is hard to believe. I remember him as such a quiet man, so content to sit and watch, you know. And yet we all saw flashes of anger and passion in him.'

She stood and walked through to stand in front of him. 'Remember him the way you do, that hasn't changed,' she said.

He kissed her. 'When he thought we were all doing something else and couldn't hear, he would sit at the piano and play. Just for the sheer love of music. That's what I will remember.'

An hour later people flooded up the steps of Sergei Valentino's Mayfair mansion. Sergei was a product of perestroika. Russian-born, he'd made his money in oil and gas and had homes in Sussex, London, New York and Monte Carlo. He was a massive man, over six foot five and two hundred and eighty pounds, but he wore exquisitely handmade clothing which hid his bulk. He was a patron of the arts, music, art, ballet, opera, and he loved the people who created the art as much as they loved him.

His home in Mayfair was a semi-detached mansion, painted white, with a black front door. Light shone from every window of the large building, and people were scrambling in all directions, putting the finishing touches to the essentials of the evening. Sergei didn't do things by halves — there were buckets of champagne on ice, and trays of canapes, and the flower arrangements were magnificent. Uniformed butlers were getting ready to take hats and coats, and others were preparing the glasses for the gold trays.

People chatted and laughed as they moved through the double doors and into the music room. At one end of the room a full orchestra sat on a platform and played. At the other end guests formed groups, sipped champagne and ate beluga caviar and oysters.

'David,' Rafael said as the family walked across the room towards him.

'Maestro.'

Gomez shared a bear hug with every one of them. 'I am so looking forward to seeing this documentary,' he said. 'You know, it was simply amazing to hear about Levi's war at Simon's funeral. And to think we didn't know!'

'We saw it this morning, you'll enjoy it. They've done a wonderful job —'

'Daniel! My boy.'

It was a roar of noise, and Daniel turned just in time to prepare himself to be engulfed by Sergei's arms.

'Hello Sergei,' he said from the depths of the Russian's Armani jacket.

'I trust you have brought her,' Sergei said, letting him go.

Daniel nodded. 'Yes I have; she's with the security guard.'

'Good, good. I haven't heard her for months, and I get withdrawal symptoms,' he said.

The Guarneri violin was called Yulena after Sergei's aunt who had been a concert violinist, murdered by the KGB when they thought she was trying to defect to the West.

'How did the ceremony go?' Gomez asked David. Before he could answer Cindy leapt in.

'It was wonderful, Maestro. He was wonderful. It is such a beautiful medal.'

David reached into his pocket and drew out the case. He opened it and showed them the medal nestled inside. 'I can't wear it, I don't have that right. But I brought it so you could have a look.'

Gomez took it from him and ran his finger over it. 'Dear Levi. So much we didn't realise, how he must have suffered,' he said softly. Sergei put out his hand, and Gomez gave him the box.

'I always liked your uncle,' he said to David, 'in his own way he was feisty. He stood up to me. I remember when he first saw the Dürer painting he wanted to know why my father hadn't tried to trace the owners if he knew it was stolen.'

David smiled at him. 'I remember,' he said. 'He came to like you too.'

Daniel looked at his watch. 'You'll have to excuse me, I need to get ready.'

He left them and walked away towards the orchestra. Gomez watched him and then smiled at Cindy.

'He's grown up, our boy,' he said.

She gave a rueful shrug. 'Sometimes I miss those days when he needed me to be there before he performed.'

'Oh he'll always need your approval, you know that,' David said, and squeezed her shoulder.

Kobi and George came through the door and caught sight of the group. Kobi gave them a small wave.

'There's Kobi with his new man. He's very handsome,' Cindy said. Gomez was about to say something, but the two men reached them.

'Hello everyone, this is George Ross ... and George, this is David and Cindy and Maestro Gomez and Sergei Valentino.'

There were handshakes all around, and then Maestro Gomez excused himself.

Five minutes later, Rafael Gomez stood on the podium and addressed the crowd.

'This evening is a celebration of the Horowitz family members who are no longer with us. Benjamin, Elizabeth, Levi, Simon and the twins Rachel and David. Four of them died during the war, and two lived to a remarkable age. All of them demonstrated extraordinary bravery.

'There is no better way to celebrate their lives than to listen to Simon's grandson, Daniel, play his Guarneri del Gesú violin. He plays this piece, a favourite of his great-grandfather's, to honour all the generations who have gone before.'

Daniel put the violin to his shoulder and tightened the frog on the end of the bow. The violin's sparkling rich varnish caught the light as it moved. He played Debussy's 'The Girl with the Flaxen Hair', the piece that Simon had played when he was first allowed to play the Guarneri. The soft melody filled the room, as smooth as a piece of silk, and haunting, achingly beautiful. His tall, lean body swayed, and his eyes closed as his fingers moved over the fingerboard and the bow swept up and down. When it came to an end, the room erupted into applause.

David and Cindy clinked their champagne glasses together.

'Here's to the past and the future and to our boy, you lovely man,' she said softly.

Kobi and George exchanged a smile.

'We should drink a toast,' David said. 'To Feter Levi … and his war.'

'To Levi's war,' they all said in unison.

David touched the medal with his finger. 'Dad's war, Rachel's war and now Feter Levi's war. An ordinary family who lived through extraordinary times.'

Cindy smiled at him. 'A family I am very proud to be a part of,' she said.

Kobi nodded. 'Me, too,' he said.

'And me,' Elizabeth said.

David's eyes glinted with unshed tears, and he raised his glass again.

'To the Horowitz family, all the heroes we remember,' he said. The others looked at him as he stood, watching his son on the podium holding the violin by its neck, his glass raised in his right hand and his left hand touching his father's St George Cross.

'To the Horowitz family,' they replied in unison.

EPILOGUE

Twenty-five years after that night, Daniel Horowitz's second son, Ben, embarked on a genealogy project. He decided to research his family tree.

Firstly, he found his great-great-great-grandparents on his father's side, Hans and Sarah Horowitz. Hans was a banker in Frankfurt. In 1925, two of his sons, Benjamin and Mordecai, had moved the family bank to Berlin and established it in the Pariser Platz. That same year, his eldest son, Avrum, had immigrated to New York.

Benjamin had married Elizabeth Silverman, the only child of Levi and Anna Silverman from Nuremberg. They had four children: Levi, Simon, and twins Rachel and David. They lived a prosperous life in Berlin, full of music and proudly German, until the rise of the Nazi party in 1933.

Everything Ben discovered dovetailed with the oral family history that had been handed down. Levi was a spy and had fought with the partisans in Italy in World War Two, Simon was interred in Dachau, Rachel was a member of the Red Orchestra resistance group and died in Auschwitz, and David, her twin, had died while still a young boy in Dachau. Their father was also recorded as having died in Dachau.

Levi, their eldest child, was the father of David, who married Cindy, and David was the father of Daniel, who was a concert violinist and Ben's father. It read like a passage from the Torah, with the same names surfacing in different generations.

But when Ben came to investigate the fate of his great-great-grandmother, Elizabeth, who was supposed to have died in Auschwitz, he could find no record. Eventually, with the help of the massive digital DNA database and a search that threw up a documentary of Shoah stories recorded in Israel in 1986, he stumbled upon Elizabeth Bernstein, a woman who had lost her family but survived the horrors of the camp, remarried and settled in Israel.

And that was how his grandfather, David, discovered the last piece of the Horowitz puzzle. Elizabeth Bernstein, née Silverman, later Horowitz, David's grandmother, was buried in Jerusalem. She had died in 1988. David took his wife, his son, his daughter-in-law and his grandchildren to visit her grave. They laid a stone for each of Elizabeth's children and her surviving grandchildren, so the circle of the Horowitz family was complete.

ACKNOWLEDGEMENTS

Some years ago, one of my friends, Dorothy, told me I should write the story of Levi's war. I was confused. At that stage I had only written *The Keeper of Secrets* and had no intention of writing any sequel, let alone two sequels. I thought Levi had explained, after a fashion, what he did in England during World War Two. She corrected me and said, 'But you and I know that his war was a great deal more exciting than that.' The seed was planted, and after much thought the story of Levi's war emerged. So thank you for the seed, Dorothy.

This book has been the hardest thing I've ever written, for several reasons. The subject matter was dark in places, and some of characters were not only real, they were the most evil of humankind. Do not underestimate the toll it takes on you to write Hitler as a character in your novel! But I have also been unwell at times, and that has made the actual process of writing hard. I am a congenital heart patient, and had my corrective surgery over fifty years ago when it was the pioneering stuff of medical legend. I have also been a diagnosed depressive since 2008, after many years of undiagnosed suffering. I owe a big thank you to the doctors who have helped me overcome my health issues, my cardiologists, Claire O'Donnell and Mark Davis, my grief counsellor, Bobbie, and my wonderful GP, Dr Nigel Schofield.

I am blessed with three older brothers, Richard, Geoffrey and Graham, who are extremely supportive and make having siblings fun. I have a whole bunch of loveable nieces and a nephew, in particular my nieces Sally and Sarah, who keep an eye on their eccentric aunt.

I have wonderful friends who offer encouragement and helpful comments — Reuben (my brilliant Beta reader), Ruth, Victoria, Mike, Dorothy, Dave, Sharon and Kimmy, to name but a few to whom I owe a debt of gratitude.

And a very special thank you to my vicar and dear friend, Jan, and to Deryck and Heather, wonderful friends and such creative people. The four of us have dissected the characters and discussed the plot of this book for hours. If it wasn't for the suggestions and the 'war stories' you shared with me, I would still be stuck!

Lastly, of course, my publishers at HarperCollins, Alex Hedley, Sandra Noakes and most especially my magnificent editor, Nicola Robinson. You guys are the personification of patience and care, and HarperCollins made my lifelong dream of being a published author come true.

I've lived with these characters for a long time, and I love them dearly. Just thinking about them brings tears to my eyes. They are combinations of all the true stories I have read and listened to, and in many ways the real acknowledgement should go to all the survivors, their descendants, the soldiers and the bystanders who have shared their experience of war with the world.

My father was a World War II Spitfire pilot, and in one of his letters home he said, 'We have a duty to ensure this never happens again.' When he wrote those words he had no idea of the scale of the horror that was to unfold in liberated Europe. But sadly we, as a species, have not stood by that duty. It has happened, to some extent, over and over again. Man's inhumanity to man. Man's inability to see people as individuals and not as a race. If you take one thing away from 'The Horowitz Chronicles' let it be this:

> *It's a simple truth. Prejudice is much harder to maintain when you break down the barrier of ignorance, my son. You see us now as individual people with talent, not subhuman vermin, and that makes it harder for you to hate us.*

Simon Horowitz to Kurt in Dachau, page 183,
The Keeper of Secrets.

Julie Thomas's first book *The Keeper of Secrets* was published by HarperCollins USA in 2013. She had written it while working fulltime as a writer, producer, director and executive producer in the media, and achieved considerable success self-publishing it on Amazon and Smashwords.

Blood, Wine & Chocolate followed in 2015, published by HarperCollins NZ. This wine crime novel revolved around a mob murder, witness protection, barrels of delicious wine and boxes of scrumptious chocolate, and some innovative murder techniques.

In 2016, Julie published *Rachel's Legacy* with HarperCollins NZ, a sequel to *The Keeper of Secrets*, which expanded on the fate of Rachel Horowitz and her part in the Red Orchestra resistance movement in World War II Berlin. With *Levi's War*, the Horowitz Chronicles come to an end.

Julie lives in the small rural town of Putaruru, where she looks out on farmland from her study window and is serenaded by cows. She is an active member of her local community and is Mum to Chloe, a black-and-white cat who rules the house.

A GRAIN OF TRUTH

All three books in this trilogy revolve around what I call 'a grain of truth'. In other words there are real people and real events at their heart.

In *The Keeper of Secrets* I used the missing 1742 Guarneri del Gesú violin as the springboard for the story and incorporated the rise of the Nazi party, life in Dachau concentration camp and the story of Soviet Russia. This was a story about possession, ownership and redemption.

Rachel's Legacy told the story of the Red Orchestra Network, a real resistance movement in Berlin. All the members of the organisation were real people, and their fate was all too true. This was a story about identity, sacrifice and nature versus nurture.

In this case, there are two different elements from World War II.

Firstly, the role that Levi shoulders as a spy, parachuted behind enemy lines, is based on refugees who were recruited to spy for the British. They were trained and sent back into Nazi-occupied Germany. Most were captured, tortured and sent to die in concentration camps. Perhaps the most famous was Violette Szabo, a French-born English Special Operations Executive (SOE) agent. During her second mission into occupied France she was captured, interrogated and tortured, and then deported to Germany, where she was eventually executed in

Ravensbrück concentration camp. Her posthumous George Cross was presented to her five-year-old daughter, Tania.

The things that Levi reports back on happened during the war at the times he encountered them. Had he, actually, been a real spy he would have been able to alert the Allies to the things he overheard. There were over a dozen assassination attempts on Hitler, and there was one at the Berghof. I took a little licence — the actual assassin never got near him.

The second thread is the story of Assisi. This captured my heart when I happened upon it while researching *Rachel's Legacy*, and I was determined that Levi would make his way there. The three major characters of that story — Father Don Aldo Brunacci, Bishop Giuseppe Placido Nicolini and Colonel Valentin Müller — were all real people and they did what they do in this story. They are three real heroes. Müller must have been a wonderful man to risk what he did, the only real German World War Two officer I've ever read about who I liked. And the Catholic clergy hid, saved and nurtured over three hundred Jews. Not one Jew was deported from Assisi.

This last book is about what makes you who you are, and what keeps you from being who you should be. Levi had a far more interesting war than we thought in the previous two books. He was on the spot for some momentous times and he survived to tell his tale.

BOOK CLUB QUESTIONS

What motivated Levi to agree to go back to Germany?

How well do you think Levi controlled his emotions and reactions?

Who killed Rolf — Levi or Werner?

What language did Levi pray and think in?

What was it about Levi's circumstances that contributed to him being such a great pianist?

Why did Levi agree to go to Italy?

How justified was Simon in his anger at not having been told the truth? Why did Levi keep his war a secret from Simon?

How conflicted did pretending to be a Christian priest make Levi?

What effect, if any, did Levi's sexuality have on his decisions?

Did Levi make the right choice in deciding to go back to England? Did Levi, in effect, have any choice?

Why had Levi refused the George Cross?

How do you think Levi would have wanted to be remembered?

Did David make the right choice in telling the family his secret?

Also by Julie Thomas

Rachel's Legacy

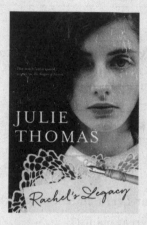

When Dr Kobi Voight is given a set of old letters by his mother, he has no inkling that they will lead him around the world and deep into his family's tragic past.

Within the letters – written in Hebrew and filled with delicate illustrations – lie the reflections of a young Jewish woman, forced to give up her baby daughter while fighting with the Resistance in Berlin. Who is the author, known only as 'Ruby', and what became of her child? And how does a priceless work of art, stolen by the Nazis, form part of the unfolding mystery?

From the Holocaust to the present day, across continents and oceans, Kobi's journey will ultimately lead him to the truth about his family – and his own identity.

'... seamlessly weaves important historical detail into this saga of a single family riven and nearly decimated by the Holocaust.' – NZ Listener